D1523132

Quixote

By Bryan Jason Lee Glass

From an original story by
Bryan J.L. Glass and Michael Avon Oeming

Illustrated by
Michael Avon Oeming

For Harry L. Glass
Who always believed.

For Ethan
Nothing is impossible.
And for Uncle Larry
...My very own Don Quixote.

The love, patience, and editorial accumen of
Judy Glass & Melissa Oeming

The following graciously provided their
professional or technical expertise at
various stages of this project:
Laurel Garver, Simon Larter & James H. Glass
Juanita and Trevor J. Hummel
at the Bucks County Academy of Fencing,
and Adam Levine.

Micah Ackley, Anne-Cara Apple, Carl Borg, Lisa Bowman,
Alicia Blackburn, Dr. Rollin (Skip) Blackburn, Craig Bracy,
Joy Converse, Roger Converse, Nathan Edmonson, Fred Foster,
Amy Glass, James Y. Glass, Patricia Glass, Rebecca Healey,
Kirsten Higley, Jean Hummel, Kristen Hummel, Jimmy Jones,
Kristen Jones, Michael Jordan, John McGready, Jonathan Olsen,
Jim Otter, Mark Sautter, Brendan Schrader, Elliot Silver,
Stacy Skinner, Tammy Smith.

Prologue

In the Year of our Lord 1605,
Spanish playwright Miguel de Cervantes Saavadra
gave birth to the modern novel with his creation
Don Quixote...

The purportedly "true tale" of Alonso Quixano
driven mad by impossible dreams of chivalry and justice.

As Quixote, Alonso rode into battle against windmills,
believing them giants...

Adored a peasant girl he dubbed Dulcinea,
whilst fighting for her virtue...

And was followed by the hapless Sancho Panza,
his devoted squire.

Cervantes assumed his hero was insane,
while history has judged his epic tale of meandering
knight errantry fiction.

But history is often born of assumption.
And assumption is very rarely fact...

Part One
IMPOSSIBLE DREAM

*How Our Hero Rescued His New Squire
and Found an Angel with a Harlot's Soul.*

Chapter One

"Do you believe?"

That was all the old man had said. His withered face was a weatherworn ruin of cracked, grey lips and dirty, creased features. Seventy years old he appeared, at the very least; ninety to a hundred-and-twenty seemed more likely. Wrinkled gouges looked like they cut to the bone. Sunken eyes sat waterlogged, deep in the recessed pits of his leathery face, reflecting back pale glimmers of light from dank, bloodshot pools.

Even on video pre-record and played back on the monitor, the old man's haunting eyes glared back from the screen, his mad conviction riveting the unwary to that terrible stare. Pure, focused intent, those aged eyes were—unstoppable, like a pair of locomotives blasting their way through a deep mountain tunnel.

"He's *perfect,* Joe. Where did you find him?" asked Dominique Angel.

"Does it matter?" answered her partner of two or so years' worth of television's Headline News. "You told me to get you 'bum shots.' I got you 'bum shots.' You ask, I humbly comply." The late-twenty-something camera-man grinned. "Now why is it that whenever I ask *you* for anything, you just say, 'Shut up, Joe'?"

"Shut up, Joe," snapped Dom, enrapt as the playback monitor further chronicled the walking car-wreck the old derelict represented. The screen image jostled slightly as the camera operator had attempted to keep pace with the old man, he who expressed his disinterest in being a topic for that evening's news by turning his back and stumbling away.

"…And tell me everything you can about this old bird," she added.

Under his official network ball cap, Joe's grin widened from ear to ear.

"That's another thing: You're always contradicting yourself. What does that say about you?"

She flicked her medium-length auburn hair from her eyes and frowned back without another word.

Joe Caparelli knew that look, and knew when to put the gags in neutral and get back to business. That was only one of the reasons Dom liked working with him so much: behind the camera, he had a good eye for the news. He knew just when and how much to lighten the mood, and most important of all, he knew when to shut up and do his job. And right now, both the reporter and her cameraman had a definite job to do.

Joe had found the old coot with the scary eyes that very morning, rooting through the trash on some ramshackle street, little more than a back alley, just north of the city's central spires of glass and steel. So innocuous was the old guy that Joe had nearly missed him. Here he was, commissioned to find bums, and he would've passed this one by—that is, until the crazy old man had thrown a clattering metal trash can lid at the side of the news-van and shouted what sounded like *"Parasites of human decadence!"* Joe couldn't be sure, but it had been far too good an opportunity to pass up.

When it came to a physical threat, Joe knew he could usually take care of himself. When the threat was nothing more than just some old vagrant hooked on the cheapest of liquor, it usually proved to be a danger only to his sense of smell. This particular old geezer met expectation on the olfactory front, but immediately after that, Joe had noticed there was something different about this one, something he couldn't quite pin down.

It wasn't just his years clinging to him, cumbersome yet threadbare, like his own unwashed clothes. The man's cracked leather face, the bent, broken body—his very bearing was madness personified. Yet his eyes were sane: those searing black pools were dark and sober, as if he alone saw what others could not. It seemed those eyes had caught a glimpse of the nightmares lurking on the cusp of our dreams, and concluded that madness was not simply a matter of perception, but was, in fact, reality.

Joe was no poet, but if the truth be told, this old man scared him as no other story coverage ever had. Dom, however, didn't care.

Dominique Angel sat bedecked in a smartly conservative light blue suit with just a splash of liberal style. Paris had declared the coming season to be an intelligent light blue one, and L.A. confirmed their enlightenment as only the West Coast could. If Dom was as smart as she believed she was, then a light blue year it most certainly would be.

Never taking her eyes from the screen, she sat mesmerized as Joe finished his tale of the morning's escapade that had captured the haunting images unfolding before her. The picture abruptly bucked and swayed as the old bum's withered hand grabbed the intrusive camera lens and shoved Joe back with a force that had surprised him. Even so, Joe claimed, he'd almost continued his harassment until a scathing parting glance from the bum withered any remaining bravado he had. And that was the only time the old man had actually spoken something clearly coherent—three words strung rationally together and posing his inexplicable question: *"Do you believe?"*

The final minute of footage was of the old bum walking away—or, more accurately, shuffling—and occasionally stopping to root through a garbage can, peer into a dumpster bin, or shout some additional unintelligible nonsense down an alleyway.

Dominique rewound the tape back to that final frightful stare that had stopped her cameraman dead in his tracks. She hummed an affirmation to herself until it coalesced into actual words. "Now *there* is a face that makes you look at yourself and think. I can hear it now: *'Is THIS the face to shape politics for the NEW MILLENNIUM?'* " And that was just how she said it: with CAPS and *italics.*

She took a sip of coffee from her steaming mug—the personalized one she kept on the job: the one inscribed "#1 Bitch."

"Oh yes…he will do nicely," she said. "We'll get him a bite to eat, prompt him on the issues, and get ourselves a scathing indictment of the current administration."

Dom allowed herself a smile of satisfaction and decided to let Joe share in the glory of his find. "You did good, Joe, really good on this one. Desmond is going to be proud of both of us."

Joe smiled back, thankful for the well-earned praise, despite its being so long in coming. The old man on the monitor didn't seem to care either way; he just stared back in freeze-frame, and let his accusing eyes do all the talking for him.

"I just hope he's articulate," Dom added. "Are you sure that's all he said?"

Joe nodded. The crazy old man had muttered a great many things, but that was all he had actually *said*:

"Do you believe?"

Chapter Two

Welcome to the Big City...

When viewed from above—by an "Eye in the Sky" rush hour traffic helicopter for instance—the grid that makes up this particular piece of urban Americana is indistinguishable from any other central to northeast city in this great land. Despite its distinctive landmarks and individual sports league franchises, these anonymous byways are the kinds of streets where the Nation and its Dream were born. And here is where it may possibly die, for these shining streets hide ugly back alleys where the dream is fading.

Along these dry, bitter tributaries, the seven deadly sins of the postmodern era thrive: *Poverty. Ignorance. Illiteracy. Intolerance. Racism. Sexism. Discrimination.* But unlike the classic vices of old, these crimes against the Politically Correct are nearly always open to inter-pretation, representing the all-too-malleable borders between the *haves* and the *forget-me-nots.*

Yet even on streets such as these, *Hope,* that elusive virtue of the down-trodden, still remains—that is, if billboards are to be believed.

The billboards in question feature a warm smile on the face of a giant-sized man who aspires to be savior of that oft-lamented American Dream. Their message is a simple one, proactive, assertive, and filled with promise:

The Choice for a Better Tomorrow—Elect Henry Devlin for Governor.

The outcome, it seems, is the people's to decide.

One particular billboard is massive, and can be seen from the city's major thoroughfare—that interstate highway that cuts through the urban *body politic* like a femoral artery. And the publicity its sheer size garners is the only thing that really matters. For despite the political posturing that accompanies any spring or fall electoral season, no one honestly cares about the embarrassing slums and the human refuse that live beneath that billboard's smiling face…

A terrified scream resounded through late afternoon shadows. It drifted across vacant lots littered with chunks of brick, broken glass, and the occasional soot-covered dolly head. It passed through broken windows, echoing in empty rooms of crumbling drywall and rotted plaster, over mildewed mattresses strewn with used condoms and hypodermic needles. The sound finally faded just as it had begun, lost in the dim recesses, the dirty corners of dead-end alleys. And any who heard that horrified cry carried on the spring breeze did nothing. In the grand scheme of things, the souls that dwelt here were considered of no consequence—unless of course, there was political advantage to be gained from human suffering.

This particular scream came from the throat of William "Billy" Sanchez as he watched his right sleeve go up in bright orange flames. He uttered the scream with such intensity because his arm was still *inside* the grey sweatshirt sleeve. He might have pulled his arm out from the burning sweatshirt had not two other sets of strong arms held him firmly in place, allowing the flames to creep along his outstretched limb and start nipping at his shoulder.

Billy Sanchez had fallen asleep far back in the alleyway, with a bottle of cheap whiskey—still half-full—cocked under his arm, fully intending to use it as a suppressant of the coming day's headache. Instead he'd been jolted from his afternoon slumber by a light kick to the head and his precious half-full whiskey bottle being poured out over him. He no longer wanted to even think about what he'd had to do to get that precious whiskey in the first place, but that memory, degrading though it was, fled his mind completely as adrenaline began to sober him up.

"I—I don' wan' no trouble," was all he could muster, the hint of an Hispanic accent filtering up through the alcohol.

"Shaddup!" was the only response. The crew surrounding him laughed amongst themselves—freshly scrubbed white faces, middle-class trash with just enough cash to keep themselves in style. Four of them were little more than boys, but should have known better. The fifth was senior enough, big enough, to attract the others' respect, and their competition for his approval—even if that meant setting another human being on fire for their own amusement.

The warm breeze made jackets optional, so the twin hulks holding Sanchez let their fine-toned muscles of youth flex in white tees. They grinned in unison, locking the skinny bum's arms out straight on either side, one each of their denim legs interlocking around Billy's knees to prevent any swift kicks. One scowled, as their leader poured the last of the whiskey over the bum's head and accidentally splashed some of the cheap rank yellow stench onto his t-shirt. The Leader ignored his scowling toady and stepped back, clutching the empty bottle in his grip.

Despite a laundry list of petty crimes lurking on the fringe of his thoughts, Billy Sanchez was at least on the ball enough to suspect that *this* retribution wasn't connected to anything he'd actually done. His soaked, stinking hair clung to his face in straggling seaweed clumps. He sputtered as he tried to shake the wet strands from his burning eyes. "Oh god, man. Jeez…jus' leave me 'lone…" He felt bile in the back of his throat.

The Leader caught the signs—the bobbing Adam's apple of original sin and the accompanying nasal snort—and backed up his large frame just in time to avoid the bum's previous meal splashing onto his pristine black leather jacket. He was proud of this particular coat, as its original vintage hide had been kept well-oiled for over fifty years—long before that Winkler kid on television had turned the previous generation's hoodlums and layabouts into popular social icons.

The Leader's most recent disciple wasn't so lucky in avoiding the bum's spew. The young punk had just turned nineteen, the eldest of the four followers, and his leather coat—in emulation of his newest idol—still creaked, groaning like a rusty hinge on a slaughterhouse gate, every time he turned around or bent his elbow. A hefty chunk of the bum's partially-digested mystery-meat dropped from the coat and onto the punk's blue-jeaned thigh.

"Shit!" Further profanity followed, bursting forth even more frothing and colorful than anything Billy Sanchez had pulled from a dumpster that morning, and hung audibly in the air, equally pungent.

The young punk drew back his hand to slug Sanchez, who was now dry-heaving into the late-afternoon air. He was stopped by a single word: "No." His stiff, new leather squeaked and groaned as he lowered his fist and turned to his mentor.

The Leader's old leather made no sound as he raised his hand, opening his fingers to reveal a vintage lighter resting in the square of his meaty palm.

"Do what we came for," he said, "…and smile for the folks at home." He gestured to the fifth and final member of their little crew: fifteen-year-old Reginald Sharpe, who, at 247 pounds, wanted nothing more than to be taken seriously, ever since he had learned that beating up elementary school kids didn't impress anyone anymore.

It was the fat boy's job to record the merry band's antics for posterity. The camera had come via the same five-fingered discount that had acquired the stiff new leather, but it neither creaked nor groaned as it operated. Videotaping crimes for later chuckles had long grown passé, but this latest generation of thuggery had been on the slow boat, never quite realizing that such trends had passed them by.

Reggie's cheap, blue nylon windbreaker stretched across the back of his overweight frame as he leaned forward eagerly. He zoomed in close as the bum spit out the last solid dribbles of puke from his mouth. The grizzled Latino didn't look quite so old close up. His life and the streets had caught up with him, probably in one swift blow of a year or two, and aged him as only poverty, guilt, and desperation can do. From a distance he looked about twenty years over his real age—anywhere from early to late thirties.

"Dutch" was the handle of the young punk in the new leather. He smiled for the camera, as he took the solid chunk of lighter into his own hand, never realizing nor truly appreciating that he now held a perverse heirloom that had set alight far more than its share of southern crosses in its heyday.

The Latino's eyes finally cleared enough to see Dutch test-fire the old lighter, and they widened in alarm as they fixed on the bright orange naphtha flame. Over the stench of his vomit, Sanchez smelled the cheap whiskey that still burned his eyes and soaked his hair and upper torso. He connected the alcohol and the fire, and started to scream.

The Leader said, "Do it."

Dutch held the lighter firmly, yet he hesitated, his eyes mirroring the small orange flame, as if weighing his own accountability one last time before committing himself to action.

The others took up their Leader's charge as a chant: *Do it! Do it! Do it!* Their words built in power and conviction, until the thug in the soiled white t-shirt on Sanchez's left yelled out, "Torch 'im already, will ya?"

Reggie started giggling behind the camera as the eldest boy thrust the lighter's flame under the bum's stinking sweatshirt sleeve. They all watched as the outstretched right arm was slowly engulfed in a liquid fire.

"For the love of god," Billy shrieked, "somebody help me!"

High above the scene, oblivious to the human drama unfolding beneath it, a pristine white Jet Ranger III traffic helicopter, emblazoned with a bold red numeral "6," made its rounds, training its dual gyro-cams on the preliminary trickle of the p.m. rush hour commute.

"Unhand that man."

Only Reginald Sharpe heard the old man's voice the first time he spoke. Instead of turning only his head away from their crime, Reggie spun the entire camera, and caught his first sight of the second bum through the viewfinder. The man stood, lanky and hunched, silhouetted in the alley's entrance.

"Hey guys," said Reggie, "we got company. Double yer pleasure!"

All but Billy Sanchez turned to look at the new arrival. Dutch was finally feeling the power of his growing role. He knew it wouldn't be long now

before he'd be confident enough to challenge Old Leather's leadership and take charge of his gang again. *The way it used to be, he thought. Back on the old corner where they used to hang out. Before the new guy had come along and taken them all under his broad wing. Before he showed them how much more they could get away with if they'd only leave the security of familiar neighborhoods.*

His new leather creaked as Dutch ordered the twin thugs holding Billy to let him go and grab the new bum, adding, "Let's torch 'em *both!*"

The two in t-shirts, not really twins, Larry "Knucklehead" Burns and Jerry "Not-the-TV-Guy" Springer were both bigger than Dutch, but not quite intelligent enough to use their size to command. As one, they dropped Sanchez and went for the newcomer.

Billy fell to his knees, desperately trying to rub out the fire along his right arm.

The Leader squinted his eyes as he took in the frail silhouette standing thirty feet away, blocking their only exit. "Wait," was all he said, and his order stopped the t-shirted duo in their tracks.

The dark shadow at the alley entryway spoke a second time, clearly, powerfully, so there was no mistaking his intent: "Leave him alone."

The Leader answered the bold challenge with one of his own. "You mind yourself, *old man*. This ain't none of *your* business."

* * * * *

Snuffing the flames, Billy Sanchez then cradled his burned arm, charred pieces of the synthetic sweatshirt breaking off like slivers of eggshell. His life had always been crap, but in this moment of seeing it all coming to an end, Billy couldn't help but break into desperate tears like a baby. He heard the younger punk in the squeaking leather jacket, the one who had torched him, try to pick a fight with his own leader. But the more experienced young man wasn't one to air their dirty laundry in public.

"Fuck it," the younger punk finally muttered under his breath, "I say we're gonna do 'em *both!*"

From the corner of his eye, Billy saw the Leader grab Dutch with one hand, the sound of the new leather screaming as his fingers clenched the black hide taut, and he pressed his protégé solidly against the brick wall with little effort. Billy could tell from the position of the Leader's head that, even while dispensing gang discipline, he never took his eyes off the strange newcomer at the mouth of the alley.

My savior, thought Billy, as the first coherent pair of words entered his brain. He would later describe *his savior* to the police—when Law Enforcement came to mop up the bloodbath the situation would rapidly become—as looking like "some hero from an old movie or something." Sanchez thought his savior looked like Robin Hood, even though he had never seen Flynn, Costner, or even Elwes, and wouldn't have actually recognized that character as such if he had. Billy only knew the name and equated it as an ancient hero from some lost time.

What he actually saw, standing at the mouth of the alleyway, was a tall man in a dark suit, cloaked beneath a flowing black trench coat, a finely-tailored vest trimmed with bright yellow piping, and a starched white ruffle that fairly burst from the man's chest—just like in old movies his Gramma had watched, the ones where everyone sang and danced. And the man wore a sword, a real sword strapped to his side like a movie cowboy would wear his six-shooter. (Billy had loved *The Lone Ranger* as a child, but that hero wore a mask and never carried a sword.)

It was definitely Robin Hood, he decided: rugged, stark, chiseled features, a bold black goatee framing the powerful jaw line of an olive-skinned Spaniard—*was Robin Hood Spanish?* he wondered, *that guy that went after windmills and sang that song?* This man was *gallant*, even *chivalrous*, if Sanchez had possessed such a vocabulary despite his limited and jumbled formal education.

Caught by a rising wind, long jet-black hair whipped across the Spaniard's face as if in a desperate attempt to hide his eyes—haunting slivers of light reflecting out of his face like the headlights of a car bearing down at 120 miles an hour.

The man spoke with a crisp, clear, solid voice filled with the burning passion of a refiner's fire. "You will cease these transgressions! That one has done you no harm."

Robin Hood and the Lone Ranger aside, Billy Sanchez later told the police that his savior *"talked like Jesus."*

Dutch had always been lean, wiry, and smart, but now he squirmed against the wall, thinking it was definitely time someone new took charge of the situation. "Whattya think you're doing?" he challenged the bigger, leaner

man he'd chosen to follow, who now held him by his collar in a vice-like grip.

The Leader's head pivoted in the young punk's direction, slowly and smoothly like a snake. As if from a forked tongue, he spat his words back in Dutch's face. "You let this old fish go. You don't go asking for more trouble than you can handle." He slammed him against the wall a second time, hard enough to bounce Dutch's head off the bricks. The young punk yelped. "Do you understand me?" the Leader added for emphasis.

"Yeah…" Dutch whined, "I understand." The lighter fell from his grip and clattered on the concrete of the alley floor.

The weird old bum spoke again, seeming to grow in stature with every word he uttered. "The goats are so easily swayed by your words. They would follow you from the safety of the shepherd's pen all the way back into Hell."

The Leader's focus shifted back to the dark figure. "These aren't yours, old man— They're *mine*," he said.

"What's he talkin' about, Vinny?" Dutch winced, still pinned against the alley wall.

The Leader's head instantly snapped back to his devotee's attention. "Ya wanna know what he's saying? Why don'tcha go find out!" he shouted as he threw his follower down onto the concrete between himself and the strange old bum. "And this is one mess I won't bail you out of if you're stupid enough to go for it," he added as he slowly, warily, bent down to recover the precious relic lighter his toady had so irreverently let fall.

Dutch got up clumsily to his knees, one hand going painfully to the back of his head. He knew his fine, new leather jacket was now ruined, scraped and scratched against the brick wall.

"Fuck this," he said as his free hand pulled a switchblade and released its cutting edge with the flick of his thumb. The new leather squeaked loudly as he leapt up and charged the old bum blade first.

Dutch got close enough to see the weathered old leathery skin, far older than the leather hide he wore on his own back. He met the old man's eyes for just an instant before the worst pain of his life shot through his arm like a runaway train. He thought he saw his own switchblade flip through the air, end over end, in slow motion it seemed, before finding himself flung force-fully onto the sidewalk outside the alley.

Billy Sanchez saw the punk that had held the lighter charge Robin Hood. But Hood never moved, his grim expression never changed. He simply caught the young punk's outstretched blade arm, and, in a twisting motion too swift to see with the naked eye, yanked it in a direction it was incapable of going. Billy heard bone snap first, followed immediately by the sound of

ripping leather; the elbow popping, snapping like a turkey drumstick—meat breaking through skin, exposing a jutting knob of joint gleaming like a juicy wet pearl.

The punk's own momentum carried him past Robin Hood and out onto the sidewalk beyond, leaving him twisting in agony as his arm dangled like a horror movie appendage.

Jerry and Knucklehead were on Robin Hood in an instant, believing brawn to be enough. Moments later, though, they too found themselves out on the sidewalk screaming over broken, twisted limbs.

The old man never moved from his spot, but he simply allowed his would-be attackers to tumble out of the alleyway on either side of him. His gaze never left their Leader. "I told you to leave that man alone," he said, indicating the Hispanic vagrant, on his knees, still gently holding his burned arm, and staring up at his savior in wonder and stunned disbelief.

Reggie Sharpe had caught none of the action on tape. He, too, stared in disbelief, but his wonder had been replaced by fear. He tried skirting his way around the tough old street bum, realizing he had plenty of room to negotiate, as long as the crazy guy didn't divert attention to him. After all, Reggie wasn't threatening, and he hadn't really done anything wrong. If only he could get out of the alley in one piece, he promised himself he'd return to the schoolyards and playgrounds to conduct his business—at least little kids didn't fight back.

The old man stopped him with an outstretched hand. Reginald whined, "Hey… I wasn't no part of this!"

The guy never turned his head, but Reggie felt the old man's yellowed eyes practically rumble in their sockets, rotating like ancient, rusted engines until their dark gaze fell solely upon him.

"Look, I just held the camera," he said as he raised the camcorder in a shaking hand.

Swift as a bolt of lightning, the old man drew a long iron shaft from the recesses of his ratty overcoat and swatted the camera like a fly from Reggie's hand, smashing it into the alley wall, pinning its shattered remains against the bricks like a prized specimen. Unfortunately for Reggie, he hadn't disentangled his plump hand from the holding strap, and his shoulder burned like fire where the socket of the joint had been instantly dislocated. The boy wailed like the smaller children he bullied.

Equally swift, the old man jerked the iron rod out of the indentation made in the bricks. Then, yanking back in an overhead arc, it dragged the twin spools of videotape out of the camera wreckage like celebratory streamers, flinging them high into the air.

Reggie screamed, but the old man made no further moves to stop the boy. His child's face was now a blur of pain and tears as he ran out of the alley and into the street.

On his way, Reggie stopped at the sight of his three buddies moaning in agony. The biggest, toughest guys he'd personally ever known lay in a broken heap—Larry Knucklehead with a shattered kneecap, Jerry's leg dislocated from the hip, and Dutch's arm looking like something gory from a "Jason" movie, only *for real*. He ran again, faster than he'd ever run in his young life, hoping, praying desperately that he never saw a single soul from that alley ever again.

Billy Sanchez heard the roar of thunder barely a split second after Robin Hood drew the fancy sword from the sheath at his side. Lightning had struck somewhere close by.

The camcorder shattered in a thousand pieces. The crackling air was filled with the smell of ozone and strands of unthreading tape. The youngest boy fled, and Billy's savior had made no move to stop him. Hood's attention—and his sword point—now focused on the Leader whose back was a mere arm's length from Billy's reach.

"This is *our* destiny," said his savior. "Leave the sheep and goats out of our battle."

The Leader sighed heavily as if resigning himself to the inevitable, and then snarled, "I ain't afraid of you."

"Then come…and may we see in whose hand the strength of righteousness prevails."

And they charged each other.

Chapter Three

"He's gotta be around here, somewhere…"

The WDVL newsvan had crisscrossed the same ten-block radius for the past thirty-five minutes with no success. A bold red numeral "6" emblazoned the sides of the otherwise stark white van, along with their locally famous motto, *WDVL 6—Making News Happen!*

Gubernatorial hopeful Henry Devlin was coming to town. Despite ever-growing accusations of bias, the local media wing of the Party was still strategizing how best to "objectively" get *their man* into the Governor's Mansion, even if that meant fabricating a political issue or two. One of the tried and true modern means to oust any incumbent from office was the rattling of a few urban trashcans until the derelict and homeless skittered like cockroaches caught in the glare of the media spotlight.

Reporter Dominique Angel, whose own media star was on the rise, intended to bait the opportunity for all it was worth, casting herself as one of those in the journalistic pool when the big fish came to town for his campaign swim. As part of her plan she had asked her ever-dependable cameraman Joe to do some extra-curricular fishing: get some good "bum shots." And Joseph Caparelli, whose sweet Italian mother had raised no *scioccos*, got her the best catch he could: the old man with the dark, enigmatic eyes. But, for some, "the best" was never quite good enough.

Now, mere passenger Dominique Angel was growing increasingly frustrated—the last expression her driver, the aforementioned Joseph Caparelli, wanted to see on the rising star's face. He didn't wish to disappoint even at the best of times, but particularly not now, after having promised so much.

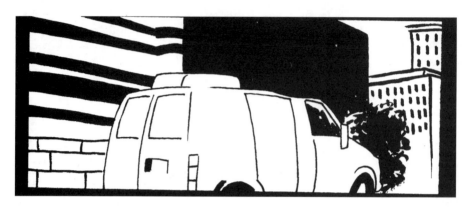

"Are you *sure* this is the neighborhood you saw him in?" she asked, demanding an immediate answer.

"I've told you 'yes' a dozen times already," said Joe. Neither took their eyes off the varied side streets and alleyways they passed. The vacant lots were beginning to look alike.

"Do you think it's possible you made a mistake?" she asked again.

The terse banter was fraying the edges of Joe's usual cool. "I am not this guy's brother, nor am I his keeper! This is still a free country and vagrants will come and go as they will!"

Dom's anger rose as she turned her attention on her partner. "Can't you just *admit* you made a mistake, Joe?"

"There's a reason they call them vagrants, Dom."

High above, the gleaming white WDVL newscopter was in the midst of its rush hour rounds. A shaft of late afternoon sun reflected off its side directly through the newsvan's windshield. A brief flare that was just enough to distract Joe from the desultory subject at hand. And the road.

"There goes Mackie," he said, indicating their airborne colleague.

"Don't change the subject," she snapped.

Just then, a heavyset teenager in a sorry blue windbreaker ran from between two parked cars, directly in front of the van. Joe would've hit him hard had he not been going easy on the gas and been able to stomp fast on the brake.

The kid bumped against the windshield, stared at the pair briefly, his eyes bleary and unseeing, before running off again.

Dom was instantly diverted from the argument as if it had never been. "That kid was crying, Joe," she said. Her eyes followed his lumbering figure as it diminished in the side rear-view mirror. She thought he looked like a hunchback, or that one arm was somehow longer than the other.

Joe honked the horn, decidedly after the fact, then gunned the vehicle forward again. Dom spun around in her captain's seat to look back in the direction from which the boy had come.

"Stop, Joe! Stop!" she shouted, as if her usually trustworthy cameraman had crushed several more children beneath his reckless tires. Joe had just cruised past a side street where several figures lay on the sidewalk. Dom's news eye had seen blood. "Back up!" she demanded.

Joe jerked to a stop a second time, shifted, and gunned the van in reverse.

"Down there, on the left," Dom harped. "Go—Go—Go! Before we miss it!"

Joe took a quick look at the street signs, then caught sight of an approaching car. "One-way street, Dom."

"Never stopped you before," she quipped.

Nodding and grimacing slightly, Joe sighed and turned the wheel to the left. The approaching car would just have to back out of the small street the way it had come.

One look at the confused expression on the approaching driver's face, his furtive left and right glances, and it was obvious the middle-aged man behind the wheel didn't belong in this neighborhood and was desperately trying to get himself out before the worst happened. Now here were Joe and Dom using one of the many unspoken rights of the press, cutting off his escape and adding to the suburbanite's urban nightmare.

The large fir-green Buick came to a slow rolling stop and the driver honked indignantly, gesturing for the encroaching newsvan to get out of *his* right of way. When the van showed no evidence of stopping, the driver readied himself to get out and have some words; that is, until he saw three writhing bodies on the sidewalk to his right, mere feet from his passenger-side door.

The driver's face turned from anger to fear, then transformed into absolute wide-eyed terror. Suddenly a fourth figure flew in from the right, straight out of a wide alleyway, landing heavily on the Buick's hood as if the body had been launched by some medieval catapult.

Upon impact, the Buick dented with a sharp crunch, the driver's view instantly obliterated by a spiderweb of shattering safety glass.

The engine stalled, but the horn and car alarm went off simultaneously, filling the little street with a shrill cacophony.

The driver thought the body was dead until he saw it move. Slowly at first, like a beached whale rolling onto its side, the body dropped off the hood by the left front tire. He was certain it had moved by its own power and not just leftover momentum. He looked out his side window to get a better view and saw the most bedraggled street vagrant he had ever seen in his life, clawing at his tire and hood trying to get himself back up on unsteady legs. The vagrant was quite an old one, over seventy, possibly pushing eighty. Wisps of long grey hair blew across his face but did nothing to hide the excessive bald pate of old, spotted, pale grey flesh that clung in wrinkled strips to his scalp.

The driver started rolling down his window to give the old coot a piece of his mind, but then the vagrant revealed an iron fence spike about three feet long, still clutched in his aged, wrinkled claw despite his brief airborne journey onto the Buick's now-shattered windshield. Then the old bum looked up and locked his dark eyes on the driver. The suburbanite's bladder let go like a standing horse.

The old man spoke loudly over the competing sounds of the vehicle, but it was his searing glare that conveyed his sharpest intent. "Get out of here—*Now!*"

The driver re-keyed the ignition and flooded the engine in one disastrous uncoordinated flick of his wrist and press of the gas pedal. That's when the driver realized he had done more than piss his pants.

The Gang Leader, his little dysfunctional band now broken and scattered, strode from the alleyway like an angry bull, his steps seeming to shatter the concrete squares of the sidewalk as he came. From beneath his smooth, silent leather, he drew an eighteen-inch machete from a hidden back-mounted sheath. His eyes glared with fire and his voice grated like it could shatter glass, its underlying bass seeming to filter up as if from Hell itself.

"Couldn't leave well enough alone, could ya, old man? This is *our* time, and the goats belong to *us!*" he bellowed. On the last word, the passenger-side window of the ruined fir-green Buick shattered inward, covering the shaking driver in a shower of tiny glass chunks.

Dominique was half out of the van when the big bruiser in the leather jacket stormed out of the alleyway and punched his fist through the passenger-side window of the stalled Buick in front of them.

Joe must have been playing around near the back of the newsvan. "Hurry it up, Joe! Hurry, you're missing it!" she shouted back to him, her eyes sparkling, her mouth unable to prevent itself from curling into an excited, adrenaline-fueled grin.

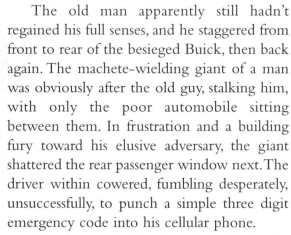

The old man apparently still hadn't regained his full senses, and he staggered from front to rear of the besieged Buick, then back again. The machete-wielding giant of a man was obviously after the old guy, stalking him, with only the poor automobile sitting between them. In frustration and a building fury toward his elusive adversary, the giant shattered the rear passenger window next. The driver within cowered, fumbling desperately, unsuccessfully, to punch a simple three digit emergency code into his cellular phone.

"I'm hurryin'—I'm hurryin'…" was the only satisfaction Joe could give the impatient Dom who dictated the play-by-play to him from her seat in the bleachers.

Finally, in what he considered a record-breaking thirty seconds, Joe had the camera out and prepped, but he was never fast enough for Dom. He ran forward, leading with his camera lens, hoping the action was as tense as Dom had made it sound over the constant bleating of the car alarm.

Billy Sanchez had seen the first blows land equally between the two combatants: Robin Hood and the evil leather knight. The thug, though, had then smashed the empty whiskey bottle over his savior's head, and then pummeled the dashing swordsman into the brick wall just above the remains of the camcorder.

The leader of the gang was huge, though not nearly as large as the muscle-bound brutes now sprawled in pain out on the sidewalk. There was an indistinct quality about him, an underlying menace. It convinced Billy that the threat posed here was greater than that of some pair of bullies who could merely break your leg or crack your skull.

Suddenly, he feared there were worse things than death. He had watched as his savior, sword and all, was hefted up in two powerful leather-clad arms and thrown from the alley like a rag doll. Billy had instinctively covered his head when he heard the distant crashing impact followed by the blaring of horns and alarms.

As his tormentor ran from the alley in pursuit of his newest target, Billy realized he'd been forgotten. While he had never been bright, he'd never been considered stupid either—general life on the streets notwithstanding. He opted to make a run for it. Maybe someday, he'd run into Robin Hood again and would thank him properly.

Billy only got as far as the alley's entry and stopped cold.

A giant red-scaled ogre—as large as the crocs Billy had seen in the zoo as a child, but standing upright like a man—stalked around the green car. It left smoking dents in the vehicle every time its flaming fist slammed into the trunk, doors, roof, hood. Steam now blew upwards from the shattered radiator. In its other massive, burnt-orange paw, it held a sword of dripping, yellow-red fire.

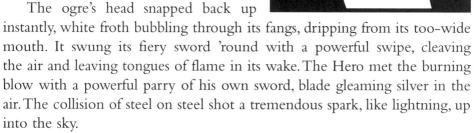

The swordsman, though, Billy's savior, his Hero, leapt feet-first through the steam, over the hood of the devastated car. One foot slammed into the ogre's face, cracking its neck sharply with the blow, and driving the massive bulk backwards with the force and momentum of his own powerful form.

The ogre's head snapped back up instantly, white froth bubbling through its fangs, dripping from its too-wide mouth. It swung its fiery sword 'round with a powerful swipe, cleaving the air and leaving tongues of flame in its wake. The Hero met the burning blow with a powerful parry of his own sword, blade gleaming silver in the air. The collision of steel on steel shot a tremendous spark, like lightning, up into the sky.

"Oh...my...god..." uttered Dom, her eyes wide, mouth gaping, uncharacteristically dumbfounded. She had just witnessed the decrepit seventy-year-old street geezer leap over the hood of an automobile with barely two steps' lead...*and kick another man in the face.*

Dom nudged Joe. The cameraman answered with a whispered, "Got it." *She didn't quite know exactly what they had gotten, but she knew it was gold.*

The guy in the leather jacket had a blade to meet the old man's fence pike, and the two now dueled as if they were gladiators in some ancient coliseum. 'Round and around the beleaguered Buick, the clatter of tempered steel against corroded iron filled the air about

them with sparks. Hunched and ducking, the hapless driver within the car appeared to have finally reached the police and was desperately explaining his plight. Again and again, deflected blows rained down upon his vehicle, battering the chassis, some of them powerful enough to crumple even the protective inner frame.

The scene was quickly drawing its share of neighborhood spectators, the gawkers and the merely curious, to witness an actual car-wreck in the making. Most seemed entertained, but one got Dom's attention. "Hey, either of you call the cops yet?"

Dom was smugly dismissive. "We're not a rescue squad, we're journalists," she said. "Keep shooting, Joe," she added as an aside to her partner, the only one of the pair actually doing the job. Her arrogance con-  cluded with an exultant flurry of justification: "…And *this is news!*"

Billy Sanchez felt the air grow colder as heavy clouds billowed in, filling the sky high over his head, arriving suddenly, as if from nowhere. The Hero and his monstrous adversary continued trading blows. Every clash was accompanied by building rumbles of thunder, each louder than the last, every strike of dual steel charging the air with lightning and fire.

Then the ogre raked a fiery claw across the Hero's chest, ripping, splitting open the ornate vest. It smelled blood and roared triumphantly into the sky. It was answered by a crackling peal of thunder and the start of a steady fine rain.

The heroic swordsman, though, shouted even louder than the growing tempest: "I grow weary of this. Let there be an end to the contest!" He renewed their battle with even greater ferocity than before. The creature's every defense was obliterated before the Hero's onslaught until, with one mighty upswing of his gleaming weapon, he hacked off the flaming sword arm of the beast, flinging it high into the storm.

The rain fell still harder, obscuring visibility beyond twenty feet, as if the torrent were building to a flood, and yet Billy swore he saw jets of liquid fire

stream out from the monster's severed limb.

Dom's expression of glee turned to unexpected horror and froze damningly on her face. She had seen a hand fly into the air. To her eyes, it seemed to hang for an eternity, preserved in brilliant sunlight as some strange testament to all that was truly wrong with humanity.

Then she saw the guy in the leather jacket fall to his knees, clutching the pulsing stump, unable to stop spouts of jetting blood, agony and horror etched on his young face. Dom heard him say, "Mercy...please!"

The old man, though, was merciless.

The bleeding guy fell forward and tried crawling away from the ferocious assault, but he barely got three feet before the old man pinned him to the ground with a stomping foot. The guy looked up briefly at the gathered crowd, noticing, then singling out Dom herself, locking his eyes with hers. She saw the pleading and the pain. She heard him cry out, begging to her alone, it seemed, "Please...help me! Get this lunatic offa me!"

The old man screamed, "Shuttup!" and then, grabbing hold of the leather coat with his free hand, yanked the young man back up onto his feet.

Billy Sanchez was now soaked to the skin, yet he barely noticed. He watched the Hero grab the giant ogre's scales, as its forked tongue screamed rage and hatred of all mankind.

Yet the Hero shouted back, "Shut your lying mouth!" With that, he flung the beast into the air with one arm and brought it crashing down onto the roof of the car that had served as centerpiece to the epic conflict. The remaining glass shattered and all four tires exploded simultaneously.

The swordsman followed, leaping onto the roof as well. "No more lambs, nor even the goats, shall heed the poison of your forked tongue!" he cried.

The ogre's head lolled over the roof's edge, dangling in where the windshield used to be. It tried rolling away, desperate to avoid the coming blow. Tears, almost pitiable, streamed from its eyes, turning into fire when touched by the rain. Saliva drooled from its fanged mouth and began melting through the paint and steel of the Buick's hood.

Billy remembered its missing hand, the one that had offered its lighter to the vicious younger punk who had wanted nothing more than to be just like his idol. Billy remembered his own arm wreathed in fire, and the smell of his own flesh burning.

Billy Sanchez felt no pity.

The Hero raised his sword high into the gale, as if challenging Heaven, or perhaps invoking it to be Witness and Judge of his actions. Lightning struck the very tip of his risen steel, and the instant crack of thunder exploded louder than any that had preceded it.

Even so, the voice of the Hero, sharp as his blade, rose above the fury of the accompanying storm, declaring an oath: "In memory of the martyrs, and in the name of the Most High, I cast you from this realm, now and forevermore. *Begone!*"

And the swordsman plunged three feet of avenging steel deep into the belly of the ogre—through its gullet, for it had no heart—and pinned it to the roof of the demolished automobile beneath.

The storm abruptly ended. The rain stopped, puddles instantly evaporating as if they had never been. One climactic clap of thunder echoed, but only in the minds of those who thought they heard it. The ogre had simply vanished, replaced by just another thug in a leather jacket. His lifeless head lolled off the crumpled roof of the devastated Buick, its fir-green hue now running red, looking like Christmas for the morbid and disturbed.

The crazy old man stood atop the entire scene, like a mad conductor still clutching his baton—the iron pole he'd rammed straight through the thug's body. It had punctured the roof, and nearly impaled the vehicle's panicked driver, missing him by scant inches.

The old man blinked his eyes, seemingly unused to direct daylight, and shook his wispy, grey-white head as if clearing his mind from the grip of some waking nightmare.

A policeman, his gun drawn and beaded on the old man, shouted, "Drop it!"

Only then did the old man appear to notice the world around him. The police officer was accompanied by three others, all in similar posture.

The old man suddenly jerked at the iron pole, trying to pull it free from the crime scene of the damned, but it momentarily caught, either on the ridges of the punctured steel roof or the hoodlum's rib cage—it was hard to say which. Then the spike yanked free and the decrepit murder suspect held it out at his side, almost daring the servants of law and order to take it from him.

"Drop it or we drop you," the officer shouted a second time, unwilling to take any chances.

The old man hesitated—weighing his options, or possibly the odds—then tossed his weapon down to the ground. It clinked twice as it hit the concrete of the sidewalk and rolled. The simple shaft of rusted iron bar came to a stop at the head of the alley, at the feet of Billy Sanchez.

Chapter Four

"And that was the scene, moments ago, as police apprehended the alleged murderer, caught in the act live by WDVL cameras."

Ever the professional, Dom stood confident and assured, microphone in hand, against a backdrop of police and paramedic wrap-up. With a simple glance over her shoulder she could direct the audience's attention to the action behind her, before yanking it straight back to herself with only the merest inflection of voice and tone. Such was the intent as her glance took in the suspect—the old vagrant, handcuffed and vacant-eyed—as he was ducked into the caged rear of a patrol cruiser. The vagrant, though, suddenly jerked back upright, as if somehow knowing the camera lens represented the eyes of thousands. He locked his dark eyes with Dom for just an instant, and then a flash of recognition showed on his deeply-lined features.

"Dulcinea!" he cried suddenly, and desperately struggled in the police officers' grip, but their experienced hands quickly resecured the old man into the rear seat and locked the door. He began banging his forehead against the window.

Dom turned back to her viewing audience, her eyes alone betraying just a hint of rattled nerve. "This is Dominique Angel, reporting live for WDVL News." Her tone remained professional.

The old man continued to butt his head against the patrol car glass, smearing greasy, black street grime from his forehead against the inside of the window. His jaw worked frantically, continuing to shout to an audience that no longer heard as the patrol car whisked him away.

"And we are...*clear*—off the air," stated Joe, signaling that their live transmission to the home studio was disconnected, thereby avoiding the potential for embarrassing outtakes going out live. "Man, that was weird," he added.

Dom's shoulders drooped. The microphone dropped into the listless swing of her arm, and she staggered right past Joe without comment, back toward the newsvan.

"What did that guy say?" he asked. "What the heck is a 'dolseneao'?"

"Dulcinea," she absently corrected him. Joe nodded, as if the jumble of syllables suddenly explained everything.

Without another word, Dom tossed the mike inside the van's side door, then stooped to pick up something near the rear tire that had caught her eye.

She steadied herself against the gleaming white exterior, her breath coming in a sudden succession of rapid pulses, as if making up for missed opportunities. Joe wasn't sure what had unnerved her so, witnessing an actual murder, attracting the old killer's attention, or whatever it was she'd seen on the ground—maybe it was a combination of the three. Dom didn't look at the object she held, but Joe saw it was a small, plastic, soot-covered dolly head that she now clutched tautly. Her eyes stared ahead, fixed on nothing. His concern rose.

"You OK, Dom?" he asked.

There were a few tense moments of silence until she finally gave him a brief shake of her head in the negative, but then caught herself. The shake became a nod. Her breath returning to a slow and steady pace, she looked up and gave her cameraman a little smile.

Detective Benjamin Saunders sat opposite the old guy—their seventy-year-old homicide suspect—both lit by the washed-out glare of overhead fluorescents. Under this light, Saunders's chocolate brown hands appeared charcoal grey as they squashed the life out of an eighteenth cigarette. The previous seventeen sat in the ashtray like little broken men.

The yellowed "NO SMOKING" sign that had hung for nearly an eternity had been replaced recently by a new, bright-plastic incarnation that stated, "THIS HAS BEEN DESIGNATED A NON-SMOKING AREA."

Saunders's face appeared to have been chiseled with long, dark lines by some mad sculptor, then patched together by grey stubble. His eyes sagged with the packed bags of a vacation that never seemed to come. He exhaled

his last cloud of nicotine with a heavy sigh, letting another breath of smoky atmosphere into the stale air of the little room. Lung cancer was a terrific excuse for early retirement. Saunders couldn't wait.

"So, it's been three hours..." Saunders muttered, realizing he was definitely talking only to himself, "I guess you really do have *nothing* to say."

The old man looked asleep, his eyes vacant under half-drooped lids. Thirty minutes ago, Saunders had witnessed the excitement of a string of saliva drooling from the vagrant's unmoving lip, then hanging by a two-inch

thread for a tantalizing five minutes, before finally falling onto the bum's ragged trench coat.

Saunders no longer knew whether his partner was still watching from the other side of the two-way mirror or not. More than likely, the much younger Detective had left the formality of this particular interrogation of his own accord and without a word. Regardless of the breech in protocol, Saunders couldn't say he blamed him.

He finally called it a night himself and left the little room, downing the

remaining rancid drops of cold coffee—poured over an hour earlier—and tossing the little Styrofoam cup onto the floor next to the little plastic trash can stenciled, "PLEASE KEEP OUR DEPARTMENT CLEAN."

The old man just stared at the little spires of smoke rising from the little broken men.

Chapter Five

In 1927, WDVL Broadcasting struck a deal with the devil. Executives in black robes performing arcane rituals against a storm-tossed night sky. Thunder. Lightning. Human sacrifice and contracts signed in blood. Thus it prospered through the lean years and the fat, and had led a diabolically charmed existence ever since.

None of that was true, of course, despite the incriminating call letters they'd been issued by the FCC. But such had been the wink-and-a-nod banter about the office coffeemaker and water cooler for over fifty years, as employees celebrated or denigrated the media juggernaut's unparalleled success.

Before the post-war boom of the 1950s, the thirty-three-story WDVL building had dominated the city skyline, due in large part to the massive steel-girder transmission tower that rose an additional ninety feet into the sky.

By the 1960s, however, the building and its tower were considered little more than an eyesore, a rust-tinged blemish on a modern city trying to compete on the national stage. Public outrage, instigated by rival media moguls and fueled by paid-off bureaucrats, called for the great tower's removal. As the debate made its way through the legal system, WDVL was cited on many charges, not the least of which was the potential danger of structural failure. Management fought back tooth and nail, as the issue rapidly became a matter of company pride versus the envy of adversaries. Once the tower was proved stable, however, it was the plaintiff's case that collapsed. In victory—and spiteful retaliation—management celebrated by having five steel-cased frames, each ten feet high and housing bright red neon spelling out their broadcast call letters and station number, audaciously bolted down the side of their now-famous, controversial fixture.

In later years, three additional sets of call letters were commissioned so that all four sides of the pyramidal structure would shine like a beacon upon every corner of the city. In time, that refurbished tower and its fiery red glow

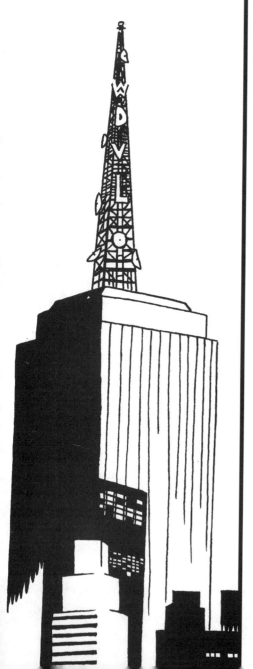

seemed to alter the very heart of the city itself, as it became the focus for all the questions, and source of all the answers, regarding life's mysteries, controversies, scandals, news, sports, and the weather.

Today, though, in the age of digital transmission and balcony-mounted satellite dish reception, there was no longer any need for such a gaudy steel pinnacle to puncture the skyline. Yet when WDVL executives upgraded the entire studio complex and decided to remove the tower and its iconic steel-cased lettering, the unexpected public outcry was as passionate as it was surprising. It seemed that an entire generation had grown up in its shadow, and now couldn't bear to lose such a precious historic landmark. From newspaper editorials to organized letter campaigns to massive street protests and national news coverage, the vociferous clamor eventually roused even local politicians to chime in on the debate.

Support our legacy—Save the tower!

In the end, the tower remained. Not the tallest structure any more by far, but high enough. It rose above the city, as staunch, beloved, and unmovable as that legendary steel assembly that dominated the Hollywood Hills. The tower and its bolted call-letter frames had become a symbol: of the city, the company, and the day-to-day affairs conducted in the offices, newsrooms, and studios beneath it…

WDVL 6—Making News Happen!

In all its long history, previous station managers had possessed bright offices with glass walls that signified their availability to all who worked for them— an open door policy that promoted trust, cooperation, and *family*. And WDVL Broadcasting had always been just that: one big, happy family, whose professional business was the news.

Current station manager Desmond Cortez, on the other hand, conducted his WDVL family affairs from the confines of a dim, mahogany-paneled office with deep-plush burgundy carpeting. One lone window gave him access to a stark sunset two-thirds of the year, and rendered his sanctum a tomb for the remainder. Currently, the office was bright with strips of light alternating with slatted shadows cast by the blinds.

WDVL network personnel was comprised of those Desmond liked and those he did not. Those Desmond disliked did not remain long, and rarely found successful employment elsewhere in the field. Desmond liked Dominique Angel.

Dom now stood in Desmond's office, treating herself to a replay, and her boss to a first-time viewing of that day's entire unedited spectacle, starting with Joseph Caparelli's aborted interview attempt, then cutting directly to the lethal afternoon battle to which Dom had been a front-row witness, and culminating with the old vagrant's attempt to get her attention as he was led away by the police.

Viewed this way, Dom thought she could process events from a detached perspective; speculate on the deeper significance, formulate opinion, every- thing her training was supposed to have prepared her for. "Live and in person," today's events had troubled her enough. Now, however, she found that "detached and distant" rattled her even more.

The old man had called her "Dulcinea," the fictional inamorata of the equally-fictitious *Don Quixote*. That was an identification she could do with- out. Dom had been called many things in her twenty-seven years, but she had never been called a "whore" with such obscure, literary eloquence before. She didn't believe there were too many other ways to interpret the old man's bizarre exclamation. She quickly decided she preferred the more straightforward approach to accusation and insult; at least that way you knew where the attack was coming from.

A little smirk sat near the very top of Desmond Cortez's six-foot-four-inch frame. He gestured to the video's climax, wherein a troubled Dominique Angel signed off as the raving, elderly lunatic batted his head against the glass window of the patrol car that finally sped him away. "It looks like you have an admirer," he said coyly.

Dom hated when her boss played these kinds of games. She pulled her still-frayed nerves together by a decisive act of will and answered him sharply. "He's a kook and a murderer, Mr. Cortez. I try my best not to associate with either."

Judging by her tone, it could have been taken as a charge against him, however unfounded or unwarranted. Desmond glanced at her sharply. Dom was like that: strong and direct—two of the many reasons he liked her so much. He let the jab slide.

It was whispered on the news floor that Desmond had been a college football star whose glory was sidelined by an undisclosed injury, but the burly station manager had never satisfied their curiosity. No one had ever actually been able to track down the college from which he'd graduated, and those who'd originally hired him had long since departed.

Dom continued, "But still, he is a bit of a mystery. I did a little quick checking on him after we got back in: no ID—doesn't match any outstanding case files, hospital or sanitarium records, Veteran's Administration. No one's claiming ownership of this old dog."

Dom stopped the tape and hit rewind. "He refuses to give a name. Won't even talk for that matter...or so my sources tell me," she added.

Desmond's eyes narrowed. "Your 'sources' tell you?" he asked.

Now it was Dom's turn to play coy. "Every good reporter has her sources...you know that." She gave Desmond that cute little smile he liked so much, the one that told him she was letting him in on her joke. He always responded with a minute smile of his own, letting her know he appreciated the inclusion. It was one of the things she liked about him.

Desmond didn't smile in return.

Dom quickly assumed that his mind must be on other matters and probably wanted to keep business as business. She changed her tack and continued into the wind undaunted. "This will work terrific with my election angle. I'd like the chance to follow up on this one, Boss." She looked him directly in the eye as only she could. "That is…with your permission, sir," she added, softening.

Desmond didn't seem able to keep her gaze—*that was new*—and lowered his face. He answered without looking up, seeming to fixate on his shoes while stroking his trim black goatee with his left hand, "*Nada*. This one is too screwy. I want you to drop it."

Dom couldn't help but break into a wide, schoolgirlish grin. "I don't believe this…you're actually worried about my safety. He likes me, ladies and gentlemen! The big, burly man with the heart of stone really, really *likes* me!"

Desmond simply turned away and went around behind his cluttered desk, perusing the various bundles of busy-work. "If you say so, Dom. But you've got too much good going for you to muddy the water with something like this. I'm telling you to drop this one. That's an order."

"And did you hear that, folks?" Dom continued, her voice chipper and playful. "He doesn't deny it! How noble. How chivalrous! My gallant knight. Who would have guessed Desmond Cortez was capable of such a thing?"

Desmond pulled a copy of that day's leading newspaper from the desk's clutter and held the front page up for her to see. The grinning visage of Gubernatorial-hopeful Henry Devlin stared back at her.

"I'm not impressed," she answered smugly. "I prefer the big one off the Boulevard—the one that says 'Hi!' to me on my way to work every morning. There's just something about that man's head, twenty feet high, staring through my windshield, that makes me want to say, '*Take me, I'm yours.*'" She giggled.

"You're not hearing me, Dom," said Desmond. "Henry Devlin is coming to town next month. Now, if you treat me right…"

He let the statement hang in the air like a baited hook.

Dom gave him a knowing glance, refusing to be so easily reeled in, encouraging him to finish with a smile that said she was waiting to be impressed.

"I can get you an exclusive with our next State Governor," he finished without flourish or fanfare.

Dom *was* impressed. But she kept the game afloat. "That sounds to me like clear-cut grounds for a charge of sexual harassment." She smiled slyly as she spoke.

"Absolutely," answered Desmond, dropping the paper back onto the clutter. Cortez was not an unattractive man, looking just a touch like a bald wrestler turned politician. His great arms, sleeves rolled up casually to reveal spectacular biceps for a desk jockey, reached across to pull Dominique forward and onto the piled mess of yesterday's news. She came willingly, and let his subtle guidance twirl her body around so that her rear end touched the desk first, before his sure grip gently lowered her onto its surface.

"You utterly evil, evil man," gasped Dom in a whisper. "Help me…oh somebody help me," she added, with little conviction of an actual plight.

She was going to keep it up until Desmond silenced her with his lips. He did just as she'd intended, and she felt the man's electricity, strength, his sheer power converge and connect in that kiss. He pinned her to the desk, but she was his willing slave.

Dom knew that here was the only man in all the world for whom she would do anything he asked. On that score, she had already proven herself beyond reproach—body and soul. She believed in Desmond Cortez and everything he said he could do for her career. It was only a matter of time. And loyalty.

She felt his weight pull away from her chest as he broke the embrace. She felt the pressure depart from her like a mother surrendering her child: she didn't want it to go.

But Desmond had already straightened his tie and was unrolling his sleeves, readjusting his prim and professional appearance before Dom could even slip off his desk. The clutter fell to the floor around all four sides, as Dom began to restore her appearance to be proper enough for general office

viewing. Suspicions abounded but the pair of them had played it carefully enough that the office family had no proof; and in matters such as these, faith without facts was worthless.

She found herself still reeling from Desmond's offer, though— *"our next State Governor,"* he had said, as confident of the political outcome as he was of his ability to grant Dom her career boon. "But…Henry Devlin?" she queried with just a hint of disbelief. "The election primary is still weeks away."

"Formality," he stated, as if concern was irrelevant.

She nodded, buying into his confidence, and smoothed her light blue

skirt as she stood, looking for all the world like far more than a mere stolen kiss had transpired. "So, tonight, then," she changed the subject, "is it my place again, or yours?"

He eyed her almost casually, as if nothing more had taken place than that

Dom had brought him the day's mail. "Just remember…you're *my* Dulcinea."

His tone was even, smooth, and landed like a solid punch to her stomach. As her prior musings had concluded, there were only so many ways to interpret such a comment, but she smiled nevertheless. Only her eyes showed the slight glint of betrayal his words had invoked.

Desmond noted the pain in her eyes and gave her a big warm smile, assuring her he had only been joking.

"My place, Dom. I'll see you tonight," he said.

Chapter Six

It had been called "The Roundhouse" for as long as anybody could remember, even before its relatively modern architecture had been designed as two great wheels connected by a large chunk axle. It was Police Headquarters for one of America's largest urban sprawls, and it housed enough riff-raff to earn its sordid reputation as a first step toward the end of the line.

As in most centers of urban blight, the Roundhouse didn't distinguish between its drunk tank—for those only spending the night—and those unable to make bail, staying for a longer haul until transfer to a more secure facility could be arranged before their arraignment and trial. Thus both the mother-rapers and father-rapers—as Arlo Guthrie had once called them, long ago and tongue-in-cheek—shared the same cells, the same benches, with shoplifters, graffiti taggers, and piss-drunk loiterers.

Billy Sanchez was sharing his cell with only three other men, and for that he counted himself lucky—except for the all-pervasive stench of urine. That, and his incarceration in the first place. He had tried telling the arresting officers how *he* was the victim, and he had the injury to prove it. But the scene of his attack and subsequent rescue had become such a mess that the cops weren't interested in listening to stories—*much less from someone who had no voice*. Billy surmised the only reason he wasn't now sharing a cell with those who had attacked him was because his savior, the Hero, Robin Hood or whoever the hell he really was, had left them all in need of serious medical attention. Of those still alive—specifically, the three who couldn't run away—he guessed they were resting up on comfy motorized beds at the end of some hospital's security corridor. Sure, they were still under arrest, but Billy considered their plight versus his own to represent the fundamental

flaw of civilization: *crooks invariably become the victims, while the victims are viewed as crooks.*

Even the black detective that questioned him had been no help. Souder, Sautter, or whatever the hell his name had been, Billy couldn't remember. He'd asked his questions all business and matter-of-fact like, nodded a couple of times, made sounds like he was agreeing with Billy's story, wrote in a little yellow pad he kept in his grey suit pocket, and lit up so many smokes that Billy was craving one for himself. When he asked, though, the detective pointed to the "NO SMOKING" sign and shrugged his shoulders as if everything was beyond his control.

Making up their own rules as they went along: just another reason Mama Sanchez's little boy hated cops no matter what color they came in.

But the one thing he still couldn't wrap his mind around was the vanishing thunderstorm. He'd seen it. He'd felt it. He'd been soaked to the bone. But then it was just gone. And no one but him seemed to have even noticed.

Billy's head hurt. Actually, it felt like his brain hurt, for, inside that sack of pickled mush that sloshed around the interior of his skull, agglutinated, dehydrated cells were making their protest known. He needed a stiff refill, a top-off of the tank fueling the spinning wheels that made the details of his day-to-day life blow by in an unrecognizable blur. Yet such engines of inefficiency are notoriously cranky, especially when their tanks of 100-proof fuel run low. Red warning lights signal first to the eyes, blinking on and off in distracting flashes that won't be ignored. Untended, the greased wheels in the brain will then ultimately seize up. The squeal of locking gears can be enough to wake the dead, or the merely unconscious. Without a constant intake (ultra or economy grade, it makes no difference), to fuel the rig and lube the works nose to tail, the pressure builds, threatening to explode the head of anyone that dares maintain such a delicate machine as the intoxicated brain. All in all, Billy just wanted to throw up.

The Roundhouse cell he occupied had been built to hold twenty, and was just one of a half-dozen others that made up the basement detention block. "A" and "B" were jam-packed with men and women respectively, but Billy practically had Detention Cell "C" all to himself.

He sat stiffly at one end of a long wooden bench, downwind of the smelliest sterno-bum he'd ever gotten a whiff of. *Talk about economy-grade.* Billy considered himself to be quite an expert on the subject of street stench—he'd often been a champion of such competitions in his own right. But this guy took the cake: he hadn't just dumped in his pants, the old geezer must have *bathed* in his own crap. Recently.

The cell's other two occupants looked like they'd been taken right off the street, right off their Harleys, and not on a mere D.U.I. or a drunk-and-disorderly brawl either—probably on more sobering charges that, if printed out, would reach all the way to the floor.  Moreover, each one of the pair outweighed Billy by three times at least. He hoped neither of them had an interest in either him or the space he occupied.

Billy soon realized his luck in this one instance, though, as the bikers' whispered exchange revealed they had their sights set on the old stink bomb polluting their air.

The shorter of the pair cruised over to the ancient bum like an alligator raised in a goldfish bowl. "Hey Grampa…you're sittin' on my bench."

The old bum gave no indication he had heard or even cared.

The larger buddy, the Great White that kept the little 'gator in line, made his wishes known a bit more sternly to avoid any misunderstanding. "Hey, shit-for-brains…you stink! Gonna have to tell you to park that stench o' yours downwind."

The old bum continued to ignore the pair looming over his frail form.

The bigger of the two was not used to being ignored. "You move that stinkin' ass of yours…'cause if I have to wash up after touchin' you, then that means there ain't gonna be enough of you left to clean up."

Finally, the old man looked at the pair. That's all Billy saw him do—look at them—and the pair immediately backed off, hands raised in peaceful diplomacy, telling the old geezer they were sorry, they'd made a mistake, and it'd never happen again.

But Billy had gotten a glimpse of that look in profile, and recognized a force there—as if every drop of water from every ocean on Earth was stored behind those two fathomless pools of darkness, waiting for the dam to burst. It was a look he'd seen in only one other set of eyes.

It took another hour before Billy sat out the pounding of his own head enough to wrestle up the courage to approach the old bum. The guy hadn't moved an inch since the biker duo had left him alone, and Billy couldn't tell if he was sleeping or simply dead—he might have laid odds on either possibility had circumstances been different.

As he got closer, inching down the bench, he noticed the old guy watching him, measuring his progress from the barest slit of one partially-opened eye. Even mostly closed, the old guy's eyes looked like they could snap open any instant and swallow him whole.

Billy's voice cracked when he spoke the first time, "Hey man…I knew it was you."

The old man was unresponsive. The sliver of eye may have blinked but Billy couldn't be sure. But unlike the bikers, the Hispanic didn't feel threatened. He tried again.

"I don't understand any of this, but…I know who you really are," Billy whispered, the gravity of his words pulling his voice down low.

At this, the old man's eyes opened fully, and his gaze fell upon Sanchez as from the Judgment Throne of Heaven. Billy didn't waver, at least not outwardly. The old man spoke over the volume of his stench. "I am not what you think."

Billy felt like he was falling straight into those dark pits, and in desperation he cried out, "You saved my life!"

The cell's other two occupants gave the scene a cursory glance, then resumed their own conversation.

Billy held up his freshly-wrapped arm as proof of his wound and identity, but moreso to prevent himself from being sucked out of his body and lost in the depths of those black pools, forever drowning, yet never dying.

"You saved my life," he repeated.

The old man closed his eyes and released Sanchez from the grip of his stare. Billy fell off the bench unsteadily to his knees. He wanted to throw up all over again. When the old man spoke a second time, his cracked, scratchy voice seemed to claw its way up from out of some dark forgotten hole where the destitute had lost interest in human speech.

"I did only that which is right...defend the weak, avenge the innocent. You owe me nothing," he said with a creaking finality that indicated the discussion had ended. Eyes closed, he let out a long, ragged, wheezing sigh.

Billy said nothing for what seemed the longest time. Perhaps the old man had indeed finally given up the ghost. He made no move nor sound, nor even seemed to expel any breath. But Billy had to confess what he'd done—not seeking absolution, nor even the approval of some late impromptu father figure lurking at death's door. It was simply the right thing to do.

Steadying himself with one hand against the bench, Billy confided, "I saved your sword."

Chapter Seven

"My angel," she'd called her...

"Mommy's little angel," she said as she took her by the hand. "And yes, you can bring along Molly Angel too," because Molly Angel was small and soft and beautiful, and had real plastic wings...

Two big arms wrapped around her as the little angel was told to hold on tight and never let go. She did just as she was told: she held on tight and wouldn't let go—her own tiny hands clutching Molly Angel just as tightly...

They were all going on a little trip—Mommy, Mommy's little angel, and Molly. They'd all fall asleep...and then, she said, the little angel would wake up in Heaven...

She closed her eyes. Mommy leaned back. And they both fell from the window...

Trying to restore as much order to her chaotic mood as she could under the circumstances, Dominique Angel had endeavored to get as many post-event interviews as possible before she and Joe had to return to the studio, but the pickings had been slim.

She had attempted an on-the-spot perspective from the driver of the wrecked fir-green Buick, but the man, one Archibald Jenkins, could barely string two coherent sentences together. Dom had quickly realized that he also smelled profusely. She decided to let that interview end abruptly, allowing Mr. Jenkins to waddle back to the police and his insurance agent who had also arrived on the scene.

Unfortunately, the actual victims of the old man's assault had been in no condition to even give the police statements, let alone grant interviews. The paramedics arriving on the scene had swooped in and barred any further access to them.

Her last hope had then been a Latino vagrant—confirmed name: William Sanchez. He was claiming to have been a victim as well—not of the old man, but of the young punks who lay about in various states of contortion and dismemberment and whom the paramedics were tending. He seemed to have a burned arm to prove his tale.

Dom had soon realized she was barking up the wrong tree, however, when Billy revealed he knew nothing about any crazy old man, but that he had been "saved by Robin Hood, who *shanked* the giant ogre." She'd rolled her eyes. Moments later, the police interrupted his rambling discourse on thunderstorms that came and went like "magic," and took the disturbed younger vagrant into custody as well.

Overall, Dom was not a happy camper. And the more she thought about the runaround, and the insult, that station manager Desmond Cortez had given her, the more stubborn and driven she became. Others could call her a cold-hearted, manipulative bitch who would

stab her own mother in the heart to get a story—*if they only knew*—but Dom considered her adamancy to be a boon and the true secret of her success. No jealous lover, implying she was a whore, was going to sidetrack her where and when a genuine story was concerned.

So now, here she was with good old dependable Joe, working extra-curricular hours in the old basement engineering department of WDVL. The first and second floor studios sat empty, disused and partially gutted. Management had recently moved the studio and all production operations to the top three floors of the WDVL building, and upgraded the entire facility with state-of-the-art digital systems.

Dom had Joe re-running the fight scene footage caught earlier, scrutinizing the taped scene of the crime as if they themselves were the guilty party. As the day had worn on, Joe's conscience was catching up to him.

Joe had seen death plenty of times—it kind of came with the territory—but he'd never actually witnessed anybody being murdered before. To finally see that act for himself, standing by like a spectator—even worse, zooming in

on the actual deathblow and catching the act on film—made him feel like a vulture. It was a feeling he was none too happy with.

Joe was also trying his best to keep the whole thing professional. He kept his 'DVL cap on, not just to hide his prematurely thinning scalp, but to maintain that distinction between the job and his private life: the cap came off every time he clocked out. That is, until tonight. This was his own time, offered up to keep Dom happy. But the cap of professionalism stayed on, helping him keep emotional distance, both from her and from what he'd recorded earlier.

On the seldom-used monitor, the old man once again took a standing jump right over the hood of that Buick, which now sat as so much junk in the police impound lot. On screen, Archibald Jenkins's fir-green chariot of middle-management self-importance lived once again, and the crazy old man was taking the proverbial flying leap just a bit too literally.

"There, Joe! Play that back again," Dom said. She could barely contain her excitement. Her cute, blue-skirted rump played teasing games with the seat of her chair—up and down, a little shake back and forth, but never a firm commitment to actually stay in her seat.

Joe kept his composure as he always did, keeping his eyes off the derrière, and invoking what he considered to be the cinema's only perfect theatrical experience. " 'You played it for her—you can play it for me,' " he wisecracked in his best *Casablancan* Richard Blaine voice.

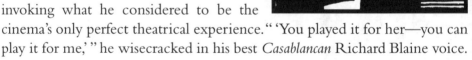

"And cut the Bogart, please," piped Dom, consumed by the video playback a little more passionately than she had been earlier that day when the old bum was merely a good angle on an existing story. "There—freeze that image!"

Joe complied, realizing the crazy old man now represented a story all his own, and Dom was salivating like a beggar at the feast.

"Didn't Cortez tell you to drop this?" he asked.

"I don't care. This one is mine!" Her eyes sparkled. Over the course of their working relationship, Joe had learned that Dom treated the participants of her stories as her property. It was as if they never existed, nor possessed any life or history of their own until she summoned them into being to support her cause.

"Now tell me, what do you see there?" she demanded.

The monitor had stolen a moment of time, a slice of the past preserved forever—or at least until the tape oxidized. There, on the screen, the old man hovered effortlessly above the Buick's hood, clutching a wrought iron fence post in one hand like a swashbuckler wielding a sword, and his foot, apparently wrapped in mere rags, outstretched and connecting powerfully with the jaw of his opponent.

"I see that the thug in the leather jacket should have been dead long before the old guy put that spike through his chest," said Joe. "Just look at how far back his head is snapped around. It's gotta be a trick of the angle or something."

"You filmed it, Joe," she replied. "Take it again, frame by frame."

Slices of flickering life inched the old man steadily forward in his flying arc, and they watched his foot now twisting the other's neck even further back at an even more impossible angle than they'd noticed before. The frame-advance finally revealed a major dislocation of the young man's jaw.

Dom's own jaw nearly dropped from her head. "That's no camera trick. That man should be dead."

"He is," answered Joe.

"You know what I mean."

"This has really gotten to you, hasn't it?"

…And then, she said, the little angel would wake up in Heaven…

Dom didn't answer, but she finally dropped into her chair. The tape continued forward again at normal speed. The kick concluded, leveling the recipient to the ground, his head doing a better Linda Blair than Joe could do Humphrey Bogart. The old man landed firmly, as if all he'd done was take a hopscotch skip, and the iron rod came crashing down in a blow seemingly intended to end the fight. But the "dead" guy rolled out of the way, and Dom and Joe watched in disbelief as his head and jaw *snapped back into place* and the battle continued to its conclusion. Joe's mouth hung open.

In the end, however, there was no doubting the young man was finally dead, an iron shaft plunged straight through his heart. They'd remained at the scene themselves for at least an hour, during which time he failed to rise or show any further sign of life. Meanwhile, the CSI boys and girls had finished their preliminaries and made way for the EMTs to take him down and zip him into a body bag.

The tape played to its broadcasted finale and Dom's sign-off. She was no longer paying any direct heed, her mind obviously elsewhere, but she deliberately turned away, eyes purposely closed, when the old man on-screen had drawn her attention with his shout. Several silent minutes elapsed, wherein Joe noticed that, in her lap, she nervously fingered the little, decapitated dolly head she'd found at the location.

For Joe, the curiosity was killing him. *It was now or never.* He ended the silence. "So, who—or *what*—is a 'Dulcinea?' "

She didn't answer right away, but stopped playing with the sooty, rubber head almost immediately. "It's nothing, Joe. She's just a character from *Don Quixote.*"

Joe nodded, again as if her vague answers were sufficient explanation, and began rewinding the tape in scan mode—history repeated itself in reverse. He gestured to the dolly head. "Is it anything connected to that?"

Dom seemed genuinely startled, more by the object in her hands than by Joe's question. "What? No," she answered herself, then called direct attention to the little fragment of discarded child's toy. Its hair was blonde and dirty. "This is nothing—memories, that's all."

She tossed it into the nearby wastebasket. Her action was casual. "A coincidental pair of unrelated issues," she added. "But why live in the past when you've got your whole future ahead of you?"

Joe knew her words were directed mostly at herself, and then realized he had wandered into dangerous territory. He calculated the odds of backtracking without triggering a landmine, and returned their attention to the incredible images flickering backward on screen. "What do you think we've got here?"

"I don't know *what* we've got. But I do know that guy must be seventy years old, at least…and he *jumped* over a car." Dom snaked out her hand and hit the pause button.

The screen filled with a frozen, blurred close-up of the crazy old man: his eyes still frightening, dark and terrible, the streak of his grimace, jagged, yellow teeth captured in a moment of snarling fury. He looked more like a rabid dog than a human being, and Joe felt the old mutt was looking right at him.

Dom continued to stare in disbelief until a little manic gleam crept up into her eyes, and her mouth curved into a tiny grin that made her look positively certifiable. Her tone changed to one of imperious excitement. "I want you to find every clear facial shot we've got of that old man, and print me a hard copy of every frame."

"But Desmond said—"

"Somebody owns this guy, Joe…and I'm going to find out what his story is."

Joe had seen that scary look on Dom's face before. He did as he was told.

Chapter Eight

"I saved your sword," Billy said again.

For the very first time, the old man appeared startled, and straightened up in his seat. His eyes bored into Billy's, asking questions his mouth refused to utter.

Billy blurted the rest, like a testimony too hot to hold onto any longer. "After you killed that giant ogre…after the rain disappeared…when the cops ordered you to throw it down…you threw it at my feet…your sword. So I took it…everybody was looking at you…or that other guy, I mean. I hid it back in the alleyway…I got this hidin' place behind some bricks…nobody knows about it…'cept me, I guess. But I hid your sword there where nobody'll find it…touch it. I felt it when I picked it up…the power… it's like…too _holy_ for anybody to touch…" His voice trailed off, and he looked down at the concrete floor, stained by the previous day's piss.

In a small voice, he added, "I'm just sorry…somebody like me had to touch it."

The old man spoke again, and for the first time in Billy's hearing, the gravelly voice softened to something more like smooth pebbles at the bottom of a stream. "This hiding place…could you take me there?" he asked.

Billy looked back up. The old man had closed his eyes again.

"When we get out…I'll take you," said Billy. They fell silent for a few moments.

"What are you called?" asked the old man at last.

"Name's Sanchez… Billy Sanchez."

A slight smile creased the old thin lips as if realizing some secret joke that only he understood. He opened his eyes and gazed down at Billy with a father's affection. "Do you believe, Billy Sanchez?"

Billy was confused, suddenly feeling as if he were being set up for some street corner con. "What? I don't—"

"Do you believe?"

The old eyes were still sadly tender, but the fire behind them that had been temporarily extinguished was sparking into life once again.

Billy fumbled, but blurted out what he hoped was the right answer. "Well, yeah…I guess…"

"Then come."

Abruptly, the old man stood upon solid legs. The other two men, who'd stayed on the opposite end of the cell, minding their own business in hushed whispers and silence for the past hour, started to their feet and

 backed against the far wall, their faces loudly expressing a fervent desire for at least ten *more* feet to separate them. The old man spoke, continuing what seemed to be an earlier conversation he'd had with someone else, his voice strong, sure, and filled with an indefinable passion burning from inside him. "…For it is by faith alone that your eyes have been opened to that which is just and true!"

The old man strode purposefully to the cell door, his gnarled fingers clutching the solid steel bars with both hands.

His stomach still queasy from his persistent hangover, Billy struggled back to his own unsteady legs. "What are you doing?"

Again, the old man simply looked at him, and for just an instant, Billy saw a flash of his savior from the alley: a gallant, handsome face, untouched by age or care, smiling back at him.

Then the lock snapped with a crack like gunfire, and the barred gate swung open upon its hinge.

The night shift officers were startled into confused action by sudden alarms and the cry of *"Jail break!"* The very idea was absurd.

The officer watching the video monitors yelled out, "Hey, I ain't kidding!" Two figures were making their way out of Detention C. The Roundhouse was usually secure, but it wasn't a prison designed for the long-term incorrigible. Its security was fairly basic and usually did the job without incident. But then, there were usually no such incidents to contend with.

The floor sprang into life. A handful of vets and a smattering of rookies unsnapped their holsters, always the first step before discovering exactly what was going on amidst an otherwise uneventful night.

The old man was upon them in an instant, a sharp kick bursting open the reinforced steel door leading out of the lock-up in the basement. The door should have automatically locked the moment the alarm sounded, but apparently had not. Obviously not: one old man came through it without even slowing down.

The room became a maelstrom of shouts, movement and sporadic gunfire. But no one could touch the old man darting mercurially through their midst. No one could draw a bead. Any who came close to the darting figure were tossed aside like small children in the way of a rampaging adult intent upon a goal they could not comprehend.

Then the second escapee—the Hispanic vagrant—charged brazenly and blindly in the old man's wake. Five-year veteran Lynn Washington nearly tackled the second, smaller figure, using her own formidable body strength to strike low and knock the younger man off balance. But desperation kept his feet steady. Pressing against a metal railing, the escaping prisoner let Washington's own momentum carry her past him.

On the brink of exit, the prisoner Sanchez hesitated and grabbed two handfuls of Lieutenant Washington's black jacket, pulling the stunned woman up with him, shuffling her out through the exit door as a human shield.

She buckled once in his grip and Sanchez lost his hold. He opted instead to push her forcefully back against the wall with all the strength he could muster. The breath was forced from her lungs. He drew back his small, bony fist, and the dazed Washington knew she'd never be fast enough to avoid the blow to her face.

A powerful voice cut across the din of shout and alarm, a voice that pealed like thunder. *"NO!"*

The Hispanic hesitated just long enough for Washington to raise her own fist. Then the old man was back, pulling the younger man's arm away from her. He spoke, "No, Sanchez. We seek only pardon. You will cause no unnecessary harm."

All that from the silent suspect Detective Saunders had called "brain dead" before he'd left for the night.

In that moment's hesitation, Lynn Washington threw her own punch and sent Sanchez reeling. Just as swift, she drew her service revolver from its well-oiled leather holster and beaded right between old John Doe's shadowy eyes. Like bottomless pits those eyes seemed to her, in the split-second before she commanded: "Freeze! Don't you so much as blink!"

She thought those eyes softened for just an instant, and the man who had spoken nothing to Saunders in three hours of interrogation said to her, "You have your whole life ahead of you. Don't make me hurt you."

She was holding the gun. Lieutenant Lynn Washington didn't have to take crap like that from anyone. She met the old man's dark eyes with a cold, steel gaze of her own.

She drew the hammer of her pistol back with a click that echoed in both their ears.

"Not another word," she said evenly.

The old man didn't speak, but his dark eyes flared instead, like the mighty firing of a great blast furnace.

Chapter Nine

"The woman is insane," Joe Caparelli pronounced as he dropped into his regular seat at the bar. Now that he was off the job completely—no more unofficial favors—his WDVL ball cap stayed off his head, back on the passenger seat of his SUV, leaving the balding young man looking a good twenty years older than he was.

He knew a decent, solid bald spot could make him look cultured and refined in the right circles. Even shaving his head completely was now not only considered socially acceptable, it was actually cool. Still, Joe couldn't seem to part any faster than necessary with what God had given him—and now seemed determined to "taketh away."

Mackie had held the seat for him, as usual, and listened to his ol' drinking buddy vent his frustrations, never once losing the wide dopey grin he kept plastered to his face.

"She's getting ready to pick a fight and she's picking it with the wrong guy. If I've learned anything since coming to 'DVL, it's that you don't mess with Cortez. I mean, I respect the guy and everything, but he's tough as nails when it comes to running the station his way—it's that or you're gone..." Joe snapped his fingers. "...Just like that. And here's Dom acting like she's got the boss-man wrapped around her little finger."

Mackie chimed in, "She's definitely got somethin' wrapped around somethin', if you ask me."

Joe glared.

"Face the cold hard truth of it, Joey, m'boy: You're in love with the broad, and she ain't got the time o' day for your sorry ass," Mackie said, the dopey grin never wavering.

Joe liked Mackie—liked him a lot actually. He and Joe had both interned at WDVL at the same time, both freshly scrubbed, just out of school, and still wet behind the ears. They'd both kissed the proper ass and made the grade. Joe was eventually teamed with the rising news starlet on the fast track to success, while Mackie got the whirlybird gig—"Eye in the Sky" traffic coverage and the occasional fire or police chase. Life was good, and neither cameraman had anything substantial to complain about. But that never stopped Joseph Caparelli.

"Believe me, it's anything but love. She knows how to do her job, she knows what she wants, and she doesn't let anybody get in her way—and I do mean *anybody*. I respect that. I respect *her*. I've got gobs and oodles of respect coming out my butt for her—but she's crazy."

"A guy uses the word 'oodles' when drinking with his best pal? Say whatever ya want…I know it's love," Mackie said, as if it decisively ended the matter.

Mackie waved to the bartender to get him and his fellow shooter their first shots of the evening—shots began and ended the night, and in between was just enough beer and peanuts to cushion the blow.

Mackie was born Macintosh McIlhenney III, fifth-generation descendant of big Irish money, which possibly explained why he had so little of it to his own name. Mackie had a big wide face, stretched that way by a lifetime of smiling. And just maybe, if you could connect all the little dots under his tousled red mop, you might see evidence of the joke that always kept him on

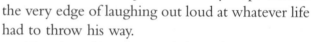

the very edge of laughing out loud at whatever life had to throw his way.

Together, the two raised their shots and initiated the weekly ritual that had bonded them for over the past three years. *Down the hatch.* Joe closed his eyes, keeping his glass raised until the trickle of burning warmth made its way to his gut.

Mackie clinked his glass down hard onto the bar. "Lay it out for me," he submitted, equally decisive. "You tell me what's got your panties in a bind."

Joe sighed, exhaling long and full, feeling the burn flare back up his throat and fill his mouth, bitter, sour, and satisfying as it matched his mood. "I witnessed a murder today."

Mackie had honestly believed Joe could say nothing to surprise him. He was wrong.

"I was there. I shot it. I did my job and never blinked. I don't even know what it was all about—some old dude put an iron spike through this tough guy. The police have him locked up. The D.A.'ll probably want our tape as evidence, but Cortez won't ever go for that—he'll fight 'em tooth and nail on the whole journalistic principle of the thing. Should be end of story, but now, none of the facts add up. This one's been weird from the get-go, and I'm not too ashamed to say I want to stay far away from it."

Joe paused, and signaled for the first of their beers. He said nothing more and soothed the burn, and his conscience, with a gulping draught.

Mackie re-primed the pump. "But Dom won't let it go."

"Correctamundo. Even Cortez thinks it's a big waste of time and specifically told her to drop it. But you know Dom, once she gets some idea in her head…"

"A bitch with a bone." Mackie grinned.

Joe immediately thought of the little dolly head clutched in her fingers, and hid his annoyance at Mackie's insistence with a shake of his own head. "She's good, Mac—really good—sometimes too good. One of these days I'm afraid it's gonna blow up in her face."

"And take a big bite outta your ass 'cause you're standing too close."

Joe nodded.

"And you're afraid your biography's gonna be written by Melville."

Joe laughed, but quickly dismissed the gag with a wave of his hand and drained his glass. "You always were the scholarly one," he added, making his statement sound like a question.

Mackie put on a thick ethnic brogue. " 'Call me…*Ishmael.*' "

Joe only smiled, searching for his intended question but unable to find it. "I mean, back in school…you were always the one with your head in a book. I'd be hosting Woody Allen Night, and you'd be in the back of the room spouting off random quotes from *Wuthering Heights.*"

Mackie agreed. "What can I say? Chicks dig a guy who knows the difference between Austen and the Brontë sisters."

"Then what can you tell me about Don Quixote?"

"*Man of La Mancha*—the Broadway musical?"

"I guess."

A man of exemplary insight, Mackie thought he knew where the question was leading, and dropped his minimal guard. "Well…my gramma had *Jim Nabors—Greatest Hits.* I grew up on Gomer Pyle crooning out 'To Dream…the Impossible Dream'…"

Mackie could not sing, but he wiped his brow from the effort nonetheless.

Joe rolled his eyes and performed a quick scan around the room to see if anybody had noticed. It seemed they were safe for the time being.

Mackie concluded his assessment of '60s pop culture. "Soul-stirring stuff. Puts that Pavarotti guy to shame." He seemed sincere, but with Mackie you could never tell.

"But wasn't it a movie too, or something?"

"Richard Kiley originated the role on stage—made him famous. It's a great play. Lousy flick, though—Sophia Loren, Peter O'Toole in the Quixote role." Mackie drained his own glass.

Joe still looked stumped.

"Unless you're asking about...the book?" said Mackie.

"Aren't they the same thing?"

"We're talkin' two very different kettles of fish, my friend."

"OK, enlighten me."

"It's like the difference between, have you ever actually read *The Bible*, or are you still waiting for the movie version?"

Joe didn't bite.

Mackie continued. "*The History of That Ingenious Gentleman Don Quixote De La Mancha*. One of the classics," he rattled off, waving his hand expressively, "by this guy, Cervantes. Written a coupl'a hundred years ago or such.

"It's about this crazy dude around the time of the Spanish Inquisition, who goes nuts from reading too many trashy novels. He fixates on this country lass, and then transforms her in his own mind into this ideal Lady, fighting for her virtue as a knight-errant, thereby justifying all his nutzoid behavior as some holy crusade. The book paints him as a lunatic—noble, but definitely loco. It's a hoot! The *musical*, on the other hand, turns him into some tragic, romantic hero in search of higher ideals. Go figure. Now what's that tell you about Western civilization?"

"What's the deal with 'Dulcinea'?" Joe couldn't get the day's events out of his head.

"Ah," said Mackie, obviously enjoying the opportunity to clarify some literary misunderstanding that was so near and dear to his heart. "That's where most people make their mistake. 'Dulcinea' doesn't even appear in the book; *she doesn't exist*. Quixote makes her up in his head. It's his squire, *Sancho Panza*, who makes the connection that 'Dulcinea' is really inspired by this peasant girl, *Aldonza*, the Don knew when he was sane but was too self-conscious or embarrassed to do anything about it.

"Sancho suspects the whole knight-errant thing is to try to make himself worthy of the gal he can't get up the courage to ask out face-to-face. Sound like anybody we know?"

Despite Mackie's teasing question, Joe still looked lost, even distant. He stared into his empty glass, watching the tiny remnants of foam bubbles popping into nothingness. *Vanity, vanity, all is…as it is,* he paraphrased in his mind, *and it all adds up to nothing in the end.*

Not one to be put off, Mackie continued, "The musical takes this minor

sub-plot and makes it the focal point of the entire show. *Man of La Mancha* takes Aldonza the peasant girl and turns her into a tavern wench prostitute to reinforce Don Quixote's noble delusion, but in the original book, she isn't.

"The Broadway version is faithful to the *spirit* of the novel, but most folks today think they're the same thing and they're not. It's like apples and oranges: they're both fruit…*they're just different kinds of fruit.* The original Dulcinea/Aldonza wasn't a prostitute, but thanks to pop-culture, everybody thinks she is. Do you get it?" Mackie was hopeful as always.

Joe really didn't care about most of his buddy's ramble, but he thought maybe it was shedding some light, some rational sense onto the odd, even mysterious encounter that afternoon. *To popular misconception, the old man had effectively called Dom a 'whore' on live TV. Mortifying. Most especially when you're an up-and-coming media star.*

Mackie brought him back to the present. "Is any of this connected to that Dom business you're going out of your way to not be specific about?"

Joe shook his head, wishing he hadn't opened his mouth, even to Mackie. "It's nothing."

Mackie wasn't convinced. "Is it about *you*, Joe? The 'crazy guy in love with the tavern wench,' searching for his higher ideals?"

He answered, dragging himself kicking and screaming back to his original concern, "You know me…I don't take a stand on anything, but I'm with the big boss on this one. If the story's too freaky, you drop it. You don't stick your nose where it don't belong…or you might get it chewed off."

"I do know you, Joey…you 'stick your neck out for nobody.'" His Bogart impression sounded more like a bad John Wayne. Mackie was smart enough to realize his friend wanted to change the subject.

"And I do a much better Bogey," added Joe.

Mackie was not intimidated in his new effort to lighten the mood and kept on rolling as, perhaps, history's worst impressionist. " 'Out of all the gin joints in all the world, she walks into mine.' " He scowled and dropped his face into the peanuts. He began exaggerated chewing, eating his fill, like a man without arms.

Joe started snickering first, but it wasn't long before the two degenerated into sputtering, laughing slobs as only two best buds at the bar can do.

Joe thumped the table and got a refill without words.

Mackie batted his eyes and intoned, " 'We'll always have Paris.' "

The two lost it all over again.

A pair of early-thirties cuties, who had been eyeing the two from the opposite end of the bar, decided to pay their own tab and leave. Joe and Mackie never even noticed them.

Joe blew his nose, deep down thankful for the opportunity to drop the weight he'd been lugging all day. He looked at his friend and saw tears rolling down the laughing, freckled face.

"That really wasn't even damn funny," murmured Joe.

That alone was almost enough to get them started all over again, but they didn't; plenty of stares that they did notice were enough to quell the riot.

Mackie simply added, "I'll be Peter Lorre to your Bumpy Hogart."

"And we all know how well that turned out," answered Joe.

Mackie wiped the tears from his eyes, finally managing to stifle the giggles. "Yeah...but seriously, Joey. I give ya my word...anything ever goes down or blows up in your face...I'm there, dude...I got yer back."

Joe smiled. "You know that goes both ways...dude."

Mackie nodded with his ever-present grin. Both friends knew that if the worst ever did happen, one or the other would even the score.

Chapter Ten

The phone call came that evening at just past 1:15. It came via the secure line, the one that could not be tapped nor traced.

Desmond Cortez had spent most of his earlier evening wrestling with an angel. His angel. Dominique Angel. The sheets were still damp. His angel now dozed softly while he sat on his side of the bed, in darkness, nursing his *Courvoisier* and a fine Cuban *Cohiba*. Through the glass balcony doors of his penthouse suite, he watched the moon arc slowly across the sky.

The moon was still riding high, bright and full, with most of its evening journey still lying ahead. Billowy clouds were rolling in steadily, though, threatening storms for sometime before daybreak. But, regardless of whatever weather was put in its path, Desmond knew that Artemis the Huntress would finish her course unimpeded. He had the benefit of seeing the big picture, and very little could rock his faith. He'd have to have some serious words, however, with WDVL's beloved meteorologist—Constance McCleary—who had forecast crystal clear skies for that evening.

Desmond looked back over his shoulder for a moment. He found he was developing a genuine fondness for "his little angel." He'd have to be careful about that. The woman was very good at both of her jobs, having proven half of that summation over the course of several hours earlier. But he'd worn her out, and she'd earned her little rest before they started up again.

Just before the phone call intruded, Desmond thought he'd heard a very distant rumble of slow thunder. That warning sound had put him just

enough on edge that he was able to snatch up the phone before the first ring
had even finished. Dom didn't wake.

"Cortez, here…" he whispered into the night, and sat himself at the very
edge of the bed to make sure his voice wouldn't rouse her.

The call was bad news from an operative sent to the Roundhouse to
confirm an earlier report. The unnamed vagrant had escaped from secure
lock-up and taken another prisoner with him. An all-points bulletin had
been issued and the pair, although unarmed, were considered extremely
dangerous.

There was little else to add to the report other than how they had torn
the place up in their escape.

"Was anyone injured?" Desmond asked, not out of concern, but for what
deeper information the answer would give him.

Beyond cuts and bruises, only one officer had been seriously wounded: Lieutenant Lynn Washington had her shooting arm broken in three places; her gun itself was snapped in two. Her story made little rational sense.

Only one seriously injured, thought Cortez, *and that was probably because the policewoman had done something stupid.* The picture he believed he saw was becoming clearer, his suspicions steadily verified.

The voice of his operative on the other end added that the identity of the perpetrator had yet to be confirmed.

"I know who it is," said Desmond. *Or, I know what he calls himself,* he mused. "That'll be all. Keep me informed. Cortez, out."

Desmond disconnected the call with the press of a finger on the remote receiver. He sat silent for a moment, his own eyes burning like two smoldering coals in the moonlit room.

Far across town, the red letters of the WDVL tower blazed like an unquenchable fire. The sky behind it suddenly flashed. For a split second before fading, heavy storm clouds glowed ominously as if lit from another world.

Desmond depressed a speed-dial code and raised the phone to his ear a second time. A click connected him to a line over two thousand miles away.

"This is Cortez…I believe we may have a problem."

The roll of approaching thunder grew closer, and voluminous clouds began to obscure the bright face of the Huntress.

With or without the light of the moon, the alley looked the same as it had earlier that day. It was darker of course, with strands of yellow police crime scene tape now whipping about in the steadily rising breeze, but nonetheless it was the same place, day or night.

Billy Sanchez had led the stumbling old man along side streets and back alleys, ever vigilant for the constant roving of patrol cars. There had been a couple of near misses. Once, the old man had seemed to forget where he was, even though he was following Billy's lead. He had looked at the younger man, not with eyes of fire but with confusion and uncertainty. For a brief instant, their roles had been reversed, and it was Billy convincing the old man to believe *him* and to follow *his* lead.

Halfway across the city and they were now back to the scene of the crime. The old man hesitated again at the entrance to the dark alleyway, his face half in shadow, half in the halo of the sodium arc streetlight. He stared

back at the empty space where Archibald Jenkins's Buick had long since been towed away, seeming to fixate upon the dark splotches on the old tarmac. Billy guessed they were oil spots perhaps, or more likely the bloody remnants of the day's battle, awaiting Heaven's tears to wash away the stain. But hadn't it already rained that very day? He couldn't be sure of anything anymore. He gently took the old man's arm and turned him away from the street glistening with broken glass, and guided him slowly but surely into the darkness.

Once back in the dim recesses of the alleyway, lit only by city light reflecting off the sky, Billy left the old man's side to push away an old rusted dumpster from the wall—officially unused, yet still filled with years of accumulated trash and junk. Billy himself had been using it to accommodate his own dumps until that very afternoon.

He still wasn't feeling any better from the hangover that had been quite literally months in the making. But the air of urgency, the sense of mission in the old man's quest, and the adventure that had brought them back to this bleak corner of the city overrode such trivial concerns as an aching, pounding skull and a pair of eyeballs that threatened to inflate out of their sockets. Activity took his mind off the pain.

Billy crouched low and began to pull a sequence of loose bricks from the base of the wall. The building to which the wall belonged had once been a bustling textile mill, abandoned long before Billy was even born. Now it served as a brick fortress safeguarding the personal treasures of the Sanchez Estate.

"Right down here, I put it…you'll see," Billy babbled on as he bent low and reached his arm deep into the crawlspace. "I thought they were gonna see me…the cops I mean…thought they'd see me hidin' it back here… or me movin' the dumpster or somethin'…"

Billy's voice trailed off, only to be replaced by a new tone of frustrated disgust. "No, man…I don't believe it…it was here…I swear to god, it was here…but…the bastards must've seen me, and taken it…ain't nothing left here, but…"

Billy couldn't finish his sentence. His head and shoulders drooped as though all hope had suddenly been sucked out, leaving him with nothing but the pain stemming from his oxygen-deprived brain.

The old man reached down and placed a reassuring hand on Billy's shoulder. "Show me," he said.

Billy slowly pulled the last remaining treasure from his hiding place. "Ain't nothin' here now…but some old metal stick."

He held the three-foot-long shaft of iron spike in both hands, presenting it before the old man like it was a holy relic; he, on his knees, his head bowed as if in shame—or reverence.

"I'm sorry," was all he could say.

The thunderous rumbles drew closer.

…And then, she said, the little angel would wake up in Heaven…

But she didn't…and they didn't fly, or fall asleep. They just fell from the window, and she didn't wake up in Heaven at all. The little angel landed hard and it hurt…

Molly Angel exploded, its dolly head ripping free from its small plush body, and leaving the little angel clutching all that was left of its soft cherubic beauty and its real plastic wings…

Dominique Angel had awakened from her exhausted doze with the ringing of the first phone call despite her lover's attempt to nip it in mid-ring. She lay there, feigning sleep, keeping her breath even and steady. For all of Desmond's vaunted perceptions, he seemed not to notice her now-fraudulent slumber.

She listened to the first strange call conclude, and nearly roused herself to question its contents. Just as she prepared to roll over, however, Desmond punched in the second call. She lay still, continuing to eavesdrop upon the one side of the odd discourse, picking up enough to know that it was her crazy old man who was the prime topic of discussion. Furthermore, they brought up Gubernatorial Candidate Henry Devlin in ways that made no sense.

In the end, she heard Desmond add the name "William Sanchez" to a list that sounded suspiciously final, followed by "Devlin doesn't need this kind of exposure."

A few more trivial formalities and then Desmond ended the call with "I'll keep you informed. Cortez—out."

Desmond set down the phone and turned, genuinely surprised to find Dom sitting up and staring at him, the red satin bed sheet wrapped around herself as if she was in the presence of a stranger. He was going to ask her how much she'd heard, but Dom beat him to the punch.

"You said there was nothing to that old bum's story," she said, her voice filled with accusation.

"Actually...I told you to drop it."

Dom dropped the harsh tact, but not the topic, and shifted effortlessly to a more playful tone. "C'mon, there's more to this old guy than meets the eye. You're holding back on me...and that's something you promised you'd never do." She gave him a pouty lip.

He didn't smile as she expected him to. Desmond's gaze was cold, almost threatening. "And I never have...held back, that is. Have I?" Then he grinned, revealing a thin line of white teeth, and yanked the sheet from her nude form.

Dom surprised herself by blushing. "You know what I mean," she said, wide-eyed and red-faced, opting to exaggerate her blush rather than hide it. She snatched up her pillow with both hands and swiped it at his back, before using it to cover herself.

Desmond grabbed hold of the pillow, mock-wrestling her for possession and chiding all the while, "Be careful with that thing—it might be loaded." He yanked it from her grasp and tossed it across the room, leaving her fully exposed on the silky spread.

"Didn't your mother warn you about leaving dangerous objects around the house?" he leered.

"My mother warned me about men like you," she said, no longer feeling quite so playful as she felt his eyes run across her supple body. Nothing he hadn't seen before, but Desmond seemed to be taking too much pleasure in reducing her to this state.

"Now come on," she said as seriously as she could muster under the circumstances. "How are those bums a threat to Henry Devlin? Ignoring, just for the moment, that one of said bums leaps over cars, and thrusts iron spikes through men three times younger than he is. Level with me on this guy: just *who* is he?"

The old man reached out and took hold of the iron shaft that Billy offered up to him from bended knee, the entire tableau ringing with medieval resonance. The old withered hand grasped it tightly, dry skin cracking, blue veins bulging.

The old man spoke in his smooth, soothing voice. "I ask you as I asked before…"

Billy opened his shamed eyes and looked up. He thought he saw a faint vestige of the earlier fire in the old man's eyes, still burning as an ember awaiting but the merest breath of wind to spark it back to life.

"Do you believe?" asked the old man again.

Billy was more honest in his second, stuttered answer to the question. "I…I don't…I don't know what I believe."

The old man replied with that strange clarity that seemed to come and go. "Do you accept only that which your eyes see…or is your mind open to a greater reality?"

Billy felt as he often had in those last few months of school, that he alone was bereft of the answers that came so easily to his classmates. "I don't…know," he said, and his voice cracked on the final syllable.

"Do you believe that a life such as yours can be worth living?"

Billy felt his eyes starting to tear up, the very last humiliation he wanted to display. But he found himself answering as desperately as he ached inside.

"I...I'd *like* to believe."

"Then..." said the old man as his frail hand re-asserted its grip on the iron spike and slowly lifted it from Billy's extended arms, "let us see what your heart and soul may show you, young Sanchez..."

Desmond stood up, revealing the nakedness of his own powerful physique that made Dom the secret envy of all those women who suspected her clandestine liaisons with the boss. He seemed to possess none of her self-conscious embarrassment, though; kneeling in the center of his king-sized mattress, Dom felt herself on display.

"I couldn't be any more serious about this, Dom," he said. "Drop it. You've got a promising career ahead of you. You don't want to go ruining a good thing by poking that pretty little head of yours into places it doesn't belong."

The last vestige of playfulness faded from his tone. Dom noticed how utterly dark he now was in silhouette. She could no longer read the subtle signs and signals on his face. But she was tired of being told what she could or could not do, as if she were still a child.

"Are you threatening me?" Dom asked coldly.

A crack of lighting suddenly split the sky, dividing the room into black and white, reducing the entire world into one split second of stark clarity.

Desmond's pure white body twitched, and a massive halfback's arm struck Dom across the face.

Dom saw a second explosion of harsh white light follow the lightning's crack, like fireworks exploding behind her closed eyes, as the solid back of Desmond's hand connected just below her left eye and sent her entire body tumbling from the bed.

Then thunder followed, sharp and distinct, signaling the end of the world, as the penthouse itself seemed to shake in the aftershock.

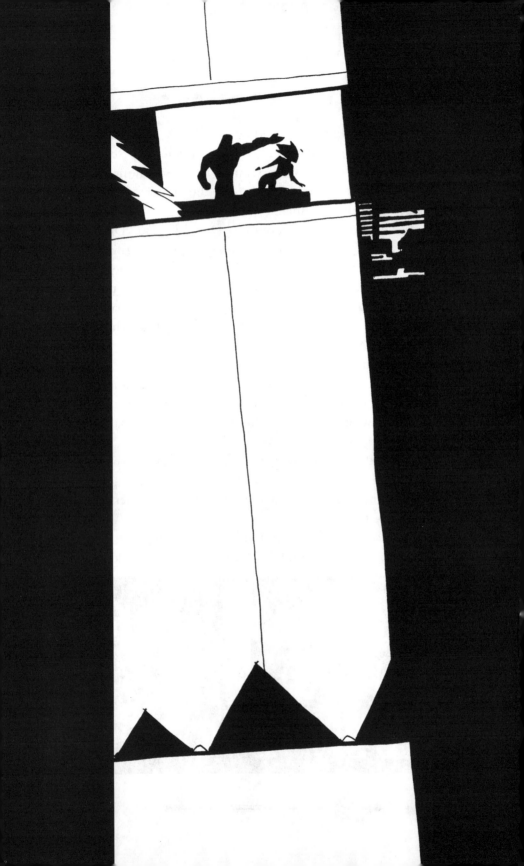

"See…hope…and believe!" uttered the old man with all the conviction of renewing an ancient pledge, and he raised the iron pike with one hand, up toward the sky.

A shaft of lightning struck downward, connecting its electrical arc to the tip of the outstretched iron, enveloping the pole in an instant of coruscating energy. Hungry waves lapped at the mortal shore, then ricocheted outward in all directions, bathing the alley in a spiderweb of dazzlingly brilliant white light.

Then Sanchez saw his savior once again. The Hero stood tall, young, powerful and proud, untouched in the shower of sparks cascading from the three feet of gleaming steel sword thrust heavenward, glowing with electrical fury.

His long black hair whipped about as if consumed by an energy all its own. His jet black eyes flashed with the reflected brilliance of nature's fire still bursting above him. His gold buttons gleamed, almost as if lit from within, the bolt of power recharging ancient and dead batteries. His sculpted features gleamed. When he spoke, Billy knew the sound of that voice was louder than thunder, for his voice was the very thunder itself.

"The conflict has but two sides. There is light and there is dark. And between them stands humanity, lost in shadow, unwilling to see the truth, unable to comprehend that it is that very darkness which consumes them!"

…And then, she said, the little angel would wake up in Heaven…

Dom staggered to her knees, delayed shock only just registering on her nervous system. The entire left side of her face throbbed with a life of its own, rebellious and seeking to flee the body that supported it. One shaking hand rose, then came away tinged with blood that dribbled from her nose.

Desmond had turned away to casually pour himself a fresh drink. She saw he was skipping his usual two fingers of brandy on ice, and going straight for a full shot of bourbon. Somewhere along the way he had taken the time to don his silken bathrobe, which clung to his form like a royal mantle.

"That's not a 'threat,' Dominique," he said evenly, just before downing the shot of bourbon. He poured himself another. "Consider it down payment on a promise."

Dom felt the weight of the blood on her fingers, and knew the explosion in her head wasn't a second round; it was simply the first still ringing, reluctant to leave.

Outside the balcony windows, the sky had become a visual cacophony of electrical discharge. It hurt her eyes simply to look at it. She vaguely remembered the 'DVL meteorologist forecasting clear skies for that evening.

She looked at the door and wondered if she could get to it before Desmond caught her.

Desmond turned, almost jovially, drink in one hand, and gestured toward her with the other. "Now get some make-up on that. Clean yourself up and come back to bed. I'll arrange that exclusive for you tomorrow."

He turned away again, focusing on the light show outside.

"Looks like a storm's coming," he said.

The first spattering of rain pelted the balcony's glass door.

"Stupid weathercasters..." muttered Dom under her breath, as she staggered to her feet and hobbled toward the palatial bathroom that adjoined Desmond's bedroom. "They don't know anything."

The Hero stood, transfixed by fire, his sword outthrust in defiance of all the world's evil.

"It is to this battle that we are called, you and I. For we see the darkness in its true form. Our eyes are opened!"

Billy Sanchez then knew his savior was not Robin Hood or Zorro, nor even that masked Ranger with his trusty six-shooter. Here stood something new, something—*someone*—real, yet stepped from out of those very same pages of legend and antiquity.

Billy slowly rose, his head clear. His own eyes now burned with the same fire and the passion of the vision before him, his face etched with equal measures of fear and wonder.

"But be warned, for darkness also has eyes to see. It sees and *fears* the name I bear..."

There was another roar of thunder, and with it, rain began to fall in a mighty torrent.

"The name...*Quixote!*"

Part Two
ERRANT KNIGHT

Of the Wise Discourse betwixt Our Hero and Dulcinea;
Of Ambush Most Foul, and of How Our Hero Was Slain.

Chapter Eleven

High over city streets, the billboard features a handsome smiling face. The face conveys both father and lover to a newly-energized female electorate—they who had fought so hard to be taken seriously only to find both parties now courting them on the grounds of their "traditional" roles. Yet the face on the billboard also suggests a rugged individualism. It tells men everywhere that here is the one man they want watching their backs should they ever find themselves crouched in a foxhole, real or imagined.

The face says "trust." The billboard itself loudly proclaims: *"The Choice for a Better Tomorrow—Elect Henry Devlin for Governor."*

In a culture where "choice" is defended and fought for as one of the classic virtues, the selection of Henry Devlin, it seems, may be the answer to everyone's hopes, and dreams, and prayers. And may Heaven show its mercy on the day the people's choice grants them what they actually deserve.

Detective Benjamin Saunders had started his day with the news that two of his collars had gotten out of jail free.

That was a funny one, he'd thought, as the old guy had seemed pretty much incapable of playing Chutes and Ladders, let alone a full-blown round of Monopoly. If anything, the old guy looked every inch the part of *do not pass go—do not collect $200.* Saunders, though, had been playing The Game of Life for far too long, and no longer had any interest in giving the little clackety plastic wheel another spin. Deep down, he really didn't care that two of his birds had flown the coop. And his partner knew it.

Detective Andy Carnahan was nearly twenty years his junior, and hated the fact that he was saddled with an old department warhorse long past his prime. Age actually had little to do with it. It was Saunders's attitude, pure and simple. As far as Carnahan was concerned, neither a natural death nor an early retirement could come soon enough for his already half-out-to-pasture partner.

Carnahan had arrived at Saunders's door that morning and dumped all the previous night's details into Ben's lap like salt on breakfast cereal.

The report was simple enough. At approximately 11:35 p.m., suspects in custody—John Doe and William Sanchez—had broken free from Detention Cell C. Eyewitness accounts, confirmed by video surveillance, revealed that John Doe had wrenched the locked gate from its hinges. The two suspects then fled—unarmed—through the midst of seven fully-armed on-duty officers. They left a swath of cuts, bruises, and one officer—five-year veteran Lieutenant Lynn Washington—in need of serious medical treatment.

The Department had tried calling Saunders at home in the wake of the fiasco, but Ben had gotten drunk on some Thunderbird whiskey and never heard the phone. There was no one else home to take the call—*at least, not anymore,* he mused sourly.

Carnahan was leaving the follow-ups for him. It was the younger man's way of saying he intended to do only just enough to keep his own nose clean, but at the end of the day, this particular nightmare was Ben's case alone.

Saunders had his work cut out for him. First stop was the Security Wing of Calvary Memorial General Hospital and a nice friendly chat with the three busted-up punks who had picked a fight with the wrong victim.

After parking his long, dark sedan in the hospital lot, Saunders planned to follow his typical procedure. He'd work his way from the stupidest on up to the "brains." He used the term loosely. He started with the muscle of the little gang: the twin brutes of Larry "Knucklehead" Burns and Jerry "Not-the-TV-Guy" Springer.

Knucklehead had a broken tibia and fibula, as well as a shattered kneecap, and, like his alleged assailant, absolutely nothing to say.

Not-the-TV-Guy Springer had complications from his dislocated hip joint and was unavailable for comment.

With no other options available, the detective went for the "leader" of the merry little band. Saunders had come to know Michael "Dutch" Waxman pretty well in the past few years, as the aspiring hoodlum had been working his way up the ranks from juvenile offender to dyed-in-the-wool adult incorrigible—and all before the legal age of twenty-one. Carnahan hated the creep as if it were a personal matter. Saunders could only hope that messing with the old guy might have finally put the proverbial fear of God into the young punk before he ended his run at the dead end of an officer's gun.

Under ordinary circumstances, the dude known as Dutch had nothing to say to any black cop. But today was a brand new day, and mere Mike Waxman was now rethinking a large majority of his life. He had received worse than a broken arm, far worse than a simple dislocated joint. His elbow was split, literally cracked in two. Future mobility was probable, though not guaranteed, and only by way of a new steel and plastic ball joint bolted onto the salvageable bone.

The man Dutch had been in a hell of a lot of pain. But thanks to modern medical miracles, *Michael* was barely feeling it less than twenty-four hours later. His court-appointed counsel, having just had the assignment dumped on her that morning, was already in the room and on the case. She didn't want to lose her legal battle before it had even started. Mike listened to her warnings but didn't care. It had all been so strange, surreal even, and he *wanted* to talk about it—at least *some* of it anyway.

"He wasn't no *old* guy," Michael started after the detective's preliminaries. "Yeah, we thought he was this old geezer at first, but—don't ask me how—he *wasn't* old, not really. He was a young guy, but older'n me—late twenties, maybe thirty or so. Long black hair and…*scary eyes.*"

Saunders felt a bolt of lightning shoot down his spine—*the same description Lt. Washington gave.* Even the vagrant Sanchez had said the same of his mysterious savior.

"*Scary* eyes?" the detective queried for clarification.

Dutch winced as a relapse of pain shot up through his arm, and a picture flashed in his mind's eye. "What are you—deaf too?" he shouted. "That's what I said. *Fuck!* Scary eyes! The dude had scary eyes and…and he carried a sword. A real, honest-to-god *sword*, like a cutlass or somethin', like what the

Marines got in all those commercials on TV. Is that what that guy was…some kind of bad-ass psycho Marine?"

"He used an iron fence spike to murder your friend."

"Hey, that piece o' shit was no friend of mine."

Saunders had no tolerance for playing word games this morning. "He died defending you. While you and the others were lying on the ground, bawling your little eyes out, that *old man* skewered your friend with an *iron pole* straight through the roof of a car like he was a damn holiday roast."

"How many times do I gotta tell you? *There was no old guy.*" Mike practically rose off the bed.

This was going nowhere. Oblivious to hospital regulations, Saunders lit up a smoke to take away the steady pain that was building behind his eyes, just a little something to keep his questions smooth and calm. "Tell me about the new guy then, the one that joined your gang."

"Is he dead?"

"Yes."

"Good. That's all I have to say." Mike closed his eyes and leaned his head back onto the pillows.

Saunders churned ahead regardless, puffing between questions, like a stubborn locomotive. "Did he have a name? Did he ever say where he came from? What was he doing hooking up with small-time thugs like your little crew? *Boxers or briefs?*"

Neither Michael—nor Dutch—bit at the chide.

The Public Defender—who sat tensely next to the bed fingering her legal pad and clicking her pen throughout the interview—now got up and flagged down a passing nurse. One bustled in and threatened to have the detective put out if he refused to do likewise with his cigarette. Saunders stifled it in infancy against the foot of the bed frame and slid it behind his ear for later use.

Michael answered no more questions. He closed his lips like a clam, apparently pondering justice on his own terms, somewhere between the pain and the drugs and his sudden craving for a smoke.

Just another lost soul caught in the system, thought Saunders, as he closed his notepad and gave the obligatory nod to the glaring P.D. But the system couldn't be all that bad when a two-bit thug with barely an honest nickel to his name could get a state-of-the-art joint repair free of charge.

No, it wasn't the system that killed you: it was all those gears behind the scenes, making the system work, that chewed you up and spit you out. And when it was grinding along at peak efficiency, that great bureaucratic machine left nothing in its wake…

Saunders pulled his earlier stifled smoke out from behind his ear.

Nothing, that is, but the crumpled husks of little broken men—men like Michael Waxman…and Benjamin Saunders.

On that cheery note, Saunders lit up as he vacated Calvary Memorial. On the city's horizon, the distant WDVL corporate tower loomed like an all-seeing eye. He hated the damn ugly thing, and couldn't think of a single neighborhood in the entire city where the red glow of that tower and its call letters couldn't be seen.

The throb growing behind his eyes felt like a migraine coming on, but Saunders knew it was just his hangover kicking into overdrive. He'd have to grin and bear it, because anything strong enough to knock it out of his head wouldn't leave him competent enough to do his job. And he still had one hell of a job staring him in the face.

Exactly where did you go in over five hundred thousand square blocks of city to find two homeless vagrants who didn't want to be found?

Chapter Twelve

"Overturning rocks in search of grubs," observed the old man.

"You could help instead of just sittin' there on yer ass," Billy Sanchez answered. He was growing desperate in both need and tone.

Since daybreak, the two vagrants had migrated from one back alley to another, the younger Sanchez claiming to know all the best restaurants that threw away the best scraps. So far, though, he was batting zip.

Other denizens of the streets seemed to be satisfying their hunger quite well this morning, but anything in the dumpsters Billy and the old man looked into was soaked.

The previous night's deluge had drenched everything. Saturating moisture had even found its way into ordinarily watertight receptacles and rendered most of the potential sustenance inedible.

The old man had followed Billy in silence, usually finding the first available surface on which to prop his frail bones each time they stopped, while his younger partner did all the digging and rooting.

Billy pulled a plastic-coated TV dinner tray from one can, poured out the murky water that had partially filled it, and scraped his mouth along an edge coated with a moist residue of a chicken and potato meal.

"Have you so little dignity left?" asked the old man, declining the offer of a second such tray.

Billy snorted. "I ain't like those bums up on 70th Street."

The old man gave a quizzical glance.

"Like a bunch'a vultures, they are," continued Billy, "swoopin' 'round, gettin' hand-outs from a bunch'a do-gooders pattin' themselves on the back for solvin' all the world's problems."

The old man straightened his back. "Is this a place where we might eat our fill?" he queried, rising to his feet.

"I don't think so," said Billy with finality.

"We must both keep up our strength if the quest is to continue."

Sanchez flared angrily. "Hey, whatever that was you had me smokin' last night, it was great, OK? You got my thanks. You had me seein' stuff I ain't never seen before. But I ain't yer Tonto so just cut all the *Kemo Sabe* crap.

Today's a new day, and a guy's gonna do whatever it takes to get through it. Y'know what I mean?"

The old man would not be put off. "Why do you go to such lengths to evade that which is so freely given?"

Billy started calculating all the ways he might ditch this hitchhiker, this new habit that now clung to his back more tenaciously than any monkey that he'd ever let climb aboard his out-of-control crazy-train. As Paul Simon had stated so profoundly, there was *no need to be coy, Roy*. Good advice, as long as Billy had sense enough to listen, and get away from the old coot before his whole life— *Heaven forbid!*—changed forever.

Billy smirked. "So what is it that yer offerin' me today?"

"I offer you life…and a life worth living." He was serious.

The old man had shown him *wonders* the day before: impossible visions of a world on the fringes of our own—a world which all his experience told him could never actually be. Billy was too much of a *pragmatist* to believe what he'd seen—though he didn't know that word well enough to ever apply it to himself, or to anyone else, for that matter. He just knew enough to get them both out of the rain last night, and they'd slept on a cushion of industrial-grade trash bags piled beneath a rusty factory awning. It did the job, and that was all Billy usually cared about.

He saw black and white, and used the handy reference manual inside his head to process his understanding of the two. Billy wanted a life where he got his facts *straight*. He wanted truth in clear-cut language—fast and sure— that he could understand without too much internal controversy.

"You got a problem wit' the way I live?" he challenged.

"You are dying."

The concise, clear-cut statement drew Billy up short. "Is that right?" he said skeptically. "I don't see no doctor plaques hangin' on your wall."

With the exception of the gaping, empty hole he felt where his stomach should have been, he was actually feeling much better. He was dry, and the pain in his head had reduced to a dull throb in his temples and behind his eyes.

The old man spoke again. "Yesterday…you saw beyond the veil. In my experience, only those close to their end see the truth with such clarity."

Sanchez reached back into the can from where the TV dinner tray had come, and he pulled out a partially peeled banana, its fruit black and barely solid. "I see what I wanna see. That's how I live my life. An' today, I see that life is doin' me just fine," he said.

"Then why are you killing yourself?"

It was a simple question whose logic could be debated. But Billy stopped in mid-bite, a child suddenly caught with his hand where it didn't belong, between issues of right and wrong that had teeth and the instinct to bite back when provoked. He locked eyes with the old man who had shown him so many things that could never actually—truly—be. His tongue rolled around the inside of his mouth, absorbing the full sensation of rotting fruit on his palate.

You are dying.

He dropped the peel back into the can and vomited up what little nourishment his shriveled stomach had managed to ingest.

Chapter Thirteen

Both political parties sought to own the issue of homelessness. The liberal Left used an agenda borne of guilt to legislate a spirit of compassion upon those who simply didn't care. The conservative Right took up the banner of personal responsibility and swung it about as a license to ultimately ignore the problem.

Somewhere in between were individuals, and the organizations they sponsored and served, who tried to meet the issue where it really mattered: on the street itself. They addressed the immediate needs of survival—food, clothing, shelter—as well as the long-term questions of personal accountability. For those serious about reclaiming their lost lives, there was always someone willing to help them.

Not an easy task. There was no shortage of charlatans to sift through, to discern those who preyed upon the generosity of others from those who were merely irresponsible, who lived for others to pay for all of their own habitual, perpetual carelessness. Then there were the mentally unstable, who'd been victimized by a judicial system that had earned "compassion" points by closing the institutions and dumping the emotionally challenged out onto the streets. All of that, however, was just what FACTS was about: doing the dirty jobs that no one else wanted to do. It reached down to the destitute, helped the lost find their way, and strove to teach all of them how to stand on their own feet again.

The name, "FACTS," was an acronym representing the principles its founder and his organization aimed to embody and pass on to those they served: *Faith, Accountability, Charity, Truth, Salvation.* FACTS didn't pigeon-hole itself solely in the realm of the homeless, either. It reached out across the wide spectrum of social ills: addictions and substance abuse, unwanted children, battered women, unwed teenage mothers—those who had made mistakes as well as those oppressed by the mistakes of others. FACTS helped the helpless, and encouraged its clientele to accept responsibility for their own futures, irrespective of color, creed, or perceptions of victim status. At least a handful were honest enough to acknowledge accountability regardless of the tragedy and heartbreak in their lives.

The plight of the homeless ultimately represented just one more sin of collective humanity that the FACTS staff sought to relieve. So, while their social services required mutual participation by those to whom they ministered, the FACTS soup kitchen was open to all without question, even to those they knew were simply scamming for a free meal they could otherwise afford.

All in all, though, FACTS received little media attention because it dared attend to and treat all these social causes—the liberal sacred cows—from the ideology of a conservative religious denomination.

Today, however, those operating *without* the official consent of WDVL Broadcasting were the lost, coming to beg at the soup kitchen door...

"God, I hate churches," moaned Dominique Angel as she gazed up at the stained glass. "They're so full of hypocrites."

"Yep," agreed her partner as he put the van in neutral and engaged the emergency brake, "and as they say—there's always room for one more."

Dom scowled at her cameraman's little jibe in a way that showed she had missed her morning coffee.

Joseph Caparelli had been raised in the church, and not the Catholicism his ethnicity stereotypically implied. There were plenty of Italian Baptists; you just didn't see them in the popular media. But the fundamentalism of his youth (and his parents) had been one of appearance over substance, and little Joey had been on the ball enough to spot the hypocrisy early on.

At the time, he couldn't believe that life was so

black and white, cut and dried, as sermons told him it was. He stopped going to Sunday services altogether as soon as he was old enough, big enough, to tell his folks "NO" and stand by it. And for the last ten years, Joe had found his own way in the world. He'd learned firsthand that organized religion alone didn't corner the market on double standards—there were always rising-star television reporters and their cameramen.

He glanced at Dom. She seemed overly anxious to get on with the job before them. She'd even abandoned her preoccupation with style for the day, trading light Parisian blue for a mourner's black pantsuit. It seemed to match her mood.

Joe switched off the ignition, and the newsvan shuddered ominously in its idle state before coming to a rest.

"That doesn't sound good," said Dom darkly, her eyes asking the questions her sense of security demanded.

Joe blew her off. "The thing's been acting up. I got it scheduled for service some time next week."

"If it *lives* that long," muttered Dom, climbing out of the newsvan's cab just outside one of the side doors of the FACTS facility.

Joe knew he could get away with blowing off Dom, at most, once in a day. After that, she kept count and usually made him pay for it. But he also knew that he, and he alone, could get away with a certain measure of brotherly protection.

"Desmond's gonna kill you when he finds out you're still after this guy," he said.

"Desmond's a pussycat," she answered.

"You should know."

Dom's glare toward her concerned cameraman was cut short by  one last quick look in the side rear-view mirror, making sure her make-up sufficiently covered the evidence of Desmond Cortez's modest regard. Just another little dab over the tender skin and she'd be ready for her close-up.

Without another word, Joe Caparelli left Dom to

tend to her personal maintenance while he went around to the back to prep his own equipment. She watched him go, her mood darkening.

Dom tolerated only so much brotherly intrusion.

Dominique actually did care about Joe. It was just his intrusive cameraman's eye and instinct that sparked her indignation when she found herself on the receiving end of them.

Simply put, he saw too much. Joe had the unnerving capacity to peer straight through the chinks in her carefully constructed armor to the small child she kept hidden fearfully within. She should have felt safe—honored even—that he could see so much and yet choose to keep silent regarding the secrets of her heart. Instead, it was the one thing she hated about him.

Dom's heart was not the business of Joseph Caparelli.

Wincing slightly, she finished her touch-up.

The previous evening, when Dom had returned from the adjoining bathroom to Desmond Cortez's penthouse bedroom, her hands were still shaking. Rain pelted the glass balcony doors. Lightning flashed. Thunder rattled the panes.

Desmond had lit a pair of candles, one on either side of the room. In the warmth of their glow, he held up her own silken robe—the scarlet one he'd given her last Christmas—and slipped it over her delicate shoulders. Then he poured a tall shot of her own preferred suppressant: the smooth edge of an Irish Cream.

"I'm sorry," he said softly as he took her quivering hand into the warmth of his own.

And that was enough. She understood the demons he had struggled with for most of his life. She certainly had enough ghosts of her own, didn't she? It certainly wasn't fair to hold another accountable for the sins for which you sought absolution yourself.

For the next hour, in counterpoint to the piercing rounds of thunder, their love was tender.

When Dom later awoke from nightmares she could not remember, it was the sure and certain warmth of Desmond's great frame to which she clung. As always, it was his undeniable, irrefutable presence in her life that calmed her fears and granted her the peace to drift off again into the uncharted realms of her own slumber.

They rose the following morning in silence.

As she applied morning makeup to start her day, she was relieved to see that Desmond's outburst had left her with minimal swelling, just a dark bruise easily camouflaged by her skillful touches.

And he would not, could not, look her in the eye.

He still felt guilty, she surmised. That was sufficient for Dom; enough to give her leverage the next time they argued.

Desmond made breakfast—a rarity for him—yet another good sign that enduring a single moment of pain was a small price to pay in order to get herself in the driver's seat. For all of Desmond's size, strength, and illusion of power, he was the true child of the pair, uncertain, fearful, terrified of the monster that dwelt within him. But Dom had a leash about that great beast's throat, and felt the satisfaction of knowing that only she could bring it to heel.

As they ate, Dom held her chin high and flinched from none of Desmond's occasional glances toward her. He kept most of his attention directed at the morning paper. When he did speak, it was merely to reinforce his promise to arrange her coveted exclusive with the would-be Governor.

The day before his offer had been a gift. Today it had become an obligation.

Dom was pleased. She then planned to spend her day following up on the leads of her own choice, namely the mysterious old man who posed a story potential large enough to unseat even the ambitions of an aspiring politician.

Did she feel the slightest regret, though, for manipulating matters best left to the natural discernment of the heart?

Absolutely. It consumed her. It cried so often in her own voice, in the privacy of her own thoughts, seeking to somehow release her from the intricate prison of her own deceptions. But the one thing Dom had vowed never to do was apologize. She would never seek absolution for anything she'd ever had to do in order to become her own woman.

Chapter Fourteen

"You want me to say I'm sorry or somethin'?"

The old man didn't answer. Two steaming bowls of hearty beef stew sat between him and Billy Sanchez, accompanied by chunks of fresh bread big enough to sop up the entire bowl and choke a horse. It was warm inside as well. Summer hadn't yet kicked in, and the spring breeze could still carry a chill when one wasn't in direct sunlight.

FACTS had taken over the old St. Luke's church property from a Unitarian congregation that, in turn, had bought it from some old Methodists after three pastors in a row had been unable to breathe any life into its dead congregation. The Unitarians hadn't wanted to sell to such a denominationally "reformed" ministry. But, from the start, FACTS had been willing to pony up a substantial sum in cash that far outbid the investors who had wanted to turn the small cathedral-like structure into a new nightclub.

Billy's energy was returning, and he now proved he could eat and speak at the same time. "I've been pretty stupid most of my life…a little slow on the uptake. Probably why I'm hangin' with you, huh?"

The old man waited until he had chewed and swallowed. "It is never too late to begin learning."

A splotch of white mixed with black landed with a smack right next to Billy's bread. He looked up into the distant shadows of the vaulted ceiling and heard the echoing flutter of distant wings.

Billy was in no position to lose an appetite. He simply removed his bread as a target and considered using it as a projectile of his own. "Two birds with one stone, eh? Whattya say, old man?"

"Unless one intends to eat the birds, I believe you'll simply lose your bread."

Billy's gaze shifted from his bread to the splotch on the table, then back again. He scarfed it down in one decisive effort.

The old man smiled softly and sipped at his broth.

St. Luke's had long had a pigeon problem. The FACTS staff believed they had solved it by sealing every access into the vast stone interior with its Gothic-revival arches that made such convenient nestling perches. But nature forced the issue—as soon as the winter freeze had come, the pigeons returned, as if to Capistrano. Who knew where or how non-migratory city birds weathered the deeper freezes farther north, but in this particular burg they moved indoors. The new St. Luke's now had until the next health inspection to solve the dilemma. In the meantime, the free meals would continue in spite of "death from above," as it had come to be known by the regulars.

When Dom and Joe entered the old building, the staff immediately assumed the news crew had come to do some kind of a hit piece on the pigeons—anything to destroy the ministry's reputation in the eyes of the public. It had certainly been tried before. FACTS's founder-in-residence, Nathan Creed, was quickly alerted. The "Big Man," as he was often called, hustled his formidable 6'7" linebacker's frame in time to keep the media opposition from advancing down the field. And he wasn't afraid to use his size when necessary.

"A big black man" was what Nathan Creed had always considered himself —rejecting the moniker of "African-American" with which the intelli-gentsia had tried to saddle him. He considered himself American, born and raised. Despite the country's often-questionable legacy, the American Dream had done him just fine as he chose *not* to embrace the restricting labels of ethnic-heritage in the name of some ethereal racial pride. Simply being an American black man had allowed him—regardless of a lifetime of hard knocks and challenges—to rise above it all and make a genuine impact in the lives of others. *That* he was proud of. And by adopting that attitude of personal responsibility, he had learned the hard way just what the "open-minded" media could do to those who would not embrace "politically-correct" policies.

"Can I help you?" the big black man asked, looming his massive bulk over Dominique Angel's comparatively petite 5'6". It wasn't an offer.

Billy had skirted the issue for most of his young life. In spite of all his mental posturing—his stance on the solid and material—he was never one to bring himself face-to-face with unpleasant realities. This was different, though.

You are dying.

He drained the last of his soup and felt full and warm within. Even his head was clearing, ever since his gut had stopped its bellyaching. So, it was now or never: he bit the bullet. Along the roads Billy had spent his years traversing, it was quite an accomplishment. "Back at that last alley…remember? You said…somethin' about…about me dyin'."

The old man merely nodded as he took another spoonful of stew slowly into his mouth.

"What did you mean by that?"

Billy watched the old man lower the spoon back into his bowl. Then, to his amazement, the largest grin the young man had yet seen on the weathered features broke across his ancient face. Billy's flare of indignation subsided, though, when he realized the old man was watching some commotion over his shoulder. He turned to see the big, black guy who ran the place stopping the pretty auburn-haired reporter and her accompanying cameraman whom he recognized from the day before. The cameraman was holding up pictures that the big guy didn't seem very interested in.

Billy turned back to the old man's yellowed grin and noticed he was missing about half his teeth. The subject abruptly changed. "You *knew* she was coming here, didn't you?"

"No. But in my experience, Providence has proven a large enough stone for more than two birds."

Joe held the crisp video print of the crazy old man's face. The intensity of the eyes had not been diminished by the medium. The young cameraman couldn't remember if the FACTS founder actually *was* an ex-football pro or merely looked like one, but he had no doubt that Dom could still take the big guy on her terms.

Dom was doing her forceful best. "But you'd remember this man if you saw him—all wild hair...crazy eyes—"

"I don't think you understand me," Nathan Creed cut in, his voice deep and booming in the wide open hall, even though he was not raising it. "So let me explain in a language I'm sure you *won't* mistake...."

His big hand closed around the printout and crumpled it right out of Joe's grasp. "I don't care *who* you're looking for, or *why*. Nor am I afraid of any threat *your* kind tries to hold over my head. We were here serving the community yesterday, and, Lord willing, we'll be here serving the community tomorrow."

"But, sir. If you'd only—"

"I want you out of here—*now!*"

Joe suddenly realized that even Dom didn't stand a chance against this guy, but was incapable of giving up a fight once she'd started one. Joe sincerely hoped it wouldn't end in blood.

A low, scratchy voice caught them all off guard. "I believe I am the one she seeks." The voice ranked just below fingernails on a chalkboard on the scale of auditory aesthetics.

Dom couldn't believe the object of her search was actually here, falling into her lap—*willingly*. She knew she was good, just not lucky. She wasn't used to circumstances coming together like this. For once, she couldn't find adequate enough words to take control.

The old man grinned widely at them, charm leaking through the gaps in his smile. "You must pardon her...she is accustomed to dictating all the answers. It disturbs her to find another usurping the role."

Though they were not directed at him, Joe saw enough of the eyes to know they had found the right man. The Hispanic guy who accompanied him looked uncomfortable, even cornered.

The old man then focused his gaze on Dom, silencing her questions—and, no doubt, expletives—with an irrefutable, inscrutable offer of his own. "Come with me. We will walk. I will tell you all that you wish to know…and much that you do not."

The old man offered his apologies to Nathan Creed for this intrusion on his work, and went out through the massive oaken doors.

Dom offered hers as well. "I'm so terribly sorry we disturbed you," she said, with less conviction, one hand on the door.

Joe couldn't believe Dom was about to follow the crazy old man. She placated her nervous partner with an open-handed gesture that insisted he calm down. Her lips silently mouthed, *"I'll be fine,"* as she deftly turned and followed the old man out into the light.

Instantly, Joe realized this was *exactly* the kind of stunt Dom would pull. He just wasn't sure what she'd want *him* to do in the meantime. Definitely something productive, though, or he'd hear about it later in no uncertain terms.

Whether he stayed close or abandoned her to fate, he knew he'd become hero or villain in an instant depending on what he chose to do in the next ten seconds. Then he recognized the one following the old guy as William Sanchez, who'd also been arrested the previous day and escaped along with their mystery man last night.

He blocked Billy's exit with his camera. "Hey! I know you. You were there yesterday. You were with him."

The small man looked nervous, his gaze torn between his departing mentor and the man who now stood in his way. Joe was reminded of a mouse he'd once surprised in the kitchen of his childhood, how its whiskers had quivered, its eyes bulging in fear.

Nathan Creed regained his authority in the situation and directed his orders at them both: "If you got legitimate business together, then so be it. But not here: you're taking it *outside*." He held the door open and gestured for them to go.

Again, the big man had no intention of having his mandate debated. Joe then realized what he needed to do: buy Dominique enough uninterrupted time with the old kook to find out any and all the answers she could.

Chapter Fifteen

Fifty years ago—a lifetime by the reckoning of some—the blocks surrounding old St. Luke's had thrived with local businesses, before the days of strip malls and franchised convenience. But a lifetime of steady deterioration, neglect, and entropy conspired with progress elsewhere to poison a neighborhood. Those who could, got out. Those who didn't, stayed behind to die slow, lingering deaths.

Although individual neighborhoods might be dying, however, the city as a whole still seemed vibrant and alive. And perhaps it was the overall life of the larger beast that kept these small cancers from killing their host.

The old man led Dominique Angel down streets only slightly more hospitable than the bombed-out ruins where young Billy Sanchez had been rescued the day before. Dilapidated row homes and closed-forever shops were just as ubiquitous, but this dying community bustled with at least the illusion of life. There were still people aplenty, bartering small favors for small dreams—hope thumbing its nose at the face of despair.

For the first several blocks, Dom remained patient and silent, giving the strange old man every opportunity to unload the wealth of information he'd promised. The blocks, however, seemed to grow longer and she felt the seconds of her life ticking away with each step she took.

The odd couple, looking for all the world as elderly father with his daughter, passed a locally known corner where women sold slices of their lives. Gaudy. Colorful. Patent and faux-leather harlequins, whose painted faces promised a brief respite from the slow death around them. These were hard women, and they carried their years like loads upon their backs.

Dom felt their eyes burn into her: jealousy, rage, lust, and longing—cries for help tangled with silent curses. This was no Julia Roberts fantasy, and Dom knew she was not welcome on these streets. She met the stares and accusations as she always did: she held her chin up proudly and ended the silence.

"You called me 'Dulcinea,'" she said.

"Yes."

"'Dulcinea'...like in *Don Quixote*...windmills and everything?"

"Yes."

"You're implying I'm a prostitute."

One of the nearby hookers gave her an even dirtier look. Refusing to be intimidated, Dom stared the woman down.

The old man looked about him with his sunken, haunted eyes. Dom realized that every hardened stare thrown his way softened, every garish eye lowered, turning away from the old man's gaze. He spoke again, his voice catching as a coat on a hook against the jagged edges of his teeth. The pain in his words lingered as if he spoke about the entire world as it spread itself out from this one desperate, angry, lonely corner.

"They sell their bodies that they may live another day. Beneath their paint, they hold their own value in such low esteem that to be used by another gives them purpose and a reason to live."

Indignant, Dom refused the pain. Never willing to turn away from a good fight, though, she accepted the old man's accusation. "You're calling me a whore."

"You sell your own for much less."

Big Nathan Creed won the day faster than the cameraman would have guessed. There comes a point when you stop arguing with someone three times your size, and that included the cameraman and Billy combined.

Now that Billy had tasted some of their hospitality, he hoped the cameraman's stubborn antics wouldn't bar him from FACTS's door the next time hunger came knocking. He had tried telling the big Mr. Creed that he and the cameraman had no business together. But the founder and administrator, while having no end to his compassion, had a very short fuse where whining stories were concerned.

The big oak doors shut with a disturbing finality, and Billy realized he didn't have a clue where the old guy had gone. But the cameraman, who said his name was Joe, still wanted to ask him some questions.

Billy had never known how to say no—not even to those in the schoolyard who had tempted him long ago with excuses to give up his life to the whims of substance and desire. Despite all of that, though, Billy got the impression the cameraman was basically stalling for time.

Once Nathan closed the door, Joe resumed his tactic with Billy: "So, you're telling me you've *never* seen the guy before yesterday? But the way you're followin' him around…what's the attraction? Or shouldn't I ask?"

Billy was flummoxed. "If I told you…you wouldn't believe me."

"You might be surprised at what I'm willing to believe."

The large, black Cadillac that slithered up alongside of them at that moment caught them both by surprise as it pulled just in front of the gleaming white WDVL newsvan. Though nondescript, it stood out in that neighborhood like the Gestapo knocking at a Passover door.

Billy felt the skin at the base of his skull crawl with the sensation of tiny insects squirming just beneath the surface. He suddenly realized that what he really wanted, more than anything else in the whole wide world, was a long, slow draught of something stiff enough to make all his problems disappear.

Impenetrably shaded windows lowered in unison, revealing just a hint of cold, pale faces within, staring out at a world that was not their own. Equally cold, distant eyes hid behind uniform, standard-issue black sunglasses. Their inscrutable gaze then fixed upon Billy and the cameraman.

Dom was thankful that their wandering course took them away from the more populated strip, and particularly from the stretch of streetwalkers to which her odd companion had dared compare her. The old man hadn't apologized for his audacity, but neither had he used his words to condemn her. He simply maintained his observation as a fact he believed—no more, no less.

"I see the burden that you carry," he said.

The old man's change of tack startled her.

"You carry the weight of many miles in too short a season," he continued.

"You don't even know me," she deflected weakly.

"I see your eyes, your bearing, the manner in which you thrust back your shoulders to show the world that you are not afraid...."

Ironically, he wasn't even looking at her. He rattled off his assessment as if he held an image of her in his mind.

"...I hear the desperate child in your voice—and she is crying."

Dom didn't accept crap insights like that from her very own good old

dependable Joe. She certainly wasn't going to accept them from this utter stranger she'd never even seen before yesterday. She felt it was time she reclaimed control of this game they were playing before one of them got hurt—and it sure as hell wasn't going to be her. "Who *are* you?"

Dom's question cut clean through the eloquent meandering, decisive enough to bring traffic to a halt. But the old man ignored her. "You run from something, and neither the miles nor the years can put enough space or time between you."

He wasn't fishing for an answer, but Dom gave him one anyway. "I'm not running from anything. Now, I thought we were here to talk about you."

"Then it is some*one* from whom you flee."

Again, it wasn't a question. Yet, against her better judgment, she found herself responding anyway, with an answer she never expected to give. "My—my father died nine years ago."

"You have my condolences."

"Save them for someone who cares," she retorted, abruptly angry with herself for the can of worms she'd just opened. He seemed startled by her attitude, though.

Score one for the professional, she mused. Dom was having a hard time keeping her building frustration from showing. *He was an oddball all right, and definitely dangerous if provoked.*

Thus far, though, he was her only lead and she needed to grant him all the patience she could muster. She changed her strategy.

"I'm not really that important, sir," she said, hoping her eyes conveyed the proper sincerity. "I'm here for *you*. I want to hear *your* story, and I want to help you in any way that I can. That's what I do." Her tone was earnest, even heartfelt.

He dismissed her insistence with a wave of his dirty hand, and asked instead, "This double-standard you employ—is it something you were taught or does it come naturally?"

It took her a moment to understand to what he was referring, and all she could manage in reply was a lame, "Excuse me?"

"You deny any insight into your own private life, yet gather 'round the misfortune of others, a carrion creature preying on the carcass of another's misery."

Dom felt her cheeks flush and her temper rise.

He continued, "Yesterday, for instance: all the while, you held yourself above reproach, for your *intentions* alone were enough and deemed good. I saw you from my distinct vantage point, before the officers took me elsewhere. For a moment only did I see you, but I glimpsed enough to recognize that soul you try so desperately to hide. It wallows in the very filth you condemn, even as you believe your own raiment sparkles as white as snow."

Her professional façade was rupturing and she inwardly cursed the old, besotted fool for getting under her skin where he didn't belong.

"Have I painted an accurate picture of the virtue of my Lady Dulcinea?"

Dom's veneer finally broke. "You dirty, good-for-nothing bastard!" *So much for mustered patience.*

He cracked a smile. She heard it. He followed it with a little chuckle that sounded too much like pebbles caught inside a can.

"My Lady feels something of the pain after all?" He nodded his own head in answer. "Yet any concern expressed for her is perceived as but an assault upon the fortress walls she's erected to protect her vulnerable heart..."

As he paused, Dom realized he was far more articulate and learned than his previous ramblings had suggested. Or perhaps, she was only now beginning to listen. She was quick to re-prime the pump. "I'm sorry. Truly I am. Please, go ahead—continue."

He seemed satisfied. "Then share with me—what was the great crime of your father's for which you still hold the rest of the world responsible?"

She had no fear of the topic. The old man couldn't pin her down with some startling, clinically-trained insight into her psyche. Calmly, she decided to let him have this round for free. "I'll tell you about my father: he was an abusive, lazy drunkard that drove my mother to suicide, and then spent the rest of his miserable life trying to atone for it. He failed. He finally couldn't live with all the guilt, and put a bullet through his head—end of story."

"Is that what you tell yourself?" he asked bluntly.

…And then, she said, the little angel would wake up in Heaven…

Molly Angel exploded, its dolly head ripping free from its small plush body, and leaving the little angel clutching all that was left of its soft cherubic beauty and its real plastic wings…

But then Daddy was there.

"My angel," he'd called her… "Daddy's little angel," he said as he took Molly's small head from out of her tiny hands. And he promised to get her a new Molly Angel—one with bigger, better, stronger wings…

But new plush-n-plastic angels are never as good as the old, never as warm, as comforting, as reliable—new angels are never as trustworthy…

There was more to the story, however, so much more. *And wasn't that the way things like this always turned out to be?*

Long before she was "making news" for WDVL, Dominique Angel had *been* news. She was only three years old when her young mother had tried to kill them both. Reporters at that time had not shied away from the word "miraculous" in reporting the child's survival of the suicidal seven-story fall that had claimed the life of her mother. Dom had spent the next several years known in the media spotlight as "the littlest angel."

Her father had waged a heroic two-year war in the courts to retain guardianship of his own "little angel," giving up most of that lifestyle which had sent her distraught mother quite literally over the edge. Finally winning the case, he then devoted the rest of his life, exclusively, to raising the child without a mother. Eventually he moved them to another city entirely in order to put the specter and spectacle to rest.

He killed himself in Dom's eighteenth year. Yet she managed to turn even that tragedy to benefit, adopting a cynicism born of her own unique adversity. Through hard work and single-minded purpose, she won herself a full university scholarship.

Dominique Angel had spent fifteen years blaming her father for her mother's suicide, and then never forgave him for taking his own life as well.

She had left all that behind her, though, and gone on with the rest of her life.

"I don't blame him—honestly, I don't." Her voice was steady and cool, as it always was whenever she replayed those particular memories. "It's just an unfortunate fact…"

She paused, then added a new inspiration she was confident would turn the tables back the way she'd intended. "A fact that I accept with the same assurance with which you made all those insinuations about me back there."

The old man conceded graciously, allowing a moment's respite before continuing. "She must have loved something in him."

Dom nearly tripped. "What?"

"Your mother—she must have loved something in him, out of which she conceived you." He actually seemed to care as he spoke.

"It was anything but love. And you'll just have to trust me on that. My mother was too stoned most of the time to care." She tried to regain her assertiveness. "Now this is supposed to be about *you*, remember?"

"Then at least you come by your moral cowardice honestly," he said.

"Dulcinea" aside, whorish insinuations she could take. But never the sullying of her mother's sacrifice.

"How dare you!" Dom said, raising one hand in an unconvincing fist.

"Why strike me?" countered the old man unflappably. She saw that frightening fire rekindle behind his eyes. "I am not your father. I am not that one you still hold accountable years after your mother has returned to dust."

Dom boiled under the surface. Here was the old man now daring to absolve her father's guilt. He did not deny that the man had indeed been guilty of many sins, but the death of her mother wasn't necessarily one of them. He hadn't said as much, but Dom knew what he was insinuating: *desperate though her mother had been, the decision—the choice—to take a life had been hers, and she had also chosen to take Dominique with her.*

She finally let the tension go, knowing that, like 'DVL's beloved meteorologist Constance McCleary, the old man didn't really *know* anything at all. She lowered her poorly-formed fist and turned away.

They continued walking, returning to the silence in which they'd started out. Although she could no longer see it from this angle, Dom knew the fire continued to burn in the deepest recesses of the old man's aged skull. After some time, he broke the quiet once again.

"You seek freedom and choice in all that you do, yet you deny the consequences of your actions, the results of the choices you make. Then you bandy about your blame, your critical judgments of others, as if bestowing *gifts* upon the unfortunate."

She let him rant, her arms folded against the chill in the air—and in his words.

He continued, "That young man who follows you, your cameraman: how often does he pay the price for your impatience? Your recklessness? Why do you blame him for all of *your* bad choices?"

She had no answer.

He *hmphed* with an air of satisfaction and resumed his own silence. At length, they came to an old iron trestle, unkept, rusted, yet still functioning with the city's blessing even though the tracks far below hadn't actually carried freight in more than a generation. Dom found relief in identifying the landmark, realizing that, although their journey had seemed long and meandering, they had actually traveled in a straight line only about five blocks from the FACTS mission soup kitchen.

She stopped at the railing and followed those disused tracks in her mind: every route brought her back to the same dead end. The city skyline framed the horizon. The WDVL tower seemed to wink at her through the afternoon haze. Somewhere within, Desmond Cortez was going about his normal routine and making all her twisted roads as straight as the tracks below. Dom sighed, realizing she was only too willing now to play this one out by the old man's rules.

"You know all these things—things you shouldn't know anything about…so, why *me?*"

It was the old man's turn to say nothing.

It might be his game and his rules, but Dom wasn't about to let him win easily. "What is it?" she prodded. "Were we *soul mates* in another life?"

His eyes seemed to cloud with her question, and he closed them, tilting his head upward as if staring at a far off vista etched only upon the insides of his eyelids.

"It is appointed man once to die, and after that…the Judgment." He wasn't merely speaking: he was quoting.

Dom was baffled. "So, we're all going to die. That doesn't exactly answer my question, now does it?"

His eyes opened again, but she knew he was still only seeing the vista in his mind. "Yes, all men die…some later than others…"

Dom addressed his faraway stare, "So, I ask again…why single me out as the recipient of all your good cheer?"

He lowered his head, saying nothing for seconds that seemed to stretch into hours. Dom saw his shoulders tremble and feared the crazy old guy might have a heart attack or stroke before she got any answers from him. She reached out and touched his quaking shoulder, telling herself that she simply wanted a story to report.

He looked up at her touch, and a tiny smile split his thin lips. "…And one day, even one such as I will grow weary of the burden and ask that it be lifted. Then shall I be taken home. But until that day arrives, I will not forsake the Call, the task set before me."

Dom felt her instant of compassion dissolve into exasperation. "You tell me everything and nothing at the same time! Why am I *bothering* with you?"

She saw a cloud pass over his face. He looked at her with no humor, just a terrible sadness.

"Because even one such as you is afraid to die."

Chapter Sixteen

Who knew how many were actually in the large, black Cadillac, but only two figures emerged. They were tall, expressionless, each looking like he could give big ol' Nathan Creed a run for his money—and win.

"Mr. Caparelli," said one.

"A moment of your time," finished the other.

There was no difference between the two voices. They each spoke as if they hid their souls behind their dark glasses. They weren't exactly identical in appearance, but Joe knew he'd be hard pressed to distinguish between the two in a line-up.

The first glided toward Joe and removed a piece of paper from inside the jacket of his crisp black suit. The paper was uncreased.

"This man was here," he said, indicating a photo on the page.

"Where did he go?" asked the other.

The crazed face of the old man threatening Joe the previous morning stared back at him.

Joe felt a sudden flare of anger he didn't understand. "Hey, that's from my shoot! Where'd you get that?!" The emotion was not conceived solely by the intrusion or apparent theft. It was something deeper. Older. An instinctive aversion that was almost primordial.

The two seemed not to notice Joe's outburst. They looked every inch the part of undercover Federal Agents possibly scouting territory for next week's campaign visit by gubernatorial hopeful Henry Devlin. But that didn't explain why, for one brief moment, Joe knew these men were the reason children are afraid of the dark.

"Your cooperation would be most...beneficial," the agent said, as if the answer had come from elsewhere and his mouth was no more than a conduit.

Thus far, neither of the agents had paid any attention to the skinny Hispanic at his side. Joe sensed Billy Sanchez tensing up, though, as he slowly backed away, whispering through clenched teeth loud enough for them all to hear, "Don't tell them *anything!*"

The second agent slowly turned toward Sanchez and fixed him with a stare. Sanchez gasped, stiffened, and stepped no further.

"Your employer—" said one, still speaking to Joe.

"Mr. Desmond Cortez—" added the other.

"...will be quite appreciative of any assistance which proves...expedient," the first concluded.

Without thinking, and still trying to quell the fury bubbling within him, Joe pointed down the street in the direction he had seen Dom follow. "He went that way." As an afterthought he added, "He's got Dominique Angel with him."

The agents were heading back to their car before Joe even finished.

"Have no fear, Mr. Caparelli," said the first as he climbed into the driver's seat.

"The safety of Ms. Angel is our paramount...concern," added the other, slipping into the passenger side.

The smoked windows rose as one, and the massive auto silently roared back to life.

Joe blinked, and they were gone: on their way in the direction he'd given. With their departure, he now felt his anger fade. He felt lightheaded and bewildered, wondering if he'd forgotten to breathe throughout the encounter. "That is—hands down—without a doubt—the *weirdest damn thing* I've ever seen."

He wasn't talking to Sanchez, but the young vagrant replied, his voice quaking, "How could you *do* that?"

Joe resorted to his stock Richard Blaine answer: "Hey, 'I stick my neck out for nobody.' "

"You sold him out!"

Joe didn't know what he'd done, but he resented the accusation on impulse. "What? No. I wouldn't do somethin' like that…"

"Didn't you see them?"

"What are you talking about?"

"They weren't human!"

Billy Sanchez screamed the last and took off running in the direction the Cadillac had gone.

Joe swiftly realized he was no longer where any story was taking place. If something big went down without his camera to back it all up, Dom would never forgive him.

He jumped into the newsvan, gunned the engine, and listened to it stall. "Damn."

Chapter Seventeen

One block beyond the dilapidated trestle, Dom sat politely on the stoop of an abandoned factory's outdoor freight platform—a man-made cul-de-sac of brick, steel and concrete—where, she hoped, the privacy might encourage the old man to finally unwind whatever secrets he was hiding.

"We are fallen, all humanity...fallen from the grace and splendor of what once was..."

The old man gestured upward at nothing more heavenly than a wrought-iron fire escape, precariously bolted to the warehouse's crumbling brick façade. Its lowest steps were balanced twenty feet off the ground to keep kids from playing atop its five stories of oxidized instability. As if realizing his lapse, he began to pace, striding purposefully back and forth, as if his audience of one was a captive congregation. Instead of secrets, Dom was getting a sermon. She fidgeted.

"We live in darkness, ignorant of our state, blindly stumbling through lives of desperation and misery. We seek solace where'er we can...in ambition, power, trinkets and the coins to purchase them. In truth, it is *companionship* we seek against the long, dark nights of this world."

As he spoke, he clenched and released his clawed fists, adding ferocity to his conviction.

"But instead, we are bitter, corrupt, turning against our brothers, our sisters, those very souls we seek to ease the pain. We are backstabbers and harlots, using what we will for self gain, sacrificing all upon the altar of our own desire!"

Then he whirled around suddenly and once again pierced her with his fiery gaze.

"And not one is immune! Not even those who cloak their ills under the guise of righteous compassion, those who cry out, 'I am better than you…see how much I care!' While all their great benevolence only leads them to hate and judge those who are not as righteous as they. We are all of us the sons of Adam and daughters of Eve. We are as sheep and goats adrift without our shepherd, grazing at the mercy of wolves."

He had hit his stride, and his gravelly voice now dropped an octave, replacing volume with menace.

"And the wolves are real…more real than you know. But your eyes refuse to see them as they are, prowling about as roaring lions seeking whom they will devour. Humanity's souls are the prey they seek."

He hesitated, seeming to have lost his place somewhere between the fire and the brimstone. Then he sat down next to Dom, catching his breath, swallowing the stones in his throat and softening far more than just his voice. "But there is hope…for our Shepherd has come and we who are His true sheep know His voice and follow Him."

Reacting to more than just the offense of his odor, Dom recalled a course she'd taken in Comparative Religions during her university days, in which she had done well enough to suspect she was now simply being fed spoonfuls of what she considered to be Christian drivel. She guessed she might still know enough to have an actual discussion, even on the old man's terms. The veil hiding her patronizing was thin.

"Excuse me, but…" she interrupted, "if you'll allow me to bypass the King James Version and cut to the chase? What you're really trying to tell me…is that life is just this game between good and evil. And all of us regular joe-blow slobs are only pawns on the great big cosmic chessboard. The 'sheep and the goats,' you call us—because we're really just a bunch of little lambs, being led to the slaughter by all of the world's lions and tigers and bears—Oh my!"

The old guy didn't catch the popular reference. He remained adamant. *"It is no game!* There is no *equality* amongst the powers that contend for dominance over this sphere. For evil creates nothing of its own; it cannot. It uses. It corrupts. It hides behind masks, distorting the truth."

Dom just nodded her head, hoping the old guy, who saw so much, wouldn't see her skepticism—not sure why she even cared. She guessed he had probably been some preacher's kid about a hundred years ago or thereabouts, who had strayed from the family faith and broken his poor momma's heart, only to come crawling back to the fold, old, broken and senile.

Sensing her doubt, he bluntly personalized his crusade. "He is using you…that *thing* you work for."

Dom should have expected it, but didn't stop to consider how he *knew* such detail before retorting, "Desmond Cortez doesn't 'use' me. We have…an understanding—that's all." Her words covered more thoroughly than did her eye shadow. "Whatever he gets from me comes with a price. From your perspective, I might be a whore…but I certainly don't come *cheap*."

"The cost is your soul."

"I'm not completely convinced I have one of those. And if it is a 'deal with the devil' as you're implying…then I'm dancing by my own free will."

"You dance upon the edge of an abyss."

Dom didn't answer immediately. She could no longer hide the incredulity blossoming across her face. The crazy old man was practically shaking with sincere urgency.

Dom could only quote his last words back at him: *"…Edge of an abyss?"* He'd made it sound oh-so-serious, so much so that she couldn't help but burst out laughing.

The old man looked genuinely startled, offended almost, that she could treat matters so obviously important to his heart with such contempt. He was like a doddering, domineering old parent who still didn't understand his children were leaving him in the old folks home for good. His quizzical expression made her laugh all the harder.

"My dear, *dear* 'Mr. Quixote,'" she chided, when she'd found her breath again, "you have no idea how absolutely *ridiculous* you sound. Here you sit in your ragged coat and smelly pants—completely out of touch with the rest of reality—spinning your little morality tale, and insinuating how I'm going to hell in a handbasket.

"I gotta hand it to you: you've got yourself a pretty good spiel—you almost had me buying what you're selling.... But I *spin* crap for a living—I don't buy it from anybody else."

"You are wrong!" declared the old man in rapidly rising decibels. "You are partial to darkness, for that is the world in which you live—a world of shadows, lies and deception. I did not call you 'harlot,' and yet you've branded yourself with the affront, as if it pays you honor. You resist the light with all of your being, with all of your lost soul.

"Truth stands ever before you, but *you do not see.*"

Dom was through playing another's game. "Truth?" she lilted. "So that must be *you*—'The Light of the World' here to free men's souls. Gimme some of that ol' time religion. I was blind but now I see. Amen! Praise the Lord...and pass the plate!"

"Does he love you?" he asked, his voice suddenly softening again.

The abruptness of the challenge startled her. "What the hell are you talking about?"

"This 'Cortez,' as he calls himself—your benefactor...*does he love you?*"

"I don't think that's any of your damn business!"

"Does he love you?"

Dom was silent.

*"Does...he...**love** you?"*

"Desmond..." Dom caressed her bruised cheek. The old man was continuing to play, forcing her back into the game on his terms. "Desmond *cares* about me...and in this life, that's about as much as anyone can hope for."

"There is *more*, Dominique. If you'd only open your eyes—" he left open the invitation.

The old man was winning, and Dom needed to end the charade decisively. *"You?"* She let her eyes and tone accuse for her. "If I work for the devil incarnate—what could a piss-stinkin' sterno-bum like you possibly have to offer me?"

There was a moment of silence and the old man turned away. *Unable to meet her eyes finally,* she mused. Then he looked back and answered, "I will die for you."

Damn the old guy! she thought bitterly. *Predictable.* And she should have seen it coming from a mile away. He'd win every time because he controlled the rules, bending them only where and when he saw fit. Her only chance was to stop playing. Immediately.

"I thought there might be a story here, but there isn't." Her tone was crisp and businesslike. "Desmond was right—nothing but a crazy old man with delusions of chivalry."

She stood briskly and dusted herself off. "Find yourself another 'Dulcinea,' Mr. Quixote." She turned and started the long walk back the way she had come.

The old man slammed balled fists into his thighs. "No! I wish I could make you…*believe.*"

Dom did not stop, nor did she slow or turn. Her decision. Her rules.

Chapter Eighteen

The black Cadillac screeched to a halt, sending small stones from the tarmac ricocheting off the brick walls of the delivery dock cul-de-sac. Even before its momentum had fully ceased, the doors flung open and four men in identically tailored black suits emerged; Will Smith and Tommy Lee Jones were not among them. They spread out like an ink stain on fine cloth, triangulating on the docking bay's two occupants, using themselves and their vehicle to block egress.

The wolves had finally come for the sheep, and the only exit from the urban slaughtering pen seemed to be the wrought-iron fire escape that creaked overhead with the slightest breeze.

Behind dark sunglasses, the pack leader intoned, in steady, measured beats, "Ms. Angel, step away slowly—for your own...protection," his growl smooth, cool and dry, not unlike a martini on ice. Three other identical voices chimed in eerily on the last word, *"protection."* As one, four mini-Uzi automatic handguns drew fluidly from shoulder holsters.

Dom had been content to leave one would-be "savior" in her dust. The last thing she wanted was four more candidates vying for the role. A fifth remained stoically in the driver's seat, hands gripping the wheel, seemingly impassive to any outside events.

Dom suddenly wished she hadn't left Joe so far away.

The old man studied the newcomers cautiously, his eyes furtively darting to each in turn and gauging intent as he deftly slid up behind the television reporter. He whispered, "You may be blind, Dominique...but soon enough you shall *see*."

He drew forth the long iron staff he hid in his ratty cloak. Dom was oddly startled—spying dried blood along its length—believing the police had confiscated the previous day's murder weapon. But then she was quickly distracted by a low rumble of thunder that slowly rolled across an otherwise clear blue sky.

The old man charged at that moment, and Dom's peripheral vision caught four gun muzzles swinging as one, targeting the old fool, discharging fire and smoke. But the old man ducked, leaping and rolling until the gunmen on each of the far sides were forced to break off or nail each other in their crossfire.

Ducking the ricochet of shrapnel and brick, Dom squatted, instinctively covering her face with her hands, but between splayed fingers she still witnessed the old man roll back up to his feet, inches from one of the two

middle gunmen, and swat aside the weapon with his own staff of iron. Bullets skittered up the brick wall of the cul-de-sac and sparked off the rattling fire escape. The old man swung his shaft back a second time, cleaving a gaping gash across the black suited agent from pec to abdomen.

Dom could have sworn she saw a burst of fire explode from within the agent, ripping its body in two, answered by a searing bolt of lightning that sizzled the very molecules of the air. She had to hold her breath to keep her lungs from bursting.

The three remaining agents dropped for cover simultaneously, two behind either end of their black Cadillac.

Lightning cracked a second time and suddenly the old man was gone. In his place, she saw a long black mane swirling around the head of one who appeared to have stepped straight from a world of both fairy tale and truth. He was a dashing figure in flowing black, belonging equally to a night of Elizabethan theater as he was to this makeshift gladiatorial arena. He glanced back toward Dom and smiled straight into her eyes—and heart.

His gold buttons gleamed, lit by electrical fire, and he held a sword, three feet of shimmering steel that looked sharp enough to slice darkness from light. He spoke, and Dom realized his voice was thunder issuing from his mouth, shaking the foundations of everything around her and all she believed

to be true. "For those without faith," he said, "*seeing* is belief!"

With a ghastly horror, the limbs of the severed agent continued to writhe independently upon the loose stones of the lot, even as they were consumed by a slow internal fire. Its sunglasses had fallen from its face, revealing tongues of flame dancing in coal-black empty sockets. The mouth screamed, lips and skin peeling back from a grinning rictus skull. The wailing of thousands poured forth from its taut grimace.

A third crack of lightning split the day in half, and rain poured from the *blue sky* as if sent from Heaven itself.

Her hands dropped from her face and for the first time in her life, Dominique Angel was completely without words.

The lone agent crouching in the far open, off to Dom's left, leapt straight through the storm that had suddenly blown in from nowhere. He didn't advance upon the swordsman, however: he charged at Dom. One powerful

hand grabbed her left wrist and yanked the reporter back up to her feet. The agent's voice never lost its smooth calm. "You are to come with us, Ms. Angel."

"I don't even know who you are," she answered.

He pulled her close to his face. Though Dom saw only her own rain-streaked reflection staring back at her from the agent's dark glasses, she now knew there was nothing but hollow sockets behind those lenses.

It spoke again. "We've been sent by Mr. Cortez." This close, she smelled its breath, and remembered flowers at her mother's funeral.

Beyond the *thing* that held her in its grip, Dom glimpsed another agent rising from behind the cover of the Cadillac to make a second attempt on the dashing swordsman, but he was waiting for just such a move. She saw the swordsman strike, and unbelievably, saw the automatic weapon fly upward in two separate chunks of black metal.

The creature holding Dom persisted, unfazed. "Your work is too important…"

"What are you talking about?"

"Mr. Devlin."

"What?" It didn't matter that these things could invoke her Desmond, or even the potential future Governor. Dom focused again on the agent before her and shrieked, "No! I'm not going anywhere with you!" She was certain she saw the swordsman turn in response to her cry.

She yanked her hand from its grasp, but the thing in agent form reclaimed its hold instantly. Dom gasped in pain as it again locked its grip around her wrist like a vice. She pulled but its arm would not budge.

This time, using the very same words, it threatened her. "For your safety, Ms. Angel—You will come with us." She spat into the sunglasses, but her ineffectual struggles merely distracted it.

The diversion proved enough, though. Behind them both, the strange swordsman from another time suddenly returned, severing the threatening agent from kidney to kidney in one mighty swing. Its upper torso fell, no longer supported by legs or trunk, and pulled Dom down with its sudden weight. She saw fire burst from its mouth, as if a spirit essence fled its body in death. Yet the jaw continued to chatter in its wake, pouring forth gibberish and obscenity.

Dom screamed, and again tried to pull her left hand free. The swordsman loomed above and struck a second blow, releasing her from the dead weight. She jerked up and stumbled backward, still screaming as she realized the chunk of

severed forearm remained clamped about her wrist.

The swordsman, her bizarre savior, his own hair matted across his face by the wind and rain, actually smiled at her plight, finding a touch of humor in her terror. But they both heard the next crack of automatic gunfire, and she saw him stagger as his left shoulder exploded from a bullet's impact. She even imagined she saw the shell pass clean through. The swordsman grimaced and, scowling, turned himself back into the storm.

He had called her Dulcinea. She had called him Quixote—and she'd intended her words to hurt him. Although he wore no armor, as a knight of honor should, he was no less brave—no less gallant—than any hero from any tale she'd ever clung to as a child, when the nights were too long, too dark, and too lonely. She realized that somehow, despite his wounds and pain, this ancient warrior fought for her virtue—and she felt shame.

Dom wobbled and fell to her knees, now desperate to pull the clamped dead fingers from her arm as she felt that malevolent hand begin to smolder about her wrist. The pieces of the agent/thing were already consuming themselves, and still the monstrous jaw screamed forth blasphemy into the gale. Its words were tangible evil, themselves bursting into flame above its head as if the storm were holy water falling from on high.

Quixote battled forth, back into the very heart of the gale itself. The lead agent couldn't draw a bead on his improbable adversary, he who danced between its fire and the raindrops. The ancient warrior possessed no fear of their blasting gunplay, as long as he saw from where their fire came. The thing in human form did smell blood though, and knew it had gotten lucky. But the entire mission was quite literally going to Hell, and the agents alone knew exactly how dire that could be. Of the four, only a single gun remained, and the warrior continued to prove he could move faster than the chemical reactions that launched lead into space.

The second of the remaining agents, that which had lost its own weapon when its device was cleaved in two, skirted around the large loading bay, avoiding the warrior's focus, and made straight for the woman. It knew she was key. The other had been right in its attempt, but had made a grave mistake and was now damned for it. This one knew better. *Use the old ways.* As it was from the beginning: use the woman *against* the man.

When the gripping claw had finally consumed itself sufficiently, Dom was at last able to wrench it from her wrist, wincing at the pain as she then held her injured arm outwards so that the rain might cool the burning she still felt. Through eyes stinging with tears, yet now rinsed by the rain, she saw the horrible red scarring she feared she might live with for the rest of her life. She wondered just *how* her ordered universe could reverse its poles in but a single afternoon of madness, violence and death.

Without warning, another of the horrific creatures descended upon her. She nearly laughed in this one's face. Her mind stepped aside from the horror for a moment as she briefly thought of over-ambitious IRS agents. *It shows about as much mercy.*

Reality rudely returned as this one snarled and yanked her again to her feet. It twisted her around until she felt both her arms held taut behind her. Its grip upon her burned wrist was sudden agony, and she cried out.

As if in answer to her cry, a distant voice howled across the bay, "We have our orders—Angel is not to be harmed!"

And Dom heard the one behind her chime in unison on, "...*not to be harmed.*"

Quixote took advantage of the agent's howling distraction and brought down a crackling deathblow. The leader of the rapidly diminishing pack swerved away at the last instant. The cutting edge of the warrior's blade merely claimed another arm, the sword continuing down through the still-running engine block of the massive Cadillac. The fan belt whipped free. Another battle-ravaged radiator geysered up, steaming into the rain-tossed sky. Sparks ignited fumes and leaking fuel. A sudden series of small fires under the hood rapidly coalesced into an explosion, blowing the warrior and the amputated agent off their feet.

The severed hand still clutched its weapon, squeezing off round after random round, pinwheeling from the recoil until the Uzi's clip ran dry

Chapter Nineteen

Billy Sanchez had run blindly for the first few blocks, then slowed to a stumbling walk as he realized he had no clue where the old man, the reporter, or even the demons in black had gone. He had simply started running a straight line in the direction the cameraman had pointed. He finally stopped completely, momentarily distracted by the corner sights he couldn't afford. The prostitutes had little interest in him anyway. He suspected a lack of bathing to be a prime contributing factor, as he held up part of his shirt for a sniff.

The more he thought about the plight of the old man, though, the less he found he cared. Billy had been doing just *fine* before the crazy old guy showed up. So why shouldn't he just use this opportunity for the excuse it presented, to heed the wisdom of Paul Simon after all? *He didn't owe the old man anything. Not really.* He probably wouldn't have even *gotten* in trouble with those punks if the old guy hadn't shown up and started the whole fracas to begin with.

But one look at the remains of his sleeve and the bandages beneath told him what a liar he was. And wasn't *that* the only skill he'd ever mastered, the only trade at which he'd ever excelled?

Billy remembered most of his years on the streets; it was only *how* he had gotten there that slipped his mind most of the time. His childhood was a fond memory: Mama and Papa, and he, the third of four children, with an older and younger brother, and an older sister. Even a grandmama had lived with the family in the days of his youth. Those had been good times: poor, but filled with love and hope and promise.

When he was ten, Billy's older brother Juan stumbled home from a gang fight covered in blood. He died before his father could rush him to the hospital.

Billy bought his first illegal substance one year later. Unbeknownst to buyer or seller, it was bought from the same young man who had stabbed Juan in the kidney, leaching the toxins that killed him into his system.

Buyer and seller became good friends, until a drive-by shooting killed that particular peddler three years later.

When Billy was fifteen, his older sister Consuela married a psychologist, moved to a larger city, bought a big suburban home that Billy only saw once, and raised the prerequisite 2.5 offspring. She simultaneously started a successful editorial career with her bachelor's in English.

Then, when Billy was eighteen, Juan Sanchez Sr. delivered an ultimatum intended to wake his middle son out of his self-inflicted stupor: get a job or get out of the house. To Billy's minimal credit, he at least tried, but soon found he spent far more than he earned. He concluded that steady employment just wasn't the life for him.

By the time he was twenty, Billy's mama wept but Papa was firm: Billy Sanchez found himself out on the street. He spent the next five years blaming his "cruel and unreasonable papa." He also cultivated a steady hatred for his "weakling mama" who had betrayed him by her inability to demand that her husband do the "decent, proper and loving thing": namely, accept Billy for who he was.

Billy's younger brother made one attempt to reach him before starting medical school after college. Billy broke his brother's nose and they never saw each other again.

At twenty-seven, he heard that his father had died of a heart attack while on the job as a night-shift security guard. Billy had been wasted at the time and was never exactly sure whether he'd really heard the news or merely dreamt it. Either way, he'd never even tried to find out the truth.

Billy became a father himself at twenty-eight, or at least that's what *the bitch* had accused him of. She died of an overdose before the baby was born. Billy considered himself lucky.

Billy should have died at the age of thirty. He'd pimped himself and was sleeping off his bottled reward when five young punks had set him on fire. No, make that four young punks—*the fifth had been a monster.*

A distant roll of thunder rumbled across the clear blue sky and Billy realized he knew from *whence* it came.

Perhaps the old man had been right and Billy was now dying by degrees, slowly killing himself for any number of reasons. He knew he wasn't the type who could stop those dice once they'd been rolled. But now, Billy realized he wanted to face that inevitable day, whenever it might be, knowing he had done at least one thing in his life right.

He did owe the old man that much.

Chapter Twenty

The stitch in his side burned, but he couldn't stop. While running across the old trestle, Billy felt the drops of rain and heard the car explode. Something told him the *things* in the Cadillac would have scared even yesterday's ogre.

He arrived at the docking cul-de-sac in time to witness a one-armed demon draw forth a sword of liquid fire. But the Hero was there. He had returned—Quixote, he had called himself. The two clashed, righteous steel against the damning fire of Hell.

Quixote was on the ground, flat on his back and struggling to his feet, his features somewhat dazed, when the demon struck. Yet, even from the ground, Quixote parried a veritable monsoon of furious blows. With a powerful kick, he ended the attack, sending the demon sprawling backward into the flames of the burning Cadillac. It seemed to consume the fiend, and gave the Hero a chance to regain an upright stance.

For a moment, the dashing man in black looked tired and clutched his shoulder, the arm wet and red. Then he lifted his face to the sky, into cleansing rain that washed the care from his features and renewed conviction without quelling the fire within.

Inside the burning vehicle, another of the creatures shrieked from behind the wheel, its own flesh consumed by the holocaust. Blackened arms flailed about its head as its claws scratched at the roof's unyielding steel.

The first demon screamed with an unearthly madness as it leapt back from out of the car's flames and renewed its own attack.

Quixote was hard pressed to avoid both the fiery sword and the flames that engulfed its infernal wielder. But Billy had faith in his Hero. *He believed.*

Dom and the agent that held her had also been knocked off their feet by the exploding automobile. Dom had the distinct impression they had both been airborne before the unyielding reality of the docking platform manifested itself beneath them. They landed hard together, like a bound bundle of newsprint thrown from a passing truck.

Dom suspected her own weight and impact weren't enough to do any harm to her captor, who had so graciously cushioned the blow by landing first. The explosion had caught them both off-guard. The agent's grip had released as they hit, and Dom rolled off with the momentum and out of reach.

The agent twitched, spasmed itself over onto its belly and continued after her, practically slithering with intent. Dom ignored the pain of her seared wrist, stumbling and crawling backwards until she reached the brick wall at the rear of the loading platform—which cut off her only escape.

The agent grinned, and Dom swore she saw fangs in its mouth.

Your work is too important...

That's when jail-escapee William Sanchez suddenly leapt screaming onto the hideous agent that seemed to be transforming before her very eyes. Sanchez landed on its back and pounded the agent's face into the old concrete. Its sunglasses shattered on the second impact, and Dom saw deep empty sockets laughing back at her as the head came up in Sanchez's grip.

Mr. Devlin...

Dom scrambled to her feet and stole a glance at the other conflict.

Quixote, pressed between the flaming agent and the burning husk of the Cadillac, leapt backwards, kicking his fiery adversary off its own feet. With a vertical backflip, he landed on the car's roof, momentarily protected, although surrounded by

flames. Despite the rain, the tongues of fire rose hungrily from the shattered windows on all four sides. The creature within was now a charred stump behind the wheel. But its moaning wails continued.

The first burning agent rose quickly and charged back into the auto's fire. Quixote dodged the sweeping blade and leapt up even higher, grabbing hold of the rungs of the ancient fire escape overhead.

The entire structure groaned with the sudden weight, the staircase shuddering. It tipped on its hinged axle, an escape route that hadn't been pressed into service in over a generation. The lower rungs shrieked on rusted joints as the base of the iron stairs came crashing down onto the car's flame-shrouded rooftop. Hot sparks flew in all directions. The other-worldly moans from inside it abruptly ceased. Quixote still hung beneath the stairs by a bloodstained arm that screamed with a pain only he could hear.

Before the swordsman could swing himself onto the top side of the iron steps, however, the flaming specter came lumbering around the burning vehicle and swatted at the dangling hero. The clash of steel started anew.

Quixote proved equally adept at hanging by but a single arm whilst dueling his one-armed adversary. Frustrated, it broke from the attack. Dom heard the burning creature shriek into the air, feeling its anger as a palpable thing reverberating within her skull.

Billy knew he had little time to do any real damage, or even—miracle of miracles—possibly kill the demon he held before it could regain the upper hand. Again and again he pounded the scaled head into the concrete. He continued even after he felt its fanged teeth shatter against the man-made stone, saw dark ooze spread out beneath the face. But deep inside, on some primordial level where men still fear the coming of night, he knew that anyone born of human lineage had little hope of slaying that which fell from Heaven, wreathed in fire and wrath. He didn't know

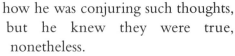

how he was conjuring such thoughts, but he knew they were true, nonetheless.

He felt the demon collecting its wits and regaining strength enough to pluck off the little gnat he knew he was. It abruptly locked its arms straight, preventing any more thrusts of its broken face into the black ichor-stained concrete. Its muscles heaved, flinging Billy from its back. A backhand blow followed. The desperate young man, who at least wanted to die knowing he had done maybe one thing right, failed to dodge and went sprawling into the muddy puddles that now filled the center of the cul-de-sac.

Dom stood by helplessly as the agent bucked Sanchez from its back like an unsecured load. It rose, the eye-less face a ruin of broken bone jutting through skin, rivulets of black blood mixing with the rain and streaking its flesh with running cracks. Its jaw appeared split in two at the chin, making the jaw line droop on either side within hanging sacks of punctured cheek. It spat out pieces of tooth and bone, and its tongue—either forked or newly split down the center—twitched as its mouth filled with an overflow of miry mucus. It whirled on the sprawled form of Billy Sanchez, stomping toward him with venomous purpose, drawing its own sword of fire from within its bloody, mud-splattered suit.

Dom screamed, "Look out!"

Quixote took the moment's respite from the broken-off attack to hoist himself up onto the staircase properly.

His enemy had returned to the burning Cadillac and, less gracefully than the ancient warrior had done, jumped onto the crushed rooftop. The fire that wreathed the creature had finally sputtered out, revealing a charred-grey hide. New scales were forming, though, even as he watched, pale and squirming worms, like mewling newborns, molting the smoking skin from its body. The new scales swiftly blackened and hardened, looking just like a finely tailored black suit sprouting itself from a skin of writhing maggots.

It leapt and mounted the staircase, hooves clanking on the metal steps. The entire structure now rattled ominously.

Quixote steadied himself on the creaking staircase and prepared for the advancing assault.

The sound of Dominique Angel's desperate cry turned his attention down to where Billy Sanchez, struggling prostrate, had no clue that death was coming for him sooner than expected.

Billy thought he heard the reporter scream something behind him. He wasn't sure, unconvinced as he was that all of his limbs were still functioning properly. He had landed hard on his left arm, and knew that a proper shakedown would tell him if he'd broken it. Billy just hoped the scream didn't mean that Dominique Angel was in trouble again. If so, he'd just have to throw himself back into that grinder a second time, and probably get himself killed in the process.

Billy turned just in time to see the misshapen thing, no longer even pretending a human form, draw back a sword of fire.

In one swing, within the space of one tick of the clock, Billy realized his head would fall from his shoulders, cleaved swift and smooth.

And not a single human being on the face of the Earth would mourn his passing.

You are dying.

Billy Sanchez was dead.

Chapter Twenty-One

Deep down, Dominique Angel knew there was nothing she could do to save the street vagrant, he who was now sacrificing his life for hers. She ran forward anyway, her scream of fury drowned out by another sudden roar of thunder that echoed off the brick canyon walls.

Rain slashed down in a torrent, the sky above utterly black. Even the storm clouds had lost all pretense of shape and substance. Darkness ruled the day.

Quixote stood, feet firmly planted upon the rickety fire escape's first landing, nearly two stories off the ground. With nary a moment's hesitation, he twisted around and threw his honed blade through the maelstrom with a strength to match the virtue of his intent.

The killing stroke had begun its arc toward the exposed throat of Billy Sanchez, when three feet of sharpest steel came from the heavens like a bolt launched by some mad god from the pinnacles of Olympus. The shaft's impact broke through skin, shattered bone. It quelled the deadly momentum in mid-swing, as its force continued to carry it straight through the demon's chest. Gouts of flame and black bile in equal measure spewed forth from both sides of the mortal wound.

The demoniac howled until its garbled voice was silenced by the blood and fire leaking from its twisted mouth.

Billy watched death hover over him, its arm outstretched in a ghastly welcome, its claw holding a glint of fiery steel that reflected streaks of the electrical lightshow raging high above them all. The demon swung its blade.

And in the very next instant, it was over.

…*dying.*

Billy was alive.

Dom saw the swordsman twist around and throw his only weapon like an Olympic-gold javelin hurl. The blade struck true and its tip passed through the hideous agent. The creature stood transfixed for an instant, teetering on the threshold of life and death before it gave up the ghost in a sudden rush of fire and fury. The body collapsed, leaving Billy Sanchez staring slack-jawed, still watching the end credits roll on the story of his life.

With the immediate threat ended, Dom's nagging professionalism intruded. She briefly considered what a mess she must now look like, with rain-whipped hair and the torn, mud-splattered remnants of her broadcast attire. All vanity aside, however, she still couldn't prevent a sudden grin spreading from ear to ear.

Sanchez looked up, finally realizing the houselights had risen, the movie ended, and he was free to leave the theater, alive and well. He matched her grin with a burst of giddy joy amidst his sudden tears.

Billy couldn't believe he was still alive! The demon at his feet didn't twitch like the others had—tormented in their passing. This one fell still and silent, and consumed itself as if untended fires raged within.

The sword of his Hero stood firm and sure, sticking up through the chest

of the creature, rain cleansing its golden hilt and gleaming steel shaft.

He saw the reporter slow her charge to a staggering walk, and then she broke into the widest grin Billy had ever seen. He heard laughing erupt above the still-howling storm and was equally stunned as he realized the laughter was his own.

He tried to stand. He wanted to hug the woman. He wanted to go home and tell his mama and papa, if the man still lived, that he was sorry for the lifetime of grief he'd given them. He wanted to tell the whole world that he was alive and that this moment had changed everything forever.

He was crying even as he laughed, and couldn't distinguish between his tears and the rain.

Then he saw Dominique Angel look up, and her smile faded.

Dom gazed upward to give her thanks to the improbable swordsman, the ancient warrior, her knight-errant, Quixote, upon his impossible quest to save the souls of men. He had indeed saved them. He had saved them all.

Only then did she see the last agent—one she had forgotten about—charging up the final few steps to ram its flaming sword through the belly of the gallant, unarmed hero.

The demon saw its accursed enemy, *the ancient fool,* turn and throw away his only protection. It flew up the remaining steps, fueled by hatred and contempt, as if all the bitter loathing its kind had ever held for humanity now burned through its veins as an unholy adrenaline.

Too late, the swordsman turned back to face it, and its blade ran him through. The demon caught just a hint of the old man's eyes looking back at it in confusion: *such was not the way 'twas intended to go…*

The demon's empty eye sockets widened into grins, exposing teeth just beneath the lids. All three of its mouths then spoke, one voice, sharing the words between three fanged maws, "Such is your weakness. And so, we win!"

It withdrew its sword in triumph, and Quixote fell from the fire escape, thirty feet to the loading zone below.

Dom saw the body strike the tarmac like a sack of wet grain, and shuddered with the impact.

Instinctively, Billy knew the reason for the reporter's despair, and he refused to turn around. He closed his eyes and heard the smacking thud

of flesh hitting the ground.

Everything has a price, Billy knew, *even lives.* He couldn't calculate how he could ever even begin paying the interest on the loan that had just now been taken in his name.

Suddenly, the white WDVL newsvan, with its striking, red-emblazoned numeral "6" stenciled on its side, came screeching, horn blaring, into the loading bay. It nearly collided with the devastated, still-burning Cadillac.

Joe had come at last, the cavalry too late to save the Alamo.

The demon took a moment to weigh its options. The mission had been costly. It cared little for losses of its own kind, but one target still remained—William Sanchez. It watched the warrior's still form, and decided the sheep was as nothing without his shepherd. The sudden arrival of the newsvan, with its intrusive cameras, confirmed its course of action.

The demon ran.

Joseph Caparelli saw the guy in the black suit run down the fire escape, land on the smashed, smoking Cadillac roof, and leap off onto the ground. He donned a pair of dark sunglasses, took a moment's hesitant glance toward Joe, then ran off in the opposite direction.

Dom and Billy Sanchez stood in the shadow of the loading bay, looking confused and disheveled, but otherwise fine.

"Sorry I couldn't get here sooner. What *happened?*" said Joe, somewhat frantic, and gesturing to the Cadillac, its flames now dwindling to smoldering embers of melted plastic and charred steel. "Everybody get out of that OK?"

Dom said nothing. Billy shook his head and dragged unwilling feet over to the prostrate form of the old man. He dropped to his knees.

Joe was absorbing detail in layers, comprehending what he saw only as veils seemed to lift slowly from his vision. Too much time behind the camera had conditioned his perception to a cognitive distance from whatever actually lay before his eyes. Anything that was divorced from the immediate story, any facts not contained within the viewfinder lens, was optional. He had moved heaven and earth and *willed* the stubborn, stalled engine of the van back into life for Dom's sake. Yet here she stood—A-OK. *Cut, print, that's a wrap, folks,* he wanted to assume. But the longer he stayed focused on the moment, the more he saw.

Grimly, Joe took in the carnage around him, part of him wondering if he should have his camera out and rolling. Around the burning automobile, crushed beneath the heavy steps of the iron fire escape, hundreds of spent shell casings littered the ground, along with twisted chunks of metal that were most probably pieces of automatic weapons. He stooped and picked up something near his feet. It was a cell phone. *Make that—a broken cell phone,* he thought, the compact piece of technology nearly falling apart in his hands. *Thing looks like it's been through a war...* Amongst the rubble, three of the dark-suited men lay, quite obviously dead. And, in the center of it all, Billy Sanchez now lay sobbing over the old man, the one who had launched the whole weird story to begin with.

"What the *hell* happened here?" he asked Dom again.

Dom couldn't believe her eyes when she saw Joe climb out of the van—good old dependable Joe. In that moment she knew she *loved* the young cameraman in a way she could never describe, much less act upon.

She didn't quite know exactly when the torrential downpour had ended, but it had. She remembered, with a hint of embarrassment, that she must

look a fright. For once she was glad Joe hadn't leapt out, camera in hand, ready for action. He was completely dry, and the 'DVL newsvan gleamed a pearly white in the sunlight.

Joe said something to her. She wasn't sure what it was. Her ears still rang from the piercing thunderclaps. Her tongue felt too thick for speech. Her skin dimpled in goose flesh chill. It had all come and gone so fast, too fast for her nerves to keep pace. In a detached sense she knew she was still dazed, observing the action's aftermath in what she'd often heard combat vets describe as the unnatural, almost super-natural, calm that could follow an intense firefight.

She was just so grateful Joe had finally come to save the day. *No. It hadn't been Joe;* she knew that much. She gingerly clutched her burned wrist, claiming a sense of reality from the pain. Then, needing to say something to address the silence and her appearance, she found her voice and blurted, "Sorry Joe…sorry I'm such a mess. I must look like some kind of drowned rat or something…"

…And then, she said, the little angel would wake up in Heaven…

Once more, she was falling from the seventh-story window and there was no one to catch her but the unfeeling ground rushing up at 120 miles per hour.

The cameraman was unfazed. "You look fine, Dom," he answered absently. Joe seemed more distracted by Sanchez than noticing her state. The Latino began helping the *dead, old man back to his feet.*

Other than a slight wobble in her stance, and a glazed expression—as well as speaking less than coherently, as if abruptly awakened from the strangest dream—Dom looked her usual self to Joe's eyes. The street bum Sanchez, on the other hand, looked every bit the role of drowned rat. The Hispanic looked as if he'd just stepped fully clothed from the shower. Yet there wasn't a cloud in the sky—a rumble of distant thunder maybe, but skies were clear as far as the cameraman could see. Besides, WDVL meteorologists had forecast clear skies all week long, and company policy maintained that they were never wrong.

Sanchez was a veritable tangle of sopping straggles, with dirty hair clinging to his scalp and face. The old guy looked far worse. He was very pale, distant and haunted, that frightening fire in his eyes extinguished. He seemed unable to focus on anything not three inches from his broken nose. Blood dribbled from both nostrils. His left shoulder was caked in fresh blood mingled with drying mud. He pulled one side of his ratty wet trench coat across his belly, as if internal organs might spill out if he let go. He staggered a step forward and Sanchez, openly weeping, took hold of his frail right arm to keep the old man steady on tottering legs.

The old man reached out then and took hold of a rusted iron bar sticking up from the ground. It wasn't until the pole was in his frail hand that Joe realized it had been yanked out of one of the black-suited dead bodies. Yet another obvious murder to lay squarely in the old man's guilty, blood-red hands. Or had it been in self-defense? Had the previous day's alley brawl possibly been just that and nothing more?

Was it possible that here now stood the only truly innocent man he'd ever known? Joe's mind whirled with possibilities and contradictions. He definitely needed a break from the heady rush threatening to unravel his objective take on events, so he looked for something more substantial.

A silver gleam caught his eye as he spied a scorched wallet lying open near the dead suit, not far from where he'd picked up the cell phone. He dropped the broken bits he still held in his hand and knelt to recover the wallet. Most of its contents were charred beyond recognition, but a silver badge still gleamed when he wiped the soot away.

Dom mumbled, "I'm dry...dry. I'm not wet," as she ran a trembling hand through her hair and then nervously patted down her clothes, waves of residual shock still washing over her. She delicately fingered a tender, red, raw band of skin around her wrist and winced. "What is happening here, Joe?" she asked weakly, parroting back his own question to her.

He looked up, his eyes dark. "Are you OK, Dom?" This was far worse than yesterday's moment of shaken silence, when she had clutched that sooty dolly head like a rosary.

She didn't answer, and seemed to take in the three dead suits as if seeing them for the first time.

"What have we stumbled into?" she asked. Her question seemed directed more at herself. The shock had sunk in behind her eyes and filtered down into the rest of her body like a misty spring drizzle, bringing a chill to her entire being.

"You tell me, Dom," he said with an edge to his voice, displaying the wallet and badge. A seared photo identification card stared back at her. "Federal Agent."

Dom shivered at his words. Her lips then moved silently as Joe had often seen her do when stringing together an unexpected connection between scattered facts.

Her tenuous concentration broke, however, when the old guy shuffled forward to extend a hand towards her. She backed away, eyes suddenly wide. "Don't *touch* me!" she said. Joe thought Dom's eyes looked like those of a rabbit caught in the head-lights of a screaming automobile. "Please…just stay away from me." Her lower lip quivered uncontrollably now as the shakes settled into her hands.

It was the derelict pair's turn to be startled, and the Latino looked at her with eyes that screamed betrayal. The old man audibly sighed and his shoulders slumped with that breath as if life had fled and he'd forgotten to fall.

"Who—*what*—are you?" asked Dom.

The old man seemingly jump-started his own heart, wincing with the pain of his effort. "I am…unimportant."

"But…how did you—I saw…I don't know what I saw—" She shook her head.

"You've begun to see…with your *heart*."

"Why me?" Her eyes filled with desperate tears, and for the first time since entering the slaughtering pen, Joe felt his own fear rise. He had never seen Dom come apart like this, and wouldn't have thought it possible.

"Was it not *you*…who sought *me*, Miss Angel?" chided the old man, as he sadly turned and staggered away, supported by the trembling arms of Billy Sanchez.

Dom's voice cracked, then rose with intensity. "You know what I mean…you, my boss, an alley filled with dead men—or whatever the hell they are—*were!*" Her expression glazed still further as the recent past replayed in her mind. "It was raining, and…and I watched those things burn to *ash*

with my own eyes—*I saw it!* One of them gave me *this* in the process!" She thrust out her wrist, the nearly three-inch band of burned skin encircling it like a red brand. "But they're all still here, aren't they? Lying at our feet...pieces of them scattered all over this alley..." She trailed off, sputtering, seeming uncertain of how to go on.

"It's insanity!" she continued, resurging. "And it's all swirling around me. *Why? Tell me the truth!*" The last she shrieked.

The old man answered over his shoulder. "I have told you all that you wished to hear."

Now the fire was in Dom's eyes, as shock coalesced into anger:

"Talk to me, dammit! No more fairy stories. *These men are dead!*"

The old man hesitated, and Sanchez whispered something in his ear before turning his head to give Joe and Dom a dirty look.

Dom's tone was suddenly imploring. Joe had never heard such agony in her voice before. "Give me something I can *believe*," she begged.

The old man sighed again. He whispered in turn to Sanchez, then released himself from the young man's supporting hold. He stood by his own strength and answered of his own conviction. "Cortez...has invested heavily in you. He plans a promising career, which he *will* deliver: fame, fortune...the respect of your peers, for whatever that is worth. You will prosper and thrive. Men will idolize and lust after you. Women will envy and hate you. But your life, your identity—your very soul—mean little to him. He will use you, then discard you and all of your dreams when you no longer serve his purpose."

Dom said nothing to challenge the silence that followed and hung in the air between them. She simply wiped the tears from her eyes. *How much of the old man's assessment of evil could be applied to her, though, when Desmond no longer served **her** purpose?*

"You asked for the truth," he added.

Joe felt an indignant stirring of his old Baptist upbringing. "And the *'truth'* shall set us free, huh?"

"So you say…so you say," the old man mumbled. "Whatever you choose to believe, Dominique, know that Cortez answers to a darker power…and his *pride* will not give you up so easily."

His eyes darkened with righteous menace one last time in Joe's presence. The cameraman never saw them again in his lifetime.

Chapter Twenty-Two

Fifteen-year-old Reginald "Reggie" Sharpe had come home the day before in his bright, plus-sized blue windbreaker and told his momma how "big kids" had hurt his shoulder really bad. Reggie's momma, bless her heart, believed every word that came out of the mouth of her over-sized child, just as she always had.

His parents immediately rushed him with his dislocated shoulder to Calvary Memorial General Hospital, where the good doctors reset the joint and gave him a prescription for the pain.

When all was said and done, Reggie knew he had only to blab some names—*any names*—and his mother's wrath would fall on them as holy vengeance. Mrs. Sharpe had often told herself that eighty-pound children were, indeed, capable of harming her three-times-their-weight son, if *he* claimed it was so. She and her husband had once tried to sue the family of a nine-year-old who had clamped ahold of their precious Reggie's forearm with his teeth and wouldn't let go. But on that day the Judge had shown the wisdom of the Divine and threw the case out of her court. Mrs. Sharpe had then wanted to sue the Judge. Reggie had been thirteen years old and weighed two hundred pounds himself at the time of the incident. His victim barely weighed ninety. All in all, the little overweight boy was growing up to make his momma proud.

This time, however, Reggie refused to identify his assailants any further than the nebulous brand, "big kids." That night, little Reggie tossed and turned in his bed, knowing now only too well that the "big kids" wielded swords and meted out justice even to simple bullies like him.

It took very little crosschecking for a detective, even of Ben Saunders's limited ambition, to connect little Reggie's injury with those of his three role models in the Security Wing, four floors above the Emergency Room entrance.

The detective's headache had at last faded to a minimal roar, like ocean waves lapping in the hollow of a seashell, when Saunders knocked at the Sharpe's residence door. Elementary school-aged kids screamed up and down the residential block, performing their after-school rituals to advance the coming of summer. The raucous activity abruptly stopped, however, when all eyes fell on the black man in the dark suit, obviously in the wrong neighborhood, calling about the latest outrage of *little* Reggie Sharpe.

Before Mrs. Sharpe opened her door, Ben dropped his latest cigarette—yet another little broken man—crushing the life from it with the sole of his shoe. Unfortunately, Mrs. Sharpe looked just like her son, and wore a blue circus tent to hide the evidence. Saunders spoke his piece but the woman's only response was to take the whole thing as a personal slight, resenting even the implication that her son could do anything to initiate a detective's investigation. Saunders could tell her resentment stemmed partly from the fact that he was an African-American man with a badge. He didn't hold it too much against her. Experience had taught him that racism was alive and well—and feeding off itself—on all sides of the ethnic divide. Politically-correct circles could argue till they were blue in the face that reverse discrimination didn't exist, but Saunders knew it was all just so much euphemized, variegated crap.

Circumstances in this case didn't justify a warrant, so if Mrs. Sharpe wouldn't help in the investigation, there was little the detective could do about it. Some old instinct, however, not yet dulled by long-term alcoholic over-consumption, saw the furtive, darting, pig-like eyes of Momma Sharpe peering over his shoulder as evidence she was covering for a child not presently at home.

Leaving the bitter woman to look after her own big top, Detective Saunders spent only nominal effort to find for himself the two hundred and fifty pound fifteen-year-old who had participated in and survived a brutal, bloody massacre—one who found no solace in the embrace of a morally-blind mother with whom he could never share the truth.

Reggie Sharpe had the locally known "Tot Lot" all to himself, the very presence of the bully frightening away most of the neighborhood kids. Despite his right arm now in a sling his presence sent a warning to concerned parents not to let the smaller tykes in unattended.

Lost in dark thoughts, like a child fallen down a dank, forgotten well, Reggie looked up dolefully from his listing swing seat. He didn't even try to bolt when the detective's long, dark sedan pulled in next to the lot just two blocks from his home. He almost seemed to welcome Ben Saunders into his own private purgatory. The rusting swing gave every impression it might soon snap under Reggie's prolonged usage, but this had been the heavy boy's favorite swing for over ten years. If he had faith in anything, it was in the hope that some things would never fail to support you, especially when you needed them most.

Saunders put on his big friendly smile, the one he reserved for kids, but which his own daughter had seen straight through.

"Hey there—Reggie Sharpe?" he asked.

The large boy nodded his head.

"Do you mind if I talk with you about a few things, son?" Saunders flipped open his wallet, flashing his badge, operating mostly on autopilot.

The boy's lost but serious expression never changed as he kicked at small stones at his feet. "You wanna talk about yesterday, don'tcha?"

Saunders had been prepared for any number of games to get to the truth he sought.

He never expected forthright cooperation. He sat himself on a low concrete retaining wall so as not to be a looming presence over the boy.

"What about yesterday?" he said.

"Are you gonna arrest me?" the boy asked. He seemed prepared to go with the detective then and there.

"Did you do anything that you should be arrested for?"

The boy was silent for several moments, as if sorting through mental notebooks instead of just looking up his answer on the Internet.

As Saunders cleared his throat to ask again, the boy nodded in affirmation.

"What happened yesterday, Reggie?"

No answer.

"Did you hurt that man in the alley?"

No answer.

"What about the old man...is he the one who hurt your shoulder?"

Reggie looked up, a hint of confusion flashing for an instant, a look that told Saunders, yet again, *there was no "old man."*

"Who hurt you, Reggie?" pushed the detective.

"The guy..."

"What guy? The guy with the *sword?*"

The boy's sudden start melted into relief, as if here, at last, was someone who might actually listen to him—and believe.

"Yeah...the sword," the boy said. "I thought I was the only one who saw him—I mean, *really* saw him."

"Long black hair? Long coat—golden buttons? *Scary eyes?*"

The boy looked down immediately, now shuffling the little stones under his too-clean, white Reebok sneakers. Saunders knew he had struck the right chord. "Scary eyes" seemed the constant, and the detective only wished that, he too, could see the man with the scary eyes.

"You saw this guy," he continued, "scary eyes and all. What can you tell me about him?"

Reggie's voice, his description and story, was an engine struggling to start. The *truth*, like an old rusty sparkplug corroded by disuse, was still able to fire if cleaned up properly. "He *saw* me, y'know?"

It was Ben Saunders's turn to nod.

"He looked inside me—right inside—and he saw everything I ever did— everything bad I ever did to anybody. He scared me…'cause I knew he was comin' after me next, and…and I *deserved* it!"

Saunders felt it was time to probe a little more firmly, and his voice ratcheted up to the next degree of authority. "What happened yesterday, son?"

"We were just screwin' around, like we usually do. I skipped school and we wuz messin' around with this camera we stole—shootin' movies and stuff—Jerry and Knucklehead trying to show how cool they were, and like, which one was really tougher.

"Then Vinny showed up and told us we could do somethin' better… more fun—he called it a 'community service.' We took this long walk across town, downtown, and we found this bum sleeping in an alley…"

Reggie grew distant and fixed his gaze far out across the playground, perhaps all the way to a plot in Easter Park where a carved headstone called him "Beloved Son," inscribed just below his name.

"And what happened?" the detective prodded once more.

"Jer and Knucklehead held him…while Dutch set 'im on fire."

"Why?"

"…Just to watch 'im burn."

"And what about you, Reggie?"

"They said I wasn't old enough yet, for the big stuff— they said maybe when I turn sixteen at the end of the summer. But it was my job to film it—to make the movie of the guy screamin' and burning…"

Reggie's far-off stare saw his own flesh aflame, blackening, peeling away to expose pink muscle, meat that browned in the fire, and plenty of white fat to sizzle as it burned.

The detective put out the fire with his words. "And that's when the guy with the sword showed up?" Saunders already knew the answer.

Reggie nodded.

"He saved the guy you were attacking?"

Reggie nodded again.

"He hurt Dutch and the other guys—"

The boy blurted, "They attacked him first."

"Then he hurt you and smashed the camera?"

Another nod.

"You boys have done a lot of bad things in your time, but you've never tried anything like this before."

"It was Vinny's idea to torch the bum." Reggie sounded a little defensive.

"Tell me about Vinny."

"Vinny Barbarino?"

The detective started, and coughed into his hand to suppress an out-of-place, out-of-context snicker. "Was that his real name?" He coughed again.

The boy was unfazed, too young and out of touch—even by late-night Nickelodeon standards—to connect with that particular piece of rerun Americana. He merely shrugged.

"Tell me about Vinny Barbarino."

The boy sniffed up the snot that had pooled in the dark hollows under his nose, and wiped at bleary eyes with his free arm. He opened his mouth to speak, but said nothing. He shook his head back and forth very slowly, and finally just mouthed the word "no," as if afraid someone might hear him.

Saunders was gentle but emphatic. "Vincent Barbarino is *dead,* Reggie. He can't hurt you if you want to tell me the truth."

The boy looked skeptical, as if gravity's existence was also under debate. "I don't believe you."

"Would you believe me if I told you Vincent Barbarino was killed by the man with the sword?"

For the first time in his fifteen years, a light bulb went on somewhere in the dim recesses of the boy's conscience. A little glimmer of truth spoke from his soul, saying that even the biggest bullies paid for their crimes in the end, sometimes at the keen edge of a blade. That same glimmer also said it was not yet too late, even for little bullies like Reginald Sharpe.

The boy spoke with a growing confidence, the engine running smoother now on a full tank, not just the fumes of desperation. "The other guys thought his name was funny too, but they never told me why. *Nobody* ever said so to his face. Vinny was the kinda guy ya just didn't wanna be messin' with. He just kinda came outta nowhere one day. Knucklehead wanted to beat 'im up, but that's just Larry. There's a reason we all call 'im 'Knucklehead,' 'cause he's always been kinda stupid. But Vinny didn't mind it at all, and instead of fightin' Larry, he got us all beers—I mean, he was the only one who could get 'em without bein' carded or nothin'." Reggie smiled, reliving how great it had all been at first.

Saunders was still taking it slow, encouraging. "How long ago was this? I mean, *when* did he show up?"

"Just a couple months ago…February, I think. We wuz all just kinda hangin' out 'round a fire Jerry had set in a big old metal can—hangin' out, raggin' on Larry, the guys bustin' on me about stuff, and just generally trying to think of somethin' to do."

"And this 'Vinny Barbarino' just came—out of the blue?"

Reggie hesitated again, his shoulders twitching from a sudden involuntary shudder. "It's like…he came right out of the fire. I mean, I know he didn't—not really. But, it's like, all of a sudden, there he was, standing there in the smoke coming from the can…standing there and grinning at us."

"And Vinny made you set William Sanchez on fire?"

The kid flared in his first genuine flash of anger. "*I didn't set nobody on fire!* I just…held the camera…" The fury was short-lived, as Reggie seemed to realize that Larry Knucklehead didn't hold a monopoly on stupidity.

"Then…Vinny made Dutch do it—torch the old bum?"

The kid closed his eyes. "No," he sighed, "Vinny never *made* us do anything. He just suggested stuff that sounded cool at the time. Whatever we did…we did it all by ourselves."

Saunders had heard enough. He'd hoped to draw some vendetta connection between the old man and his young victim but, just like media acknowledgment of black-on-black crime, his perp just didn't seem to exist in the real world.

"I want to thank you, son…for your honesty," the detective said, as he stood up and brushed city dirt from the seat of his pants.

"Am I under arrest?"

"Not this time. I think you got off lucky, wouldn't you say?"

Reggie nodded and bit his lip.

"And I also think you've been given a lot to think about...about where your life might be going. You're not too old yet, Mr. Sharpe. There's still time to turn that course around; get yourself a new direction...and some new friends."

The boy agreed, but his head still seemed elsewhere, preoccupied by a stronger memory or thought that he needed to let go while he had the chance: one last item for the confessional.

"Y'know...I looked at 'im one time..."

"Who?"

"Vinny..."

"Yes?"

"I saw him this one time..."

"And?"

"...And he *didn't have any eyes.*" Reggie's voice was a whisper.

Wind whipped up the scatterings of trash in small cyclones of dirt and grit, miniature dust devils wandering across the desolate playground.

Suddenly, the Doppler roar of a WDVL newscopter ripped by, high overhead, the noise of its gnashing-teeth rotor escalating, then fading as it sped across the sky into the setting sun, and straight toward parts unknown. Reggie shook at the sound.

To Saunders, as he glanced up at the fast-waning echo, the rising wind and rays of red sun shafting through the dark, billowing clouds looked like the end of the world was coming: hard, fast, and, conveniently, just in time for the evening news.

Chapter Twenty-Three

For some, the last night of the world was bringing yet another evening of steadily building clouds—thunderheads, their crests bulging and black against the deep crystal blue of the steadily darkening sky. Unlike the previous night, however, this particular storm pattern was actually witnessed by WDVL's beloved meteorologist, Constance McCleary. She fully intended to do her job by forecasting the coming storm, regardless of how it contradicted the National Weather Bureau's official report.

Desmond Cortez was watching the 5:30 p.m. Early Edition weather report from the control booth. Amid the swirling professional bustle around him, the beefy station manager was still a little unnerved that no one else at the network had noticed the previous evening's electrical display and accompanying storm that had seemingly blown in from nowhere and been accounted for by no one.

When he'd queried Constance McCleary about it, the old cow retorted that she knew her "damn job well enough," and added that if she needed "any help predicting the weather or the future," she'd ask him. She'd then wrapped her tirade with a strong recommendation that he "leave forecasting to the professionals."

Desmond privately "predicted" she'd be out of a job before week's end.

At that moment, though, McCleary's televised façade was sternly warning the home audience that "none but the bravest" should risk going out that evening into what was sure to be "one humdinger of an unexpected nor'easter."

Desmond couldn't stand the homey banter. He found himself wanting to strike the barometric chatter right out of her mouth, along with the teeth

behind those wrinkled lips. Constance had been nothing but a constant thorn for over thirty years, but where TV weathercasters were concerned, *constant* equaled *ratings*. Desmond opted to let the indignities slide—as had generations of station managers before him. He then berated himself for letting recent events get under his skin deeper than they should. Constance might be a pain in the ass, but she was still *his* pain in the ass.

Desmond found his meteorological musings cut short by a call on his secure line. He took it in his office. It was an update on the afternoon's festivities, which, he was told, had ended with a "spectacular gutting" followed by a "thirty foot drop." With such a report, not even the "collateral damage" they had sustained was enough to dampen Desmond's newly-joyous spirits.

"Excellent news! No—witnesses are not a problem. William Sanchez is no longer of any consequence. No one is going to care about the rantings of a vagrant. As for Ms. Angel and the cameraman—they belong to me. They'll believe what I tell them to believe."

Desmond allowed himself one smug smile and briefly admired his physique in the office mirror. He found it amusing that Dom actually believed that it was she who led their little dance. But all it took to maintain control was learning when to apologize, and by how much. She could only make it so far on her own, and he knew it would be just a matter of time before *his* Dom came flitting back to the roost begging to know the truth as only he could enlighten her.

Just one tiny, nagging thread of uncertainty lingered.

"But are you absolutely certain the target is no longer a player?" In his business, Desmond had seen too many apparent victories turn to disaster, more than he cared to remember. So, it was with a grim and dark authority that the General sent his soldier back into battle.

"Listen to me and listen carefully…my neck is on the line just as much as yours—compromise on any level is not an option. If I take heat, *you will burn*. Understand? I want you to go back there. Make sure this is over—done—completely finished."

Half a city away, the surviving, one-armed agent understood the underlying threat. It confirmed the new orders, even though it considered the mission already ended, and the return assignment a mere formality.

Annoyingly enough, the agent had lost its cell phone as well as its arm, and was thus forced to find a functioning pay phone—a greater challenge in that particular neighborhood than one would have thought. It despised its current reliance on the technology of this world. It finally found a phone outside a Chinese take-out joint—open all night, yet barricaded as if against the coming apocalypse.

The thing in human form hung up the receiver, amusing itself with an image of the owners strung up like Peking duck—still alive as their entrails spilled out to foretell their deaths. It smiled thinly in satisfaction.

Then its own internal organs exploded.

The agent felt bile rise up its throat until flames burst from out of its mouth and empty eye sockets. Its sunglasses melted back into its head. Three

feet of righteous steel ripped through its ribcage and jerked upward, cracking the sternum, and then went for the throat. Deft handling of the sword severed the head at the neck. The blade withdrew from between split shoulder blades. Internal fires began to fiercely consume the flesh, damnation claiming yet another of its own.

The old man was still unsteady on his feet, and there was far more blood loss than Billy thought safe. Still, he'd stood firm enough to ram his iron pike straight through the demon agent's back.

Its death shriek was nearly deafening, but seemed to draw no attention.

The old man stood over his foe and watched it dissolve into ash. Only when every trace had scattered on the breeze did he let his shoulders sag again, nearly losing the grip on his spike.

They had left the reporter and her cameraman blocks away. Despite their inquisitiveness, the pair had done nothing to hinder their exit. Regardless of his own history of *betrayal*, Billy realized he had never really understood that word until he'd stared into the face of Dominique Angel there at the end.

With all that they'd seen, witnessed, and fought together—the victory, the sacrifice—she'd turned her back on them. On *him*. On Quixote.

Yet, even then, she'd believed herself entitled to answers.

"She's not worth it," Billy had muttered in whisper.

But the old man—the Hero—had answered, "She is…as *you* were."

You are dying.

The old man had turned back into the face of his betrayer, the very mouth of the accuser, and spoken words of truth, of love, of things the harlot had no desire to hear. He offered her forgiveness for all of her past and a chance to start again.

She'd rejected him.

Billy now believed he understood, not in any way he could ever articulate or even explain to himself, but in his own mind where thoughts and feelings didn't need tangible substance. As the old man had told the woman—*that media whore*—it was possible to see with the heart. And when such vision was used properly, it could reveal far more than mere eyes of flesh and blood might conceive. Just as the filthy rags he wore had been washed clean in the sudden storm that hadn't really been, and yet was, so Billy felt that he had been born anew. They had both been wet, but the reporter's soaked garb had evaporated the instant the battle had ended. The answer to that seeming contradiction was simple enough for even Billy grasp: he believed; she did not. He vowed in that moment to follow the old man and his wisdom until the end of his life, whenever that might finally be.

Now, however, Billy was convinced that the police, as well as other *things*, would soon be prowling the streets in numbers too great to evade for long.

The old man seemed lost yet again, and Billy took him by the arm. Together, they hobbled into the shadows of the setting sun.

Chapter Twenty-Four

"What is that *noise* you keep making?" asked the pilot, over the staccato roar of the Jet Ranger engine.

For the last hour, in between ground traffic reports and air traffic communications, Macintosh McIlhenney III had serenaded the beautiful pilot of the Bell 206B newscopter with a steady dose of blissful humming, partial and off-key lyrics, and enough *fa-la-la-ing* to drive any sane mortal to the brink of pondering eternity.

" 'To Each His Dulcinea,' " Mackie answered her. "*Man of La Mancha,* original Broadway Cast recording. The irony is Dulcinea doesn't even show up in the original novel. I was just telling Joey yesterday—"

"Never heard of it," the pilot cut him off. She knew the trouble she was instigating, but anything was better than Mackie's continued attempts at singing.

"You've got to be kidding me." He was truly shocked, but he milked it for whatever meager comedic value he could, as if his recently refreshed trivia was common knowledge on the tip of the tongue of all. "You've never heard of *Man of La Mancha?* Adaptation by Dale Wasserman? Music and lyrics, Mitch Leigh, Joe Darion? Tony Award winner for Best Musical, 1965?"

"That was before my time," she said with a smile, her full lips parting to reveal a surprisingly tiny mouth.

"You need to get out of this whirlybird more often and live—expand your cultural horizons!" Mackie gestured at the spectacular skyline with its oblong pinnacles of mirrored-glass high-rises, now reflecting striking red and orange streaks of early sunset, framed by a horizon of indistinct dark menace.

Before Mackie could continue, though, the pilot hushed the traffic cameraman with a wave of her hand as a new command came over their headsets.

With his usual devil-may-care demeanor, Mackie was patient to let official business run its course, biding his time to jump straight back into whatever conversational thread he was currently unspooling. He sat back content and simply enjoyed the ride, patched into the onboard communication system himself via a homemade headset and accompanying mike. Like many of his personal idiosyncrasies, the makeshift contraption drew attention to itself every time he arranged the tangled mess of cables atop his sandy red mop of hair. Yet he insisted it possessed greater audio quality than anything the studio provided.

Under her white helmet, the pilot was Madeline Jeunet—as French as her dear widowed mama was grey, even if her first name was spelled like the children's book heroine. Yet every time she opened her mouth, one would swear she descended from the 1980s Mets, and possibly straight out of Shea Stadium itself.

Mackie never wore a helmet aboard the airborne Bell Jet Ranger. Pilot Jeunet didn't approve and considered it dangerous. But the mad Irishman always assured her that, short of going to war, no one wore helmets aboard 'copters any more. Other networks' chopper crews certainly didn't bother. Logic suggested that any crash requiring a helmet would most likely be from such a height as to render the scant protection useless.

Madeline still maintained her stance that such negligence was going to get him killed one of these days, but that was Maddy, more like her mama than she was willing to admit. Mackie, however, boiled it down to a personal desire to "live dangerously."

Ever the professional, she acknowledged reception of their new orders: a factory fire on the city's northwest edge could use some "Eye in the Sky" coverage for the six o'clock news.

"Duty calls," she said as she banked the newscopter around.

As they passed the WDVL building, Mackie gave a sudden involuntary shudder.

"Are you OK?" Maddy asked, seeing his momentary tremor.

He had viewed the iconic transmission tower from this angle over a thousand times, but for just an instant what he thought he saw *was **not** a structure of rivets and steel...*

"Yeah...I'm fine," he said distantly. "I just had a weird thought, that's all."

He shook the odd image from his mind.

The massive tower's giant red neon call letters flickered into life just as they wheeled by. Leaving their home base behind, the news team saw a steady plume of smoke rising ahead of them on the far horizon.

Mackie seized the moment to pick right back up from where they'd left off, as if there'd been no interruption at all. "Y'know, I had that album spinning all morning."

Madeline tried to keep a straight face. "They make these new record albums today," she said. "They're called CDs."

"Heaven forbid," Mackie said, mortified, laying a hand on his chest for emphasis. This was old conversational territory for the pair. Following in his father's footsteps as a cut-rate audiophile, Mackie had remained an analog slave to vinyl and tape, actually believing his discerning ears alone could pick out the Compact Disc and DVD digital encoding coming straight through the speakers in a steady series of beeps and boops. Many considered this snobbish foible to be just another quirk of his flamboyant Irish charm.

Mackie was too easy a target, Madeline mused, and opted to steer the eccentric cameraman clear of the established controversies between them.

"So, what has you in a tilting-at-windmills mood?" she asked.

"Aha...so thou dost know aught of which I speak?"

"I know enough to know Don Quixote didn't go around talking in some hackneyed British accent."

"I'll stick to me native tongue then," he said, switching to a thick Irish brogue, the only intonation he did well.

Madeline liked Mackie. Hell, *everybody* liked Mackie. His disarming manner made it difficult for anybody not to like him, although there were always those who tried.

"'Tis due in part to the lovelorn Sir Joseph Caparelli. He of the wandering newsvan, traversing the length and breadth, the hills and dales, of this fair urban kingdom seeking the favor of his dulcet Angel."

Madeline smirked at the insinuation.

In the past two years, Macintosh and Madeline had endured more than their own fair share of romance-laden innuendo. The only thing that prevented childish *"sittin' in the tree"* lyrics from ever gaining validity was Maddy's own staunch and outspoken belief in the separation of home and work. Like Joe Caparelli's ball cap distinction, she left all thought of her co-workers back on the job when she went home. Sometimes, though, Mackie's ineffable appeal made it a tough resolution to keep, but definitely not tonight. After a day of his tuneless blather, this coming evening was one of those rare times she was glad this wasn't the man she was bringing home to meet mom.

"So, is our Joey ensnared by anybody I know?" Madeline asked, having her own suspicions.

"Probably. But if I told you, Sir Caparelli would, more than likely, have me skinned alive, and feast on my bones."

"His secret's safe with me," she said, banking the chopper again, straight into the glare of a spectacular, storm-wreathed sunset.

Mackie loved it up here in the sky for these few brief hours each day, away from the woes of everyone on the ground. It was liberating, and never failed to touch deeper chords within his carefree spirit.

"God clouds," he said softly, dropping the brogue and indicating the extraordinary brilliance of the diminishing day sky. "That's what my Aunt Amy always called skies like that. Those streaks of sun shafting through black clouds, breaking them apart—they look like the light of Heaven is about to burst through onto the Earth."

"Never took you for one of those religious nuts, Mack," Madeline snickered.

"I wasn't being religious, I was attempting to *wax poetic*." Amid his wistful eloquence, Mackie became suddenly, surprisingly, indignant. "Y'know, that's one of the problems with today's culture…. Everybody's *search* for truth is treated like some holy pilgrimage, but the moment anybody claims they've actually *found* what they were lookin' for, they get dismissed as some close-minded religious wacko."

Maddy wasn't going to get caught up in such a debate, and kept her response focused on Mackie himself. "Does that include you?"

His negative tone was as short-lived as it had been unwelcome. "Like my man Bono, I'm still looking." Mackie sighed, the strange vision having re-entered his mind: *a great and mighty windmill sitting atop the tower of WDVL.* "Unfortunately for me, my idealistic soul's got too much of a practical heart. I'd like to believe in something, but I got this problem with anything I can't actually put my hand on. Y'know what I mean?"

"You are one mixed-up ball of wax. Anyone ever tell you that?"

"I prefer the term 'professional conundrum.' "

Madeline just shook her head, while Mackie started humming another verse of sixties' nostalgia. Together, the pair set out to chronicle one more slice of human misery, themselves untouched from their vantage point in the heavens.

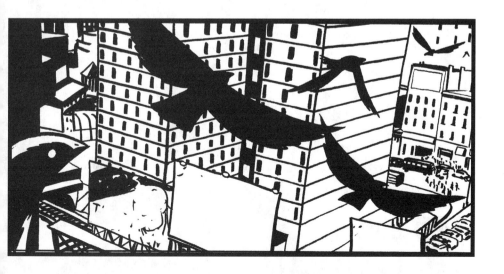

Chapter Twenty-Five

Joe thought he heard the rumble of distant thunder, a sound that had now become an ominous undertone to all the strange events that had entered his life in the past 36 hours. During the six o'clock edition weathercast, WDVL's Constance McCleary had said something about an approaching storm front due later that night. The young cameraman guessed it must be coming early, and possibly from straight out of the mouth of station head Desmond Cortez.

The barrel-chested manager gave an uneasy glance over his shoulder toward the slatted window of his mahogany office, where the final rays of sunlight still shone through from the west, despite the growing overcast blanketing the city.

Cortez dismissed Joe's testimony with a wave of his hand and a smile that was either bemusement or contempt—it was hard to tell which. He opened his mouth to clarify his expression but Dom cut the boss off, in defense of her young partner.

"But you weren't there, Desmond. You didn't see what happened…what we saw…"

Joe lowered his head, dropping his eyes into a slot of shadow, the better to keep watch on this man about whom they had been so recently warned.

The boss's desk was cluttered with what minimal evidence they possessed— scattered still-prints of the scary old man performing the impossible, images of the perfectly sliced automatic weapons, the charred wallet, and of one gleaming government-issue badge—dumped in a heap upon Desmond Cortez's well-ordered world of newsprint, magazines, and wire-service transcripts.

Dom was frantic, and the only working theory she'd been able to cobble together since leaving the ill-fated loading bay, the only premise that made any sense whatsoever, she knew could be easily filed under the kook-fringe category and discarded. Still, she had to try. "Those things—those men that came after us—were *undercover Federal Agents!* They're working for Henry Devlin—they've got to be. They practically said so themselves. And there's a connection with that street bum…but he is far, *far* more than just some simple panhandler!" She knew she was bordering on certifiable, buying into old Quixote's world, yet she still argued with all the passion of a high-priced lawyer.

Joe couldn't concur with everything Dom claimed, particularly about the sudden downpour—which made no sense—as well as her bizarre theory, but he had seen enough the previous morning to know there was vastly more to the old guy than appearance suggested. Joe thought of him as part wise old eastern sage, part fiery Fundamentalist preacher from his youth. And yet, there was something a little more genuine, a bit more heartfelt about the crazy old bird than either of those allusions suggested. Joe also believed this particular old man could kick his ass any day of the week.

Dom finished her appeal. "There's a story here that could blow the entire governor's race wide open!"

Cortez turned away and stared out through the blinds, keeping track of the sun's setting and the encroaching storm. His words were delicate, slowly measured, and soothing. "I understand what you *think* you saw…but the two of you have to realize the delicacy of this situation…"

Dom slammed her hands on the same desk that had played host to their brief romp the previous afternoon. "My god, Desmond—*This is news!* We—*report*—the *news!*" She firmly enunciated each word, complete with dashes—and *italics.*

Cortez turned slowly, as if to bestow fatherly wisdom to the rebellious child, she who truly believed her new boyfriend held the secrets of the universe. "Of all people, Dom, *you* ought to appreciate our position. It is not our job to simply 'report the news'… you know our motto—we *make* the news. Don't tell me that amidst this cloak-and-dagger novelty of *perceived* conspiracy, you've forgotten why you went into journalism in the first place." His tone was patronizing. She hated being patronized.

"I was taught to be objective," Dom said, clutching her burned wrist, now salved and wrapped in white bandage, "the first rule of journalism is—"

"Objectivity, my ass!" bellowed Cortez. "You wanted to change the world, Dom. Now I'm giving you that chance—an opportunity to fulfill the dream of a lifetime. And you're willing to throw it all away because some moralizing, self-righteous *con man* tugged on your heart strings—pushed some

buttons—got you all weepy for a cause…suckered you at your own game. Give me a damn break!"

Cortez scattered their evidence off his desk in a gesture reminiscent of the previous day's tussle, only now fury bubbled just

below the surface. He punctuated each point of his argument by testily holding up the various print media in turn, each piece adding to his growing vehemence.

"We build the heroes and we tear them down. We elect their kings, and we point the fingers of blame. We declare which wars are the righteous cause, and which get conveniently blamed, overlooked or forgotten. It's our hand that shapes public perception. Our side tells them what to eat, what to wear, what to hear, see, *feel*—our kind tells them what to *think!* You want to change the world, Dom? You want to make a difference? Then make a *choice*."

His rage hung in the room like a preamble to the coming storm, but then he softened his voice. Joe thought of him in that moment as good-cop/bad-cop all rolled into one. "The people are like *sheep*, Dom. They need somebody to protect them, guide them…*and that's us*—you and me, and even our ever-trustworthy Mr. Caparelli…"

He gave Joe a grand smile.

Joe shot back, "And we cull the herd when it gets out of line?"

"When necessary." The grand smile never faltered, though it seemed to harden a bit. "It's a terrible burden, being the caretakers of humanity's conscience. But it's a responsibility I and my associates take very seriously."

"Right…" countered Joe, unable to prevent his own grin from emerging. It wasn't a happy grin. "You and a bunch of goons in a dark, smoke-filled room on an X-Files rerun?"

Cortez said nothing but let his smile fade as he took a nonchalant seat at his desk and began re-organizing the various papers, prints, and documents.

"So," Joe continued, "who died and left you in charge?"

Cortez answered, "Believe me when I say you wouldn't understand."

Billy barely got the staggering old man into the alley before a police patrol car turned the corner. At least they were drying out now. But the old guy had definitely lost a lot of blood in that skirmish, and the continuing flow showed no signs of stopping any time soon.

Billy realized that what he really wanted was a drink, a smoke, a toke, any kind of fix that might take him away from this world of ogres, demons, and impossible dreams. He wanted any escape he could get from the rational, concrete reality that all those visions now represented to his mind: circumstance and consequence—the old man who'd saved his life, now dying in his arms. He was worried—old habits, as well as abusive desires, it seemed, died hard.

The moment Billy let go of the uninjured shoulder, the tottering, aged legs buckled. The old man collapsed onto his hands and knees.

"We gotta get you to a hospital…" Billy croaked, even more scared now than he'd been when facing the very spawn of Hell.

The old man was defiant, even as his voice wheezed and rasped. "No… a long time I've lived. Perhaps too long…perhaps it's time another…takes my place…takes the mantle—Elijah to…" The voice faded off into silence.

Billy fell to his own knees, and steadied the old man's trembling shoulders.

"No…what're you talking about? Who's Elijah?"

"A life worth living," gasped the old man, clinging to his own life and breath, and smiling his gap-toothed grin. "It was no…*accident*, Billy Sanchez…that I…found you…" He sputtered and a mouthful of blood coughed up over his lower lip. "…*When* I found you—I understand now…you remind me of another…long, long ago. The dream…is now yours."

Billy shook his head.

The old man nodded. "I bequeath to you…*the quest.*"

He held out the iron spike.

The last rays of direct sun vanished. All that remained was gathering twilight and the threat of storm.

Cortez shifted his focus from Joe back to Dominique. "Now tell me, Dom…whose side are you on?"

She said nothing, as if pondering the weight of all the options before her. She watched as her boss gathered the still-prints of the old man into his hand. In the end, after all had been said and done, all of the arguments and their counters weighed, Dom finally convinced herself that it was the crazy old man who was the impossible dreamer.

"OK, Desmond," she said, arriving at her own surprise verdict in the case she had argued. "What do you want me to do?" Her tone was flat.

Desmond grinned, and it was genuine this time, knowing all along that the "littlest angel" would come around eventually. Dom was smart, and she was going to go far. The cameraman on the other hand, was another matter altogether.

Joe was outraged. "You can't—you *can't* go along with him on this, Dom. I admit, there's plenty of times we both turned a blind eye to things that were staring us in the face—we did what we were told—but *this?!*"

Dom was still somber. "Aren't you the one who prides himself on 'sticking his neck out for nobody'?" she said. Her flat tone was tempering.

"Dammit, Dom—don't play that game with me. That old man probably died saving your life! Don't sell him out like this!"

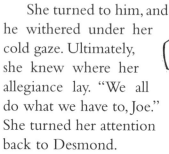

She turned to him, and he withered under her cold gaze. Ultimately, she knew where her allegiance lay. "We all do what we have to, Joe." She turned her attention back to Desmond.

The station manager gave her a sad but reassuring smile in return, and handed her a folder. "I took the liberty of having the whole thing pre-prepped from your notes," he said. "Everything you need for the eleven o'clock show is right there."

...And that's all it really is, mused Dom. When all was said and done, everything came down to *the show.* Truth no longer mattered when all one had to do was present the "facts" in a pretty package. You could make the masses buy anything you had to sell—any *story* you had to tell—as long as it was properly spun. "News" wasn't the same as truth: it was market-tested, commerce-driven, slick, polished, hi-tech info-tainment. Dom was simply the latest shiny ribbon to adorn that pretty package. She had only to re-dress her wound, don fresh and smartly-hued attire, smooth her hair, and apply a fresh coat of paint to help her look human under the bright lights. The magic of television...just a few cosmetic changes, and she'd be ready to play her part in the grand illusion.

She held her chin high and Desmond, escorting her to the office door, practically fawned over her with a sickening display of contrived gratitude, the Prima Donna wooed back to the stage by her appreciative manager. Dom hesitated at the threshold, the guilt she was trying to choke down stubbornly imploring her to say *something* to alleviate the dark cloud filling the room.

"We've all got priorities, Joe," she finally said, "and this girl's got to take care of her own."

Dumbfounded, her partner through thick and thin stared incredulously, his respect for her panned away, as worthless as fool's gold.

Desmond smirked. "My little angel knows what's best for her." He patted her on the backside, and gave an encouragement dredged up from *Father Knows Best* reruns: "Now get out there, and do the right thing. Make me proud."

With a grim concession, Dom realized that the crazy old man had only one fact right: *she really was a whore after all—but at least she was a damn good one.*

The weight of the iron shaft was suddenly too much for the old man, and it teetered in his skin-n-bones grip, faltering muscles straining beyond the strength of a broken heart to bear.

Billy protested feebly, his own Judas heart skipping beats with every syllable. "But...I can't...I'm the reason they got you..."

The old man cut him off with a charge uttered in blood. "Protect her, Sancho...*Billy.* Protect our...Dulcinea..."

He fell forward, at the last instant only barely supporting himself above the ground by clutching the spike in desperate, dying hands.

With Dominique's exit, Cortez closed the door behind her with a decisive click. Joe heard it lock. *What kind of game was Desmond up to?* he wondered.

Cortez ignored the young cameraman for just an instant, gazing off into space and seeing alternate paths. "My 'Dulcinea'...she had me worried for a moment there." He turned and grinned again. His mouth was full of teeth. "As for *you*, Mr. Caparelli...you've thrown away much more than a career."

Joe might very well be doing just that, but he no longer cared; *some things were worth fighting for.* He held his ground. *Some things might even be worth dying for,* he believed, if it came to that.

Joe didn't know how he was going to break all this to Mackie; he was still trying to figure it out for himself. His and Dom's brief glimpse at the six o'clock edition had revealed that his buddy was up in the air. The "Eye in the Sky" team was covering the factory disaster across town, set in motion, allegedly, by a trio of street vagrants who had touched off the "out-of-control" blaze to cover the evidence of their crime: an apparent murder victim that

firefighters had been able to recover. *It seemed that not all denizens of the streets were as tragically noble as the media often painted them to be.* But then he remembered all that he'd witnessed in the past two days.

"You don't scare me, Mr. Cortez," he said. "You won't bully and manipulate me the way you do her."

"Oh, but I *will*, Mr. Caparelli…"

Joe turned away to grab his coat and bag. "There are plenty of other stations in town not in on your racket…plenty of networks that'll jump at a story like this."

"Just give me time…and I will make of you a *true believer.*" The voice never changed, never wavered, as Desmond Cortez split from his human skin like an over-ripened fruit.

What emerged *stank* as something that did not belong of this world. Or perhaps it had taken its first steps here, lived and died, and then crawled up again from the ground, rotted, like putrid meat. Nausea washed through Joe before he even saw the thing that would soon rip the very muscle from his bones while his voice still screamed in agony.

Joseph Caparelli had one chance, one hope alone, as he found himself swiftly returning to the abandoned faith of his childhood.

Welcome back to the fight, Monsieur Rick…

He remembered a small boy offering up a prayer he barely understood at the time—and prayed again, that, despite a lifetime of preoccupation, he might still see his Lord on the other side of Paradise.

…This time I know our side will win!

But as station manager Desmond Cortez finished with him, there was nothing left of good old Joe—nor his cinema fixation with *Casablanca*—except what the Dragon picked from his own teeth to keep them clean and sharp.

Where was the Hero now, the dashing swordsman in black, who had slain ogres and demons? Was he merely a figment of imagination, now to die along with the mind that had created him?

The old man had finally closed his eyes and fell the final few inches to the ground when Billy refused to accept the rusted spike of iron.

...And wasn't that all it really was? Just an iron bar taken how long ago, from what dilapidated cemetery or condemned schoolyard that had never even missed it?

"I'm the reason... I'm the reason..." Billy muttered again and again, as if the chant had become a litany that could somehow absolve him of all his sins.

A bolt of electrical fire quickened across the night sky.

In the end, though, the old man had one thing Billy did not: someone to weep for him as he died.

Part Three
LIFE WORTH LIVING

*What Happened Atop the Tower,
And How All Was Made Right in the End.*

Chapter Twenty-Six

High above the vast urban canyons, a god looks down upon his people. His eyes see all that transpires beneath his gaze, for his image and effigy, his shrines, dapple his kingdom in all places, from the great heights to the bustling thoroughfares of commerce and transport.

He declares that he cares for the children. And once such a statement is proclaimed, there is little else—beyond assurances for their comfort and prosperity—with which the sheep and the goats concern themselves. Yet in time, none will escape his inevitable wrath, not even the lowest of the low—the destitute, those without any voice save that ascribed unto them from on high.

He is a jealous god that concedes no equals, brooks neither pretenders nor usurpers of the crown that is his, and his alone—his destiny preordained before the foundations of the world. In six months' time, he will demand that his people set aside their false deities and worship only him as the one true god of heaven and earth.

The Choice for a Better Tomorrow—Elect Henry Devlin for Governor.

Detective Benjamin Saunders had never much liked FACTS's founder, Nate Creed. He considered the administrator one of those holier-than-thou, rabble-rousing troublemakers. But *like* and *respect* were two very different things. Saunders *respected* Creed more than any other human being in the entire misbegotten city. Like him or not, Nathan Creed told you up front where he stood and what he believed, and he wouldn't take crap from nobody, regardless of race, faith, or political affiliation. Integrity like that had to be respected.

Likewise, Nathan Creed had never much liked Detective Ben Saunders, and had long considered him merely a jerk wearing a badge. Yet when the detective's wife left him and gained custody of their only daughter, something broke the detective's spirit. He was never the same. He still did his job—punched the clock, 'round the clock, as those in his profession so often did. But now he also smoked too much, drank too heavily, and was slowly deteriorating his way toward death or retirement, whichever came first. And for all of that, Saunders garnered Creed's sympathy.

So, somewhere between *respect* and *sympathy*, each man thought something mutually profitable might come from cooperating with the other.

"Yeah, they were both here," said Nathan Creed matter-of-factly when the beleaguered detective came knocking on FACTS's door after ten o'clock, waving about his black-and-white mug shots of the old guy and his younger partner in crime.

The FACTS shelter shut its doors promptly at 9 p.m. From then on it usually took about an hour to get everybody settled down for the night. Winter or summer, Creed took the nine o'clock deadline very seriously. He was dealing with men and women with no sense of boundaries or limits and, as a result, had lives spinning out of control. The nine o'clock curfew was one big, immutable boundary that the people of the street could count on. Some in the media had called the practice "unrealistic," "barbaric," "inconsiderate of the social lives of the homeless," and simply "cruel." Nathan Creed sat in his stone and mortar refuge for the lost, and responded to the charges with an attitude that said, *let the little wolves blow.*

On this night, the administrator led the detective into his office where

Nate, at least, could put his big feet up on his own big desk.

A large, framed embroidered sampler hung on the wall behind the desk—a hand-made gift from one of the first recipients of Creed's charity, long before there'd ever been a FACTS organization. It featured a ship at sea, and stated " '...Follow me and I will make you fishers of men.' — Matthew 4:19"

Saunders glanced at the decoration cynically, then pushed such unproductive thoughts to the back of his mind before speaking. "I understand the impracticality of what I'm asking before I ask," he said, adding his justifying caveat as he sat down opposite the big man's feet. "I just want you to know that. But can you tell me anything about what those two did while they were here? Anything they might have said that sticks out in your mind. Did they meet anybody? Leave with anyone? What time did they leave? And heaven help me, could you just solve the whole blasted case and tell me where they went and what they're planning to do when they get there?"

There was a note of desperation in the detective's voice, even though his dead eyes said he'd rather be in bed, maybe even six feet under, anywhere but on the job. Saunders could tell himself he just didn't care anymore, but his anxiety for the issue at hand betrayed the truth.

Nathan sized him up with a keen, clear discernment born of experience. "I just need to know one thing, Ben: are you genuinely interested in seeing real justice done? Or are you just out to hound these two boys—balancing out that internal department racial quota?"

The detective decided then and there that he wasn't going to get anything from the self-righteous Nathan Creed. "Always holding out for some higher cause, aren't you, Nate?" he said. "What's it gonna be about this time: basic police brutality, or are you going to accuse *me* of some kind of racial profiling now?"

Their mutual brown eyes locked on each other until one or the other would give up his ground.

Creed finally said, "You know I'm not one of them bleeding hearts. But I do need to know where *your* heart's at in all this before I consent to lending you a helping hand."

The detective's eyes were weary and cold. "I could charge you... obstruction at the least; aiding and abetting at the worst—"

"And I will fight you every step of the way. You know as well as I do those charges would never hold up."

"Then maybe I'll just do it out of spite—teach you some kind of lesson. I'm serious."

The administrator didn't budge. "You tell yourself different...but I know you're a better man than that."

Saunders looked askance in an attempt to avoid being the butt of the inevitable joke.

No joke followed.

Saunders dropped his eyes and sighed heavily, letting the younger, bigger man win the moral high ground. His tone changed to one of defeat. "I really don't know what to make of this one, Nate. Near as I can tell, William Sanchez has been a product of the streets. Other than a handful of misdemeanors over the years—and slowly killing himself—the guy's clean. And it *does* look like *he* was the victim in all of this, jumped by a gang of local kids that tried to set him on fire—*kids*." His grin tasted bad. "If Sanchez hadn't broken out of custody last night, he'd be a free man today."

"What about the old guy?" said Creed.

"That's a mystery all by itself. I've had some tight-lipped customers in my day, but I've never had anybody say absolutely *nothing* through *three hours* of interrogation. And I'll tell you this, I couldn't dig up one scrap of information on the guy. I can't say for certain *he'd* be a free man today, but it looks like the chump he wasted was in self-defense, provoked by his saving Sanchez."

The detective suddenly looked around the sparse room with a spark of uncharacteristic animation, possibly looking for hidden cameras, as if he was about to unload state secrets. Seeing nothing overt or suspicious, he leaned forward, getting conspiratorial with Nathan Creed's big shoe. "But that's the other thing I can't quite figure out. You tell me what're the odds of one guy with no name killing *another guy with no name?*"

"You're kidding," said Nathan, as he removed his feet from the desk, making himself slightly more approachable to the burdened detective.

"You know me better'n that, Nate. I'm too fried to make jokes any more. The dead guy had no identification...his friends say his name was 'Vincent Barbarino'...can you believe that?"

Without thought, Saunders lit up the last of his on-board smokes. FACTS was a no-smoking facility but Nathan let the infraction pass. Compassion came in many forms.

"You look tired, Ben," said Nathan.

"I *am* tired—*tired* of slogging my way through crap like this twenty-four hours a day, seven days a week, fifty-two weeks a year. I mean, I don't even know what I'm gonna do with this guy when I find him, Nate. A couple of black-and-whites catch him in the act of ramming an iron spike through a guy's belly and down through the roof of another guy's car—not to mention this is after trashing the whole car to begin with. We've got this old dude, dead to rights, end of story, lock him up till the end of time. But then I learn from his partner that he's really the white knight saving the day, rescuing street vagrants from alleyway barbecues. He does things no man half his age can do, and caps it all off by breaking out of lock-up—and I do mean *'breaking out.'* He broke a locked steel gate right off its hinges.

"And that's just for starters…"

Saunders stood up and began pacing as his frustration bubbled into anger in his blood. Industrial-strength drags on his last cigarette had burned it down to the filter in half the usual time.

"Here's where all the stories start falling apart. Nobody can identify him. I've got the man's victims—not the dead one—telling me how the old guy we had in custody wasn't even at the scene of the crime. No, sir. I get to hear about some lunatic avenging the righteous and putting the *evil Vinny Barbarino* to death on the tip of his sword. And you know what? *There is no sword.* There's no iron spike—the one arresting officers saw him with. There's no murder weapon. No leads. No motives. No identities. The only suspects I have are the *victims*…and I don't even have *them* anymore. There's no story here that makes any kind of sense. Nothing fits. It's like we all took some weird turn into the Twilight Zone or something. My own partner doesn't even want to hear it any more—hangs up on me after I start talking about the 'swordsman with the scary eyes.' "

Saunders finished his rant but had difficulty calming down. Early in the tirade Creed had slid an ornate, inscribed metal bowl across the desk—some community service award he'd received—to help the detective with his ash.

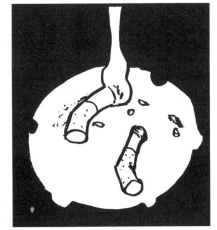

After smoking his cigarette down to the filter and stifling the embers, Saunders anxiously patted down his pockets looking for another, deathly afraid he'd burned down his last.

Creed didn't make any further moves, but assessed Ben Saunders' plight with serious eyes. "This isn't about the case anymore, is it?" he said calmly.

Saunders stopped his pacing and rummaging through his pockets, and hated the big man even more. He hated him for looking underneath all the crap and seeing him for what he really was: a burned-out, washed-up, sorry-ass excuse for a cop, partner, husband, father, *human being*—take your pick.

Saunders sat back down with a heavy sigh. "No…it's not."

"This is about trying to get Margaret back…"

"No. Not anymore. Nothing's changed. All I know how to do is my job, and that's the way it's always been. I don't know *how* to do anything else. I had no business gettin' married…becoming a father. I'm married to that desk downtown, but I'm not even a good husband to the force no more…just ask my partner about that one. And I still don't know what the hell I'm doing with that damned keyboard. They took away all the typewriters over ten years ago, saying the computer would be easier—clear up all the paperwork—get us back out on the street faster, doing our job—but nothing's changed."

"When's the last time you and Margaret talked?"

Saunders started picking at the untended scraps of his growing grey beard. "Last year, if you can believe it. And she said it was the last time *she* was making the call. She said next time, it had better be *me* picking up the phone and dialing. A year and a half later…well, you get the picture. I drove her away—there isn't any doubt about that. And I've got no business now making up excuses trying to take that guilt away."

"How about April? How is she doing?"

"Haven't seen her in over five years." Saunders took a moment to relive the seven years he'd actually had with his daughter before Margaret took them both out of his life. The memories were brief. "All grown up now, I'd expect. We don't talk. She's got herself some *African sister name* now, trying to get back in touch with her roots…or get back at me, more'n likely. The worst of it is, I probably couldn't pick my own daughter from out of a line-up—not that I'd ever have to, mind you…. I'm pretty sure Margaret's raised her better'n that."

"That isn't your fault."

"Yes it is."

"You're guilty of a lot of things, Ben—I won't take that away from you—but *her spite* isn't one of them."

Saunders glanced down at his watch, and then weighed the manila envelope containing the mug shots of the damned. "It doesn't matter. None of it matters anymore. I spend all my free time nowadays with my nose buried so deep down a bottle of whiskey, you'd swear I lived in it."

Nathan leaned back in his chair and stared up at the white tiles of the drop ceiling. He had a crazy idea he knew the detective would never go for, but he had to try. "How about you take some of that free time, Ben… get your nose out of the Thunderbird…and come down and put in some volunteer work here at FACTS."

"You know I can't do that."

"This is still a free country. Nobody can tell you how you can spend your free time."

"Conflict of interest."

"My customers aren't going to care about your real business, Ben."

Saunders answer was decisive. "Your customers *are* my business, Nate. The big machine chews them up, then spits them out. They land at my door or yours…usually both."

Nathan dug in, equally stubborn. "And we *both* do what we can, Ben. You take care of your end, I take care of mine, and we do the *best job we can.* We're not gonna change the world…and that's OK. Who could? Nobody ever said it was our job to change it. But we both do everything we can, take care of who shows up at our respective doors. Just imagine it, Ben, if *everybody* did just that…"

The mission founder let his words hang in the air, his charisma like incense. This was what fueled his passion.

…*Fishers of men.*

Nathan grinned as he baited the hook. "Y'know what…we'd change the world after all. Then, maybe we'd both be outta work because there'd no longer be any reason for either one of our two doors."

"Yeah, that'll be the day." Saunders licked the roof of his mouth and found the taste as bitter as his smile.

"And you know what we'd do if that day ever happened?" continued Nathan Creed, casting his line.

Saunders could only stare in disbelief at what he considered to be nothing more than the manic, wide-eyed dreams of the big man.

"Me an' you…you and I…we'd both go *fishing.*"

"That isn't ever going to happen."

"Our fishing together?"

"No. The world. It isn't ever going to change."

"Probably not," said Nathan, knowing the big fish always put up a fight as you reeled them in. "History says it never has, and the Good Book says it never will, because the real problem isn't the world…it's the *people* in it."

Saunders put his weary head in his hands, counting himself as one of those billions that made up the problems of the world.

Nathan was incessant. "So, how about when all this is over, you and I... we go fishin' anyway?"

Saunders couldn't believe that the holier-than-thou big man was being *genuinely* sincere, not just the kind you put on for company. He was actually asking him to spend leisure time together.

"But you don't even *like* me," the detective said.

"And you can't stand my sorry butt. We'll have a great time." Nathan's eyes gleamed with amusement.

Saunders's mind filled with faded images of him and his grandfather out on distant mountain lakes, the water still and crystalline, snapshot fragments from long-forgotten summers past. They were few, but still some of the warmest memories he had. He answered Nathan from inside the reminiscence of that boat out on the sparkling, long-ago August lake. "I think I might like that." He yanked himself back to the present, though, and straightened in his chair. "But that's later. What do we do in the meantime?"

Creed could tell that Saunders still meant business. "I help you find these guys," he said. "You make sure you do what you can to get them legitimate justice, and I'll do what I can to help them get cleaned up and off the streets after everything's said and done."

"Deal."

Nathan leaned back in his chair again, relishing the afterglow of winning the big catch, even as he was getting his own head back into the gears of business. "I'm gonna guess they got here about eleven or so—that was this morning. We open up the lunch line at noon and some folks'll start lining up as early as nine, as soon as we shut the breakfast shift down—but most show up about eleven. Then it was about...ten after one when the news crew showed up."

"News crew?"

"Channel 6—WDVL—that Dominique Angel who's gonna be doing that hit-piece series on 'homelessness and the ideological evils of our abusive political system' tonight." He waved his hand with annoyance.

Saunders knew Dominique Angel—everybody in town did—but possessed a rather nebulous comprehension of whatever her latest investigative report might be.

"I was gettin' ready to put her out myself," Nathan continued, "when it turned out she was looking for your boys. She and the old guy walked out of here together...I'd say about 1:20. Don't know which way they went—sorry."

The detective understood, but still felt a sliver of the old excitement creep back into his veins at the prospect of a new, high-profile lead. Rising stars like Angel always gave a 50/50 option when it came to cooperation. They either clammed up completely, or bent over backwards, giving you a big ass to kiss while simultaneously spilling their guts out in their eagerness to be seen in a helpful light. It all came down to showmanship and sales. Saunders liked the even-split odds.

Creed had a bit more: "The other one hung out some with Angel's cameraman. I finally told them to take their business elsewhere. You know me—I've got nothing to hide—but I won't make it easy for the media to come swooping in here like buzzards looking for a fresh kill."

Saunders nodded in agreement, jotted down the minimal facts, and was already planning his visit to 'DVL as he rose with Creed and clasped the big man's hand like they were two old pals making a pact, minus the spit on the palm. Saunders added a genuine smile, one that didn't taste so bad this time. "Thanks."

"And you and me, Ben, who knows…?" said Creed, not relaxing his firm grip on the detective's hand, "we work together on this, we just *might* help change the world."

"I'm taking odds on how soon we'll be forced to kill each other."

"Well…at least that's a start," and the big man laughed.

The camaraderie was short-lived as Bridget Foster—the cute, buxom blonde volunteer that everybody wrongly assumed was having an affair with the big Mr. Creed—came bursting into Nathan's office. She didn't knock because the administrator never closed his door. There were very few secrets in the FACTS facility.

"Nate!" she cried, "You gotta see this—all *hell's* breaking out over at WDVL!"

"What have I told you about language, Miss Foster?" Nathan said, as if she were merely bringing in the day's logbook for him to review.

"Sorry boss—my bad—but you gotta see this. It's on the news—*Live!*"

The trio, along with the rest of FACTS's staff who had dropped everything and come running, caught the chaos that, through the magic of television, was engulfing the WDVL building downtown at that exact moment. The action centered on the old transmission tower that was broadcasting the incredible images that held them in spellbound fascination.

Bridget continued, explaining what the men had missed. "We were watching the news, and the signal just cut out, halfway through the broadcast—no explanation. That Dominique Angel was on, and we were tuning in to see what she was gonna say about us, after being here today and everything…then it just got *weird*. She started babbling stuff, looking like she was about to cry, and then the station just went off the air—that's it—zippo! Then, not even ten minutes later…it comes back on with—*this!*"

The images were shaky, coming from a helicopter in flight, but Creed recognized their crazy old man battling his way across the studio rooftop, spike in hand. And they all saw reporter Dominique Angel held hostage at the end of a gun.

Saunders only needed thirty seconds' viewing to prompt him to take action himself—and he felt that his current case was getting *stranger* with every passing minute.

Chapter Twenty-Seven

Several hours earlier, William "Billy" Sanchez, who had no clue that pardon and acquittal awaited him if he'd only surrender himself and claim them, had sat face to face with the end result of all his failure.

The old man lay lifeless, his face resting in a stinking puddle of yesterday's sewage. The eyes had closed, and his right arm still held the iron spike out toward Billy, as if the old man's offer was still valid.

The sun had set long ago, but Billy had lost all track or interest in time's passage. He sat curled in a ball, arms wrapped around damp, shaking knees, staring at the peaceful old face that had given *everything* so that Billy might live just one more day. Twice now, the old man had saved his life, but when he'd asked no more of him than to follow in his footsteps, Billy had refused.

"I'm the reason," he muttered to himself again, oblivious to how incriminating the entire streetside tableau appeared. "I'm the reason you're dead."

Tight tendrils of guilt finally unwound from his heart, only to take root in his soul. But at least they moved him to break his stupor. Releasing his trembling limbs, he reached out shaking fingers to take the iron spike. It was something solid, something physical that he could put his faith in. Somehow, he believed the old man might live again—live and walk through Billy's heart and mind as before. All he had to do was take up the sword, hidden as it was from mortal sight, he guessed, until wielded by hands of faith. But were *his hands* enough? **His faith?**

Do you believe?

What a joke it must be when he couldn't even bring himself to accept what his eyes had shown him to be true. *No!* He *did* believe. And because he believed, he knew he could never be good enough to follow in footsteps

he'd never be worthy enough to fill. It seemed that *belief* and *faith* were two very different things. Definitely, a *belief* came first, but that served as only a steppingstone to *faith* which followed. Billy just couldn't keep up, one stone to another. He never could. So, it turned out to be a joke after all—one whose punch line came at his expense.

"No...I *can't*," he moaned.

Billy believed, yet still had no faith. Belief was worthless without faith to give it power. He could not take the weapon. His hand closed into a fist instead, and he pounded the ground in shame.

But this was his chance. The last opportunity to finally make up for all the evil, the bad, the flat-out stupid mistakes he'd spent a lifetime making. Here was his chance to show them all, everybody, that he wasn't a joke, that Billy Sanchez could do something right.

No, no, and still **NO!** He knew he was responsible for far more than he could ever atone for with his own action. Only now, to take up that holy blade and die in some vain attempt to prove his worth would bring nothing but dishonor to everything the sword stood for, *everything the old man had died for. Guilt could never be the motivating factor for doing something righteous. Pride was worse.* He really wanted a drink.

Yet Billy would not bring shame to the Hero's memory. He realized the only right thing he could do, the *only* good deed he could ever perform, was to do *nothing*. In accepting that truth, impotent rage tore away at the fraying edges of his soul.

He stood up, intending to run away as far as his own strength—and the law—would let him go. He took only two steps, though, and found he could run no further. He'd never outrun the old man lying there dead in the alley. He had carried his dying body long enough to be awash in the old man's blood, and blood carried a stain you could never truly wash away. Blood alone washed away blood, and an eye for an eye was immutable truth.

You are dying.

He could never escape the allegory.

His back to the still form, unable to face it, Billy finally spoke to the old man, words that he should have said long before they became merely sounds echoing off brick chasm walls. Only later did he realize he actually spoke them to himself, to his own heart. "It was just...yesterday, thirty, maybe forty hours ago...I was dying, man. Inside...I was just as dead as you are now. But...but, *what* d'ya say to the guy that saved yer life? You should'a let me die, 'cause..."

I offer you life…and a life worth living.

He turned around. "Because I don't know what to do…I don't know

how to pick up the pieces. I just know that I can't…"

Billy dropped to his knees, into the puddle at the old man's side. "I can't go back to killin' myself. So, what do I do? What d'ya want me to do? What am I s'posed to do with my life now?"

His tears flowing freely, Billy found his answer. "You said 'Protect her…*protect our Dulcinea.*'"

He wiped at his face with a grimy, alley-stained

hand. "All right, I'll protect her. I'll try—I promise ya I'll do my best…I hope that's enough."

He reached for the iron pole one last time, yet still stopped himself. "But I can't take the sword, man—do ya hear me? *I just can't…*"

He stood and wiped at his nose. "I'm not good enough."

Billy turned and ran into the night, finally believing he had found a course that was clear and true. No guilt, no doubts ran through his head—except one: *Y'know, if I took that thing, I'd probably hit myself in the head with it…and that'd just be really stupid.*

Chapter Twenty-Eight

Rising from atop the WDVL corporate headquarters, the steel girders of the landmark signal transmission tower drew the usual share of lightning to its heavy-mounted, steel-cased, red neon call letters—in the form of controversy. Tonight, however, the lightning that struck was real.

Despite appearances, lightning was never supposed to harm the functioning of the tower. Building codes and electrical contractors had long ago assured that the strategic placement of copper rods would channel the energy of any ozone-conjuring strikes through the great tower itself, and down thirty-three stories to the grounded safety of mother earth, with nary a hint of transmission interference.

Not so tonight. The sky above the tower was alive with a veritable chorus line of dancing electrical fire. And every bolt, it seemed, found its home atop WDVL. Network engineers were scrambling overtime to ensure the 11:00 p.m. newscast would be glitch-free.

But the glitches upon that evening's broadcast had barely begun…

WDVL news anchor Steven Dúmas had perfect hair. Some suggested that the *piece* might be a little *too* perfect, but those were the jealous ones, he believed. He flashed brilliant blue contacts directly into the camera and rattled off this installment's opening teaser.

"Good evening, and welcome to the late edition of WDVL news. On tonight's broadcast—The heated race for Governor grows hotter—Our very own Dominique Angel begins her controversial Special Report series—In

sports, Freedom's Belles stage a dramatic comeback on the field—And meteorologist Constance McCleary provides some explanation for tonight's unexpected precipitation…"

Another lightning strike scrambled the signal, and the floor manager gave Steven a *pause* gesture. All felt the building shudder as the lights flickered briefly.

Dúmas planned to remember this particular night when contract renewal came up. He felt the evening's broadcast had begun under a cloud of shoddy unprofessionalism for which he held management responsible—just as he also still blamed that first Stephen King prison movie, rerunning endlessly on cable TV, for an ongoing slight upon his name. Dúmas resented the ignorant, blue-collar working class that consistently called him "Dumb Ass" at public appearances. But neither the common masses, nor management, had ever prevented him from doing his job with all the arrogant condescension that he could muster, and most certainly not tonight. No mere atmospheric *Act of God* was going to stop him from doing the one thing he did best. *It was probably all that damned Constance McCleary's fault anyway.*

The floor manager gave him an *all clear.*

Dúmas continued as if he'd never paused, "But tonight's top story: An abandoned factory fire still rages unchecked, and our Eye in the Sky team has the latest coverage…"

At exactly 11:17 p.m., returning from a commercial on feminine hygiene, and then an update on the factory fire that had, at last, been declared by authorities as "under control," reporter Dominique Angel turned her serious face to the camera. Her makeup hid all trace of doubt and fear—as well as the lingering evidence of Desmond's affection.

She caught her intro from Steven Dúmas with professional aplomb, betraying no hint of the disdain she personally felt for the man off-camera. She began her prepared pitch to the masses, one that was particularly ironic in the wake of the broadcast's lead-in feature. "Good evening, ladies and gentle-men…this is Dominique Angel bringing you the first installment of my latest investigative report…'Homelessness: the Forgotten Priority'…"

In the shadowed depths of a forgotten alleyway, the old man stirred. He did

not open his eyes, but his cracked lips moved nonetheless.

"Please..." he mumbled, "let me sleep...just a little longer..."

The eyes finally did open, though, releasing rivulets of tears collected beneath the lids. The eyes were old, and tired from too much living.

"Forgive me, Lord...I understand...You are not finished with your old servant just yet."

Slowly, painfully, the old man pulled his arms close in and, gripping the iron staff, used it to raise himself from the stinking puddle and up onto his knees. He felt pain in his left shoulder and vaguely remembered being shot. Yet it was of no importance. When the Creator of Heaven and Earth told you to get up, get up you did, and you let Him worry about all the little aches and pains.

It was as simple as that.

"I obey...I obey," he rattled through his throat as he staggered to his feet.

The stench of garbage in which he'd lain, clung to him and brought itself to even *his* attention. He sniffed and made a face. "Goodness...I hope that's not me."

He suddenly teetered, agony burning through his abdomen.

"Just a little unsteady, that's all..." he said as he clutched awkwardly at the gaping wound in his gut. "...Loss of blood will do that, I'm told."

He gently placed the iron shaft against the nearest wall, never once troubled by Sanchez's refusal to take it, then used the brick face to hold himself up.

"...Just going to be a little harder than I thought..." he mused, and the old creases of his face cracked back into his warm and familiar gap-toothed smile. He methodically tore long strips from the lining of his ragged trench coat, and wound them tautly around his bloody abdomen.

"But...I am *yours,* Lord..." The old man narrowed his eyes, and the convicting fire within rekindled from the embers.

"...And whether the strength be mine or Thine...whatever the cost... I shall be faithful to the Call."

Chapter Twenty-Nine

To reinforce the dire sobriety of the issue she was now champion-ing, Dominique Angel had switched styles for the evening to a drab, yet fashionable, tan blazer and skirt combination, with a trim white blouse, complementing the freshly-set auburn locks that framed her face and high-lighted her oft-publicized "angelic beauty." Even the grimmest of tidings needed a bearer who looked her best if high ratings were to continue. Dom continued her special report, for the most part, as originally planned: seeking to place blame everywhere except where it truly belonged.

"It has been over a decade since this nation was last forced to look in the mirror and brought face-to-face with the darker spirits of our nature. What is it, we ask, that compels humanity to cast off our lesser selves into segregated ghettos of poverty and despair?"

As if in answer to the rhetoric, Billy Sanchez burst through the main studio doors, utilizing strength that was not his own. He stormed onto the sound stage floor, a crowbar in his grip and a gaggle of uncertain security guards bringing up the rear. The official station rent-a-cops were armed but, apparently, could never threaten lethal force without advance authorization passed through committee. Like everything connected to the news program, their weapons were only for show, but this intruder gave no indication of buying whatever threat they had to sell.

Dom didn't recognize the disheveled intruder at first, and simply did her professional best to keep her voice from faltering on-camera. "...Consumed by ideologies, the victims of right-wing political agendas..."

Another on-stage security guard leapt forward with a *sotto voce* shout, "Hey! You can't come in here!"

Sanchez threatened back with a wave of his crowbar. The guard, like his brothers in arms, backed off. Amid the confusion, the vagrant worked his way between Camera Three's operator and the floor manager—both of whom were now calculating the extent of their contractual obligation to WDVL Broadcasting.

Dom lost her train of thought as her eyes darted between the intrusion and the camera lens—her direct link to the eyes and ears of an estimated six million viewers. "...Uh, my apologies, ladies and gentlemen..."

Sanchez stared her straight in the eye and smiled. "Miss Angel...I'm here to protect you."

The camera operator had abandoned his post, leaving Camera Three fixed on Dominique's beautiful yet dumbfounded face. She still wasn't making the visual connection with her memory, or perhaps the vagrant's new demeanor of confidence made him unrecognizable to any who may have previously known him. He raised his weapon again toward the guard who had just changed places with the uncertain floor manager. The guard held his ground.

Sanchez continued, "He's dead, Miss Angel...a few hours ago, after we left you. I'd have been here sooner, but...well, I had some trouble gettin' to the station," he added with a wash of shame. "He did it for us, y'know...for me an' for you. We're like...I don't know how to say it—like different sides of the same coin...or somethin' like that."

"I...I don't quite know what you're referring to, sir..." Dom said, her lower lip quivering, betraying her stated denial. She now knew who the man was, and of whom he spoke. She felt a tear build in her left eye and willed it to stay where it was.

Sanchez saw the spark of recognition flash across her features, and his own assurance bolstered. "Don't let them win! Tell the truth, Miss Angel...*believe*."

The only satisfaction Desmond Cortez had to ease his troubled mind was that the threatening storm, promised all evening, had never actually manifested. Yet there was small comfort in the storm's uncertainty.

A full moon shining through clear skies should have been confirmation that the old fool had finally passed from this world. But his last contact had failed to report back. Thus the dark clouds and the station manager's doubt had remained as the hours ticked by.

Three minutes earlier, he had received his first notice of the commotion down in the building's sub-level garage. The description of "dirty, scrawny Hispanic" did not match that of his ancient adversary, so he'd told security the problem was *theirs* and they were to deal with it without bothering him again.

They hadn't, so their problem was now *his*.

With the sudden intrusion into the studio, Cortez—who had watched "his angel's" progress on his own office monitor, even as he kept track of the terrible reception the electrically-plagued tower was inflicting on the home viewing audience—barged onto the sound stage floor himself, bellowing, "What the hell is going on out here?!"

The problem appeared to be nothing more than the vagrant William Sanchez, and, as such, should have been no problem at all.

Cortez signaled and the security detail drew their side arms, now with officially-sanctioned confidence. He barked, "Somebody get that son of a bitch the hell off my damned sound stage!"

Sanchez took one ineffectual swing at the enclosing circle of armed security who swiftly knocked the crowbar from his possession. Even with their guns drawn, an actual weapons discharge by any of the rent-a-cops was a lawsuit waiting to happen.

Up at the broadcast newsdesk, Dominique went on with her segment, now desperate to form a new story right there on the spot, "...I—I must confess...this has *not* been my prepared report—I don't know how long I'll be allowed to continue broadcasting, but—I have uncovered evidence linking this station and its management to a conspiracy to manipulate the outcome of the upcoming gubernatorial election..."

Cortez made his way swiftly from the stage floor into the control room. "Cut transmission," he ordered coldly.

"But...we're on live," said the director.

"Cut it *now!*" And he snarled like a rabid dog.

Moments later, Sanchez was handcuffed and pinned to the studio wall by a pair of guards, while another of them now held his crowbar and playfully threatened to hit him with it.

The floor manager quickly reasserted control of his sound stage. He drew his index finger in a cutting motion across his chin, but Dom paid no attention and kept blurting out her impromptu exposé.

Finally, he stepped in front of the camera she stared so intently into. "I'm sorry, Dom…but it's over," he said.

The building tear in her left eye finally broke free and trailed down her disbelieving face. "But… b-but I wasn't finished," she stammered.

The heartbreak was visible on the floor manager's face. "We're *off* the air, Dom."

The voice of station head Desmond Cortez broke over the master intercom from the control room: "Security! You will escort Ms. Angel to my office—*immediately.*"

Dom didn't move even as two security guards, wearing faces of apology, mounted the blue chroma-key backdropped staging platform and took hold of her by either arm.

"Come with us, Ms. Angel," said one, almost gently.

"It's for your own safety," chimed the other, both ignorant of what their dull monotone sounded like to Dom's ears.

Suddenly animate, Dom shouted toward the internal microphones she knew were still operational, "You can't do this, Desmond! You can't kill a story this big just to protect your own political candidate!"

But she struggled in the grip of the two rent-a-cops to no avail, and just once, she locked eyes with Billy Sanchez. Both of them realized in that moment that everything they had lived for was coming to an end. Even worse, they now knew that every wrong choice they'd made along the way had been nobody's fault but their own.

The rest of the studio floor staff exchanged embarrassed glances at the manhandling of one of their own.

Constance McCleary looked angry; her chance to explain the odd weather would have to wait until tomorrow when it would no longer matter to anyone.

Anchor Steven Dúmas sat incredulous, unmoving, slowly coming to the conclusion that no one cared what he thought about the situation.

The studio lights suddenly dimmed, and the studio floor shuddered. All knew the old tower far above their heads had somehow taken a direct hit. This time the dimming lights flickered, then burst into showers of sparks, plunging the studio into unexpected darkness, lit only by the minimal glow of monitors and exit signs.

The main doors burst open a second time, spilling an abundance of emergency lighting into the darkened studio. A hunched figure stood silhouetted in the double-door frame, barely standing, seemingly supported only by the iron stability of a three-foot pole. A pair of guards lay unmoving, unconscious at his feet. Wisps of long grey hair and dangling scraps of clothing identified him to the few who might recognize him.

Far across the sound stage, at the opposite end doors, Cortez had met the guards escorting Dominique, and taken her into his own personal custody.

The old man cried across the chasm of darkness, his voice an arrow straight through the station manager's burly chest wherein his heart was supposed to rest. "Unhand her *this instant* or, with God as my witness above, I'll send you to Hell *before* the appointed hour!"

Cortez shouted to security, "Take care of *that*—Get rid of them both!" Then he bustled Dom out into the dim hall.

Dom struggled, and her protest rose with a steadily growing boldness, "What do you think you're doing?"

Cortez ignored her and pulled out the cell phone, his secure line, without losing his solid grip on his incidental captive.

"You're *afraid* of him, aren't you?" she challenged. "Somehow that old man terrifies you!"

She saw his eyes flare with anger and he slammed her against the wall, right next to the clearly-marked exit door of the emergency stairwell. His voice was hissing propane awaiting a spark: "I'm not afraid of *anything* your kind threatens me with!"

He muscled her into the stairwell, brightly lit by emergency floods, and punched a rapid key sequence into the phone. His hostility toward Dom now seemed an afterthought to where his true fury lay: "You had a chance to be someone,

Dom—a chance to step into the spotlight and actually become somebody who mattered...but you blew it!"

Under the harsh flood glare, she looked at her boss, her lover, with new eyes. "He's right, isn't he...everything he said about you is true! You're terrified that if you lose me— all the hard work you've put into *my* career—then you'll look like a failure to Henry Devlin, or whoever the hell it is that's pulling your strings— and *that* scares the piss out of you!"

"Shut up!" He slapped her. Unlike last night, however, she did not cower, but glared back as harshly as the floodlights. His own gaze bore straight back into her newly emboldened eyes. "I don't know why, but that old fool actually thinks you're worth saving."

He turned aside abruptly and spoke into his cell as if the signal had only just connected: "Unit A—I'm coming topside—target will follow...and I want a *clean kill* this time."

Dom suddenly understood. "I'm the bait."

Cortez smiled back as he dragged her up the staircase. "I think he actually *loves* you, Dom. And he's going to go to his death to prove it."

The old man limped unhindered into the deathly quiet studio, feeling every eye upon him despite the gloom. He locked his own eyes upon every stare in turn. He saw Sanchez against the wall, now held by only a single guard. The others were slowly forming a steady circle around him, a tightening noose of seven gun barrels pointed at his chest.

The old man spoke. He spoke as the ancient warrior. He spoke as Quixote: "The *first* man to pull a trigger—"

There was a sudden flash of movement as one finger tightened on a trigger. Instantly, the security guard who'd held that pistol fell to the floor, clutching broken fingers.

Quixote now held the pistol along with his sword. "The *next* man to pull a trigger…will join your fellow upon the floor."

The guards exchanged nervous glances and then stared at the fire of conviction behind the old man's eyes. Without another word, they lowered their weapons and parted.

Quixote passed through the silence. He gestured toward the handcuffed Sanchez, adding, "…And release that man. He has done you no harm."

Witless, the guard complied, while Quixote, with nary a second glance, hurried for the exit through which *the Dragon* had taken his Dulcinea.

Chapter Thirty

It was not the old man whom Dom saw come crashing out onto the rooftop of the thirty-three-story WDVL building, but the ancient warrior she had come to know as Quixote. He now leapt out to stand tall and proud before her. He was not *old*, nor withered and weatherworn, but vibrant and alive, a defender of righteousness carrying Heaven's vengeance in his eyes. In his hand, he now held a pistol to complement his trusty sword.

The old man might be as dead as Billy Sanchez had said, but this angelic avenger raised his new weapon and seemed to point its barrel straight between Dom's eyes. In that moment, she knew that she deserved whatever retribution he had come to deliver. But then, as she visually traced his aim, she was reminded that Desmond Cortez stood a full head taller right behind her. She desperately hoped the Hero's mark would be as true as his gallant spirit.

A hands-free receiver was now attached to Desmond's secure line and he barked orders without flinching or loosening the grip upon his hostage.

"Take him!
Take the bastard— *NOW!*"

In answer, a cacophony of rapid, sequential thunderclaps riddled the night air, released as a hail of gunfire and swept downward by the rotary gust of a black heli-copter gunship.

Without a moment's hesitation, Quixote ran for the rooftop's edge, discarding the pistol as bullets ripped up a trail behind his feet. The Hero leapt over the chain-link security fence around the building's sky-high perimeter

and clung precariously by the lowest links, off the side, over five hundred feet above the street. The chopper buzzed in a straight line over his head.

The pilot of the black chopper brought the craft to a halt and spun it around to give the onboard marksman a clear shot at the little insect clinging desperately to the wall. But as the black beast was reorienting itself against the night sky, Quixote hitched himself up with one free arm and let the rotor's draft blow his body back over the fence and onto the rooftop proper. He landed firm and sure, as impotent gunfire ricocheted off the fence.

Cortez shrieked at his agents' incompetence. "He's just one man! Can't you do anything right?" Dom could feel Cortez's musculature tense like over-coiled steel bands screaming to explode.

The black chopper held a pair of black-garbed things in human form, empty eye-sockets occupying the void behind the dark visors that lowered from within their dark helmets. Flak vests covered Federal agency identification. The implements of human ingenuity were awkward, yet effective in administering death, and the marksman filled one of its all-seeing  empty sockets with the targeting scope of an M-16 automatic rifle. Its eerie monotone carried an edge of concern. "He's fast…can't get any bead worth a damn."

The pilot parroted the monotone assessment and radioed their lack of progress to their superior down on the rooftop—one who could possibly do far worse than simply dishonorably discharge them, should things end up officially FUBAR.

The ancient warrior stood tall and proud, seeming to taunt them in their failure. The pilot recklessly swung the chopper back around to rise above the roof—only to come face-to-disastrous-face with the last thing they needed on top of everything else.

"Damnation!" it shrieked, swerving the chopper violently to the left of the transmission tower to avoid the sudden arrival of the WDVL *traffic helicopter* that came swooping in on the right, all cameras blazing.

Nearly falling from the chopper's open side hatch, the accompanying demon echoed the curse. It almost lost its rifle in the scramble for a handhold. Almost.

Far below, the swordsman took advantage of the near-collision and made his way back to Cortez and his hostage.

On the other side of the tower, the black chopper pilot finally recalibrated and the marksman climbed back in, chest heaving more heavily than its human training and spectral experience permitted.

"Mr. Cortez…we have another problem up here…" the pilot relayed, " a very *serious* problem."

The newly-arrived traffic 'copter gleamed as white as the WDVL newsvans. The bright red numeral "6" blazed on its side like a beacon, letting all the world know that where that 'copter flew, *news followed*. With only one refueling stop, the "Eye in the Sky" Jet Ranger had spent most of the evening airborne, chronicling a bird's-eye record of the city's biggest blaze in years. It had been a doozy, pulling in firefighting crews from seven neighboring districts. But almost immediately on the heels of its crew's last "under control" update, all contact with the studio had gone cold—dead air.

It had been Madeline Jeunet's call, and Macintosh McIlhenney III had promised to back her up. They'd hightailed it back to the studio only to discover, upon their return, the fiercest of opposition. This wasn't the trivial rivalry of another network looking to scoop, but a more dangerous breed—

the deadliest of competition, already on the case.

Their near miss of the black chopper was a little too close for Maddy's comfort. "Did you *catch* that?" she radioed to her cameraman, who had changed seats and now hung partially out the side of the Ranger's cabin.

Mackie had the twin on-board gyro-cams rolling on automatic. But under the circumstances, he also clung to his shoulder-mounted unit to make full use of manual tracking and zoom-in close-ups. He placed his faith and trust in a safety harness and pilot Jeunet's capable hands.

"Better than that, my dear..." Mackie grinned in answer as he realized he was now covering traffic and disaster of a far different sort. "I got us some great blackmail material on the boss! Looks like we're both gonna be in line for some raises!"

Mackie's viewfinder was full of the threatening visage of Desmond Cortez.

Chapter Thirty-One

The gyro-cam footage of station manager Desmond Cortez, re-covering a security pistol and using his own reporter as a human shield, relayed instantly to the WDVL news studio. The director and control room staff sat dumbfounded as they witnessed not only the gun being held to Dom's head, but everything else that was unfolding in the bizarre scene upstairs.

The transmission circuit continued directly onto monitors in the darkened sound stage proper. News anchor Steven Dúmas felt his stomach sour. He had always despised Cortez, but for whatever reason, the burly station manager seemed to like him. Dúmas knew his job rested squarely in those large hands, one of which now held a gun. He despised Desmond all the more for jeopardizing the prize anchor's career with such a series of boldly stupid decisions.

The rest of the studio was silent. Even Constance McCleary had found something new in the boss's behavior to stew over privately. She had known all along that *this* was exactly the kind of thing Cortez was capable of doing, but now, nobody would care that *she* had known it first.

Most of the studio staff, including security and Billy Sanchez, who was no longer considered a security concern, had migrated to the control room looking for some kind of an answer. Officially, the network was still broad-casting dead air, its "Please Stand By" signal transmitting into the charged night sky, even as the extraordinary coverage of things above continued to beam down to them from Mackie and the Jet Ranger. One by one, all eyes turned to the director in the command hot seat. He had nothing to offer and seemed just as lost as the rest. The conflict of *instinct* versus

direct order had reduced the lot of them to a state of paralysis in the face of actual crisis.

"We *can't* go live with this…" explained the director defensively, "that's the *boss*."

There were murmurs of assent, as each weighed their own culpability in the wake of such a scandal going public. But the voice of Billy Sanchez resounded through them all like a gong, "No, man, that's *NEWS*…you guys *make* the news—*run it!*"

The murmuring that had agreed with the director moments before now turned to support Billy Sanchez. Each participant came to the conclusion that the director's head alone would roll if there were any negative consequences, although there'd be praise enough for all if the decision proved fortuitous.

The director looked around the roomful of expectant faces, and steeled his courage to keep pace with his professional instinct. "OK, run it," he said through clenched teeth.

There was hesitation in the hands of the technical director at his side.

The director looked his T.D. straight in the eye. "This is *my* call, and mine alone. We run it—live feed—*Now!*"

Unaware that his actions were about to make national news, Desmond Cortez continued to keep the swordsman at bay. He'd retrieved the gun the warrior had dropped and now aimed it at the side of Dom's head. Quixote circled around them, a slow and deliberate dance, much like the twin helicopters above that hovered around the great tower.

Dominique rationally concluded that the gun wasn't really to threaten her, but its implication was to keep the Hero from swiftly ending the stand-off with his blade. Spying the multiple lenses aboard the newscopter trained on their drama, Dom chided her—one way or the other—*former* boss, "This picture's going to look great as tomorrow's lead story."

Cortez saw the cameras too. He could barely keep his rage from splitting his skin, exposing to all the true spirit within. In that moment, he wanted nothing more than to twist the reporter's head from her spine and ram it down the old fool's throat.

That was the least preferable course of action, but Cortez feared it was going to end there regardless. If so, he'd have a hell of a time covering his ass. It wasn't impossible yet, but grew more difficult every minute the newscopter continued to chronicle his exploits.

"Take that traffic bird down!" he shrieked into his headset. "I don't care that it's one of mine. Take it down, and that's an *order!*"

His only consolations now were that he'd already ordered transmission to be cut, and that everyone on his staff knew better than to disregard a direct command.

As Desmond ordered the aerial strike, Dom felt the coiled springs of his muscles loosen. She chose that moment to attack, bringing the point of her heel sharply down through the bridge of his shoe leather.

Desmond howled, loosening his grip on her, and she used all her strength to break free.

Quixote leapt forward in the instant Dom broke away from Cortez's hold, his sword plunging through the right lung of the larger man.

Desmond fired back, a copycat wound upon the ancient warrior, trading lead for steel. The impact forced the swordsman backward, pulling his blade from Cortez's chest. The station manager immediately started coughing up blood. Quixote recovered more swiftly, though, than his burlier adversary. With another sure strike of his sword, he disarmed his opponent of the pistol, along with three of the fingers that had held it.

Another mighty bolt of lightning struck the rooftop, the accompanying thunder nearly deafening them all. Then rain began to fall.

Down in the WDVL control booth, a cheer broke out as the studio crew watched the broadcasted image of the old guy with the spike running Cortez through. Even Constance McCleary and Steven Dúmas realized that something

was transpiring here that was definitely bigger than themselves or their opinions thereof.

Then, all watched with bated breath as Dominique Angel, her escape route blocked by a pair of apparent madmen dueling to the death over something as nebulous as principle, ditched her heels and began climbing the steel transmission tower itself in a desperate bid to escape them both.

Billy Sanchez chose that moment to duck out and head for the roof.

Chapter Thirty-Two

The best friend of the late Joey Caparelli couldn't believe his good fortune, and, unaware of his fellow cameraman's earlier fate, Mackie couldn't wait to share this incredible story with his best bud over a drink when all was finally said and done. That is, if the mad Irishman lived to tell the tale.

Neither of the young cameramen had ever much liked station manager Desmond Cortez. For Mackie to now catch that old pit bull with his proverbial pants down, crapping on the public trust, was like a dream come true. But Mackie knew his camera had caught far more than downed pants when Cortez and the swordsman exchanged blows. He suddenly entertained visions of Pulitzers and Emmys, swirling about like the sugarplums that were said to fill Christmas Eve dreams. He snapped out of his mental chorus line revue when he heard Madeline curse up a blue streak, right before the Ranger practically lurched ninety degrees onto its side.

The other chopper, with which they'd been dancing their bizarre aerial ballet, now opened fire upon them via two strut-mounted M-60s under the dark pilot's control. Bullets ripped through their own chassis and canopy. Mackie caught one in the arm.

"I'm hit!" he yelled to Maddy.

The young woman at the throttle now realized just how high the stakes had become. The voice of her mama rang in her head, telling her to get the pair of them out of there. But these were the legendary moments that showed the world *who* you were and *what* you were made of. This was her career, her passion. This was Maddy's moment to do or die.

The two 'copters continued weaving in and out, back and forth, dosey-doe-ing their way around the old tower. Lightning filled the sky like the Fourth of July while the traffic 'copter's cockpit filled with fireworks, though the competing rotors churned up the night sky louder than any professional-caliber bottle rocket.

Then the clouds opened, releasing a sudden deluge, roaring downward as if all the tears of Heaven were pouring out at once. Yet neither bird was willing to abandon its true calling. The dark agents had their orders, underscored with the dread of failure and its consequences. As for the two newshounds, they discovered what countless war-veteran journalists before them had: that covering such a story was never an issue of personal safety, but a matter of pride, ambition, and the sacred honor of chronicling such human moments of unadulterated truth.

Cortez staggered back, hacking up great lungfuls of blood and phlegm as he wildly looked around for his fallen firearm. All he saw, though, with a detached, fascinated horror, were two of his three missing fingers awash in the sudden downpour.

Heedless of his own wound, Quixote lunged forward, and Cortez barely made it behind one of the four massive support legs of the mighty transmission tower before the swordsman's blade connected bluntly, steel to steel, and sent shudders up his arm. Cortez delivered a staggering kick to the warrior's thigh, and Quixote slipped to his knees on the newly-wet surface. Unable to ignore his injury any longer, he gritted his teeth against the most recent pain in his chest and *willed* air into his collapsing lung.

Reluctant to press the moment's advantage without an actual weapon, and with nowhere else to go, Cortez took hold of the lowest girder of the massive tower, grimacing in his own pain, and began to climb. He reasoned it might be easier to avoid the swordsman's blade from above it. In the interval, he'd buy some time for his marksman to *finish* the ancient warrior once and for all.

The black chopper swung around the upper tip of the tower and swooped down like a hawk upon the less-maneuverable bird.

Maddy tried to compensate, but her sparking instrumentation betrayed the skill of her hands, and her ship's whirling blades caught the building's rooftop service entrance.

For one brief instant, Mackie thought it might have been a good practice to have worn a helmet after all.

Trailing smoke, the Jet Ranger III jerked and spasmed its way onto the WDVL roof tarmac, exploding into the rain-swept night with a spectacular gout of fire.

Excess fuel spouted onto the surface, spreading out like brimstone beneath a witch's cauldron. The rooftop instantly became an inferno.

From where he lay, Quixote barely dodged the spinning rotor blade of the falling 'copter, its edge catching just a sliver of his scalp, enough to draw blood. He dove and tumbled across the ground, then rolled to avoid the flaming jet fuel that spewed out where he had landed. The fuel burned white-hot, far too great for even the torrential downpour to quench.

He looked around for his enemy. His grip upon his ancient blade was slick from a blend of his own blood, rain, and the slippery gel of fuel. Two girder-lengths above him, he espied the Dragon climbing toward his Dulcinea, who ascended even higher up the tower, far above them both.

The black chopper now reappeared with the ancient warrior again in its sights. It swooped around the flaming tower like a locust of Revelation, harbinger of the Apocalypse.

Quixote heard the whine of its bullets before the first three strafed up his back, tearing his long coat and ripping his flesh. It seemed only blind luck had set him running so that the burning lead merely bit yet did not

penetrate. But the warrior did not believe in luck. He knew better.

His options were limited: the rooftop had become a holocaust of elemental fury—storm, flood, and fire. So he ran across the flames, long black wisps of his hair singeing, and through the wind and the rain.

The rotary demon pursued him, chewing up the burning rooftop in its hunger for the blood of the righteous, the devil's shot ever at his heel.

When the chopper's target ran out of room at the rooftop's highest edge, Quixote scaled the fence and vaulted out into space. Unfortunately for the chopper, its malevolent guidance had never anticipated such a suicidal move. At the last instant, its dark pilot had spurred its demonic engine forward, intending to cut around the fleeing prey who was then leaping into the night.

Quixote caught the bottom runner of the chopper in mid-air, having ascertained its trajectory, instinctively calculated the higher math in his wizened head without really thinking about it, and now clung unseen to its landing carriage.

The pilot frantically initiated a visual search for the intruder it realized was somewhere aboard, clinging like an insect. The great whirling beast spun itself into a steady revolution around the massive tower, where the call letters still glared forth into the night, despite the storm, in ten-foot-high, steel-cased, red neon blocks: WDVL 6

Chapter Thirty-Three

Dominique Angel felt she was on top of a world that was falling, fast and furiously, toward oblivion.

It wasn't her fault. She hadn't asked for any of this; nor would she allow herself to pay the price.

The climb up the slippery steel was now a blur—a crazy enough endeavor in a medium-length skirt, but she'd already passed her own self-inflicted point of no return by the time the rain had begun to fall.

The crash of the news 'copter confirmed the evening as an ongoing nightmare that would not release her from its tenacious grip. She wanted so desperately to wake up in her own bed, in her own apartment—and not in the satin sheets of Desmond's penthouse suite. *Never again* did she want to awaken in the arms of the brutal monster she now knew him to be, that monster who, even now, she saw, pursued her ever higher up the rain-slick girders.

Cortez had paused to wrap his tie about the bloody mess that had once been his left hand. But even as he did so, he continued to hound her with his tongue, as if he could run her to ground by the dominating force of his will.

"We were visionaries, Dom—you and I—made for each other," he said, calling to her, as he reached up with his remaining good hand onto the beam upon which she now stood. "Prophets of the New Age…we spoke for the gods of this world—do you understand that, Dom?" His mangled hand reached up next to secure his hold. "So why'd you do it? Why did you have to go and ruin everything?"

Incredulous, she defied the pursuing nightmare. *"You're insane!"* she screamed.

She could have crushed his remaining fingers even then with only her stockinged feet, inflicting further pain upon the devastated hand. But all Dom really wanted was to run far, far away.

She was already on her way up to the next beam, steadying herself along the edge of a cross support when she chanced another look over her shoulder. He kept coming. She slipped on the slick steel, and fell back onto her previous perch. Like a fearful child, she clung desperately to the crossbeam support, realizing just how close she had come to plummeting nearly fifty feet to the burning fury below.

"It isn't about *me,* Dom," Desmond said, as he pulled himself up onto the very beam to which she still clung.

"This is about *you* and it always has been. Have you any idea what I'll have to do—how much *ass* I'm going to have to kiss to get all this swept under the carpet?!"

He rose to his feet and steadied himself, standing on the precarious, six-inch width of the girder. Then he suddenly grinned, as if they were merely out sightseeing on a fine day. In actuality, he was following the progress of the chopper that spun around the tower, and especially the tiny figure that clung helplessly to its under-carriage.

"But—you're the *cause!*" Dom screamed.

"Don't blame me! Show some respect…by the end of tonight, I may be the only excuse you have left!"

"You used me!"

"Only as much as you used me *first,* Dom. I took you no farther than you were willing to go. I was just your steppingstone on the path to success. I did whatever I had to do for your sake, while you turned a convenient blind eye away from anything you didn't want to see!"

She stopped and considered his words, the echo of Joseph Caparelli ringing in her memory. He'd been right of course, back in the station manager's office, but the cameraman had *spun* the facts in support of the old man. Now, the same argument came from the mouth of Desmond Cortez himself, the same charge, the same facts, only this time *twisted* to suit the cause of another. *Perception as reality, molded by agenda.* Dom felt she had no choice but to embrace the only truth she'd ever depended on: the utter *malleability* of truth.

Any fears, any concern she may have had for the crazed swordsman, engulfed by the raging inferno below, now slipped away. *After all, hadn't Quixote and his mad crusade been the true cause of this entire nightmare in the first place?* She had never *asked* for his help. Before his arrival, butting into her business with all his castigating charges of personal accountability, she had known where she stood, knew all she needed to know about right and wrong, and all the grey areas in between. That was what really mattered: knowing what she could get away with in a world where foolish, childhood rules no longer applied. And with that knowledge, she'd bent all things to serve her career, her life, her future. She'd never needed any old man to help her see clearly before. She'd known who was—and always had been—to blame. And there were no *windmills,* nor *giant ogres, demons,* or *dragons to be slain* on behalf of her ephemeral virtue. Quixote? *Let the fucking lunatic be damned.*

She just wanted to go home.

Chapter Thirty-Four

Aboard the black chopper, the marksman searched for its target, leering out and peering down and around. Striking like a wise serpent, the ancient warrior snagged it by the throat with his blade and yanked the body straight out, sending it down uncounted feet to the hellish fury below.

With one enemy ejected, only the pilot remained to be dealt with—and Cortez still to come. The swordsman pulled himself up from beneath the undercarriage, now clinging to the outside of its front canopy. The pilot seemed to panic and sent the chopper into a sudden spin, hoping that centrifugal force would fling his unwelcome guest away. But Quixote smashed his fist through the cockpit glass and seized a handful of the pilot's flak vest to anchor himself. The thing immediately ripped free of its shoulder restraints as natural law exerted its mighty pull.

The dark pilot felt one joint pop, but, despite the physical pain, it fought to retain control as its mechanical beast spun around recklessly, ever closer to the tower that would spell its doom. Up, down, north and south, left and right, every diametrically opposed direction—save right and wrong—went askew, as the entire world tumbled around them. Still, Quixote held firm, and the pilot's black-helmeted head snapped back and forth, again and again, colliding with the safety glass until both helmet visor and tempered canopy shattered together.

Then all motion and momentum came to a sudden, jarring stop. It was the landing gear's hooking onto the massive transmission tower that jerked the spinning chopper to its abrupt halt, securing the chattering metal insect within its steel web of old girders and aged cross beams.

The entire tower shuddered, the shock waves rattling through the building itself, and a great and mighty windmill now loomed far over the city skyline in sheer defiance of the storm.

And where the *Windmill* challenged the gale, *Giants* and *the Dragon* could not be far.

The entire tower shuddered, and Dom fell.

Desmond caught her.

He had inched his way ever closer to the cowering reporter and was within a single yard of her when the raging mechanized demon that had swirled around them, hooked and anchored itself to the steel barely another forty feet above them. Only seconds before, the corner of his eye had caught sight of a figure falling from it.

Dom slipped from the impact, as had Cortez. But the burly manager had been able to drop immediately to the beam at his feet and so kept himself from falling. Dom, however, was knocked loose from her own hold, and fell toward him. His good right hand grabbed hold of her jacket and blouse, thus preventing her from plummeting to the fire far below. She didn't scream until he'd actually caught her.

There, the two of them hung from the tower, the massive power of the chopper's rotary blades swirling vertically above them, the flames

beneath in seeming competition with the electrical
fire high overhead, lighting the clouds of
the storm-shrouded night.

Still the rain fell in thick sheets.

Desmond looked down
into Dom's face.

She stared back, but her own
eyes were no longer focused on
anything. History had a way of
repeating itself, and she realized
that the past would always
come back to haunt her.
Just as with the swords-
man's recent intrusion
into her life, she had
never *asked* for a
miracle all those

long years ago—*she should have died along with her mother
and not given her father a chance to screw up any further.*

Maybe the confusion of recent events was telling her that she'd built a
life on borrowed time, and the hour had finally come around to pay the
balance. "Just let me go," she said quietly, her voice dead.

"I should let you fall…" he answered. "I really should. But I won't."
He flashed his teeth, and they were as bright and jolly and carefree as she'd
ever seen them in their mutual afterglow. "You're important, Dom…you
matter to me."

Dom didn't want to hear any of it. She just wanted all her fear, doubt,
and pain to go away.

But Desmond shook her from her musings with a twitch of his good
hand. "I won't expect you to understand this…but I'm asking you to
trust me."

She said nothing, but her head gave the slightest nod.

"Then use your hands...pull yourself up," he continued. "Remember...God only helps those who help themselves."

Working together, they were able to get her back up onto the beam, where Dom regained a modicum of stability on her bent knees. All the while, the gale blew around them, soaking cloth to skin, and skin to bone, the whole tower shaking as much with the vibration of the chopper's engine as from the storm.

He steadied her, but then she broke away, crawling toward the nearest steel pylon leg. As he let her go, he found even *he* needed better support upon the trembling tower against the onslaught of the elements. He made his way in the opposite direction toward the next nearest leg.

At fifty feet above the rooftop, only a scant five yards lay between them, corner to steel corner of the tower's pyramidal frame. All the while, at any moment, it seemed that the aged tower itself might collapse, twisting and crushing them beneath its tons of steel.

Now, with something to hold on to, Cortez stood tall again, satisfied that, by saving the woman's life, she was *his* once again. Dom needed only a moment to wrestle with that fact for herself and reach the same conclusion. With the ancient adversary gone, fallen to his doom, Desmond could afford now to be gracious and give her that moment. *Life was good.*

He grinned maniacally into the wind and rain. "Helluva night, wouldn't you say, Dom?"

She had also gotten back to her feet, her head swirling with all of the inescapable absolutes: life, death…and how consequences had a way of catching up to you. The sudden brush with mortality had yanked her back to conceding the old man's noble intent, however misguided. And the strange vision of the dashing Hero demanded at least some acknowledgment. "But what about—"

"He's dead. I saw him fall. He was just a nightmare anyway—some fairy tale madman you made up in your mind to give you answers to all the things that scared you, everything that goes bump in the night. But he's gone now and you're awake, Dom. It's just you and me."

He laid it out so matter-of-factly.

Could it be as simple as that, she thought, *some twisted wish-fulfillment born out of all the uncertainties of her past?* Everything connected to the improbable swordsman was a mystery: his words, his actions, his very identity a conundrum of impossible duality.

Desmond, on the other hand, had come into Dom's life without questions or judgments, a physical savior who offered a tangible future. Again and again, he delivered on the dream of success she had wished for long ago, when her mother lay dead in the ground and her sorry excuse for a father tried to make everything all better again. Doubt had always whispered that she deserved no better than that sorry legacy her unfortunate parents had left her. So, when the path ahead finally looked clear, her ambition on the very cusp of fulfillment, *fear* had conjured the moralistic madman and made the ambiguous guilt he represented real. That felt like a truth she could live with.

But hadn't she just been longing to join her mother in the grave? And now, only too willing to let a monster put her career back on track? **She** *was probably the crazy one.*

Amidst all the seeming contradiction, though, it was Desmond alone who provided the only answers that made psychological sense. The choice was hers. Take his truth and claim it as her own, embrace the peace it promised, or continue muddling through all the regret and solitude that filled the world.

No choice really. At last, she'd found something she could believe in.

Chapter Thirty-Five

The "madman," actually alive and well—and quite physically tangible—dropped from the jerking chopper high above. He seemed to ride the current of the wind itself down to the girder where Cortez gloated and Dominique cowered at opposite ends. His black boots landed hard between them, finding firm and sure footing upon the slick, wet steel. He then leveled his sword and his fury toward the startled station manager, who kept himself just inches from the blade's reach.

"Your mouth is ever full of lies, Prince of Devils," the swordsman cried in his voice of thunder, the power of it rattling Cortez, and forcing him back toward the next perpendicular strut. "Does your forked tongue know nothing but deception?"

Cortez regained his balance and composure. Rapidly calculating how to now shift gears in order to ride out this inevitable confrontation, he answered with a grand smirk, "This was never your concern, *Old Man...*"

Though he was beaten and torn, the jibe never altered the features of the gallant young hero whose eyes seemed to reflect the burning fire from far below.

Dom couldn't bring herself to look at him, even though he wasn't facing her. His mere presence rocked all of her convictions and knocked the foundation right out from under her grand determination of moments ago.

Cortez persisted, even as he put further distance between them. "...And in her heart, *'my angel'* knows I'm the only man that's ever played her straight. *Me!* Not you—not some decrepit old phantom who's stubbornly lived on past his own relevance!"

"Enough!" commanded Quixote. "Show yourself!"

Cortez flinched as if he had been struck, an involuntary spasm of taut muscles beneath the skin, but he recovered swiftly, grabbing hold of the next support leg, and countered the challenge: "I make no excuse for what I am. But *you*, at least, could be sincere. Are we not—*all three of us*—creatures of deceit?"

Dom started to shake her head, but whether she was denying the past or the present, it was hard to tell. Cortez felt his newly restored hold over the woman slipping.

Quixote dismissed the accusation. "As it was from the beginning, the serpent plies the craft of reason so well—"

Dominique stopped him. "He's right," she said, looking around and indicating Cortez. She was finally able to face the swordsman she'd convinced herself had only been a product of her own subconscious. "He knows me better than anyone…and everything he's said is true."

Quixote answered her, his tone still boldly defiant of Cortez. "Such creatures use truth only to destroy. He slips poison between the cracks. You are closer to salvation than you know—and *that* is the substance of his fear."

She listened, but her eyes were still fearful and haunted, filled with memories leaking straight from her oft-disputed soul.

"Did you catch all that, Dom?" shouted Cortez, disputing nothing, but making enough allowance so that the ideological contest might end decisively, the ancient warrior finally hanged by his own logically twisted noose. Dom looked anxious to participate—anything to clear her head—and, in this instance, full disclosure might just be what was needed to win the day. "Look at him," he gestured toward the swordsman,

even as he then inched his way toward the next support leg, the opposite corner of the tower, now quite far from the warrior's striking range.

She didn't want to look any deeper, but with Cortez as far across from them as he could go without coming back, Dom had an unobstructed view of the swordsman's profile. Black hair clung to his head and face in long soaking strands. Half of his hairline dripped blood from a scalp laceration. His features, though, were staunch, finely chiseled as if by a Renaissance master, an embodiment of true nobility granted physical form and burning with undaunted purpose. He was *Ulysses, King David* incarnate, *Arthur, Robin Hood,* and *Quixote.* He was *every hero* of *every age,* one who never took his fierce eyes from his opponent, nor the tip of his sword from his enemy's direction. Despite the contradiction his reality caused in her mind, Dom felt hope stir in her breast once again. She couldn't help herself.

"I mean *really* look at him, Dom," Cortez reiterated, adding emphasis to reclaim her heart. He had only words to fight with now, as the warrior had withstood every other physical weapon in his arsenal. "...And see him for what he is..."

Dom knew Desmond's insistence couldn't change what she saw with her own eyes. The Hero was real, true flesh and blood standing before her, undaunted. Yet even so, there *were* more wounds than she'd noticed before, most of them fresh and untended, bleeding freely through the scraps of his once-dapper garb, now washed by the rain. She saw his shoulders sag, just a little, and Dom realized that he *was* old, just as Desmond had been saying all along, far older even than the seventy years she had first guessed. His eyes, recessed into bony sockets, were deep and dark. His crooked nose had been broken in countless skirmishes. Bloodstained blotches of tattered grey beard narrowly defined his angular jaw line.

Desmond was merciless. "What do you *see* standing

there? Nothing but a faded old dreamer whose ideals are obsolete!" And with those words, the last vestige of the Hero vanished.

In that moment, the old man nearly fell from the tower. Yet then, as if awakening from a long, deep sleep, he shook his head sharply and the visage and bearing of the Hero returned in an instant.

Dom wiped at her eyes, convinced the rain had blurred her vision in

precise conjunction with the slices of Desmond's scything tongue. For just a moment, her Hero had appeared as the decrepit old man who, apparently, had lived, died, and yet lived again more times than her sanity was willing to grant credence.

Quixote then spoke to balance the scales in her mind, "In my action there is no guile. I am old, yes—far older than you might guess—but this face is no illusion nor mere façade…"

For the first time since landing on the tower strut, he turned away from his adversary to look at Dom. He smiled, and she saw the fire behind his eyes had dimmed, yet only enough to make them warm. He continued, "The countenance you see before you is but a projection of my heart, and it is my *true* face. The soul behind these eyes is as one now unscathed by the sin of this world—a redeemed and righteous soul, still burning with true conviction and the very fire and vigor of my youth."

Cortez laughed across the chasm between them. "Have you ever heard such a stinking load of crap before in your life, Dom? You *really* plan to go along with all that—letting him play Clark to your Lois?"

The swordsman's eyes spoke truth, and they told her that Desmond lied. Yet she had spent a lifetime shaping words to twist emotion, altering memory to suit desire, drafting her own lies to hide the pain. The Hero may have embodied hope for the lost, but she herself wasn't ready to believe.

Cortez could feel the battle within her. There was yet still a chance for

Desmond to be proud of "his little angel." He lay down his final challenge to the avenging knight, "Tell her *who* you are, old man. Tell her the *truth*… if you dare."

Dominique held onto the steel girder as if it alone had proven to be the only reliable, substantial truth the world had to offer. Now even *that* foundation was trembling beneath the vibration of the spinning rotor—a veritable sword of Damocles it was, and every bit as tenuous—hanging far above all their condemned heads.

"What's he talking about?" she begged the warm eyes of her would-be savior, "What truth? Please! I don't even know your *name!*"

He turned away from her, just as in the freight alley—an eternity ago it now seemed to Dom—unable once more to meet her eyes. "I am only that which you see—a Knight of the Sacred Gospel, and a Keeper of the Code…" His gaze wandered off into space, across the yawning chasm of Hell beneath them, then straight into the eyes of Desmond Cortez. He finished with a stoic certainty. "…And I have lived nearly five hundred years as a servant of the Most High God, and He has not finished with me yet."

Cortez received the gaze without concession, actually smiling in return. "Don't stop there, old man—tell her the rest. Tell her *all* of it!"

Quixote appeared unsteady again, as if only one revelation away from falling into the abyss. His free hand returned to the earlier wound through his belly, and discovered mortal pain there. He turned back to Dom, suddenly desperate for someone, anyone, to believe him, to bolster his own sense of fading conviction.

Dom simply stared back, pleading with equal desperation, "Please… I need to believe in *something!*"

How far, he mused, *had they both come since that afternoon when her fervent desire was simply to pad out a pointless story?* Too far, it seemed. His enemy's strategy had now left him with humble admission as his only recourse.

The warrior's shoulders drooped further, and the fiery eyes extinguished under the heavy lids of a mottled and wrinkled face. The sword wavered unsteadily in a spotted, blue-veined, quivering hand. It gained weight as it assumed greater substance, fine-honed steel transmuting back into mere iron, the enchanted relic revealed as nothing more than three rusted feet of absconded fence spike from some old church's gate.

"I am…" A tear rolled from the warrior's ancient eye as he spoke, this time uttered in a voice nearly drowned out by the storm. Yet there was no denying each word he said, as if the wind carried the whisper from his lips

to her ear. *"I am…Alonso Quixano de la Mancha…"*

A heavy sigh, rasping like a mortal soul's final breath, escaped his thin blue lips. Yet the old man attempted to regain some semblance of his former posture, an effort to restore the glory of what once was. He filled his lungs to capacity and let them buoy his chest. He straightened his bony shoulders, and bolstered the muscles of his thin, sagging arms, straining to hold forth the weight of the shaft by sheer effort of a will born of righteousness. His old voice cracked as it slowly rose in volume, regaining some of its former passion and power. "…And I will *go on* heeding the Sacred Call as long as breath remains within this body…until I am called home—*and not one hour before!*"

Cortez's smile widened from ear to ear, knowing that victory was finally his. "Do you hear him, Dom…he thinks he's *The Man of La Mancha.* Any minute now he's going to start singing!"

With a spring in his step, despite the elements, Cortez left the security of his support and continued his journey around the steel beam perimeter, closing the gap back toward Dominique.

"He can barely stand! Is *that* what you gave me up for, Dom—is *this* who you've put your faith in—some crazy old bastard with an impossible dream?"

The old man staggered as if from physical blows. He reached out a clawed hand toward Dom, one now red with the blood of his re-opened wound.

She rose to her stockinged feet, and maneuvered around the support leg just as Desmond had, to avoid the swordsman's reach.

Tears now poured from the old man's deep December eyes as his gnarly voice added to the melancholy season: "It was not faith that gave you eyes to see—no…not this time. You saw the truth of my heart through the eyes of *his* fear." He raised his shaking hand in an accusing claw toward Cortez who steadily worked his way closer.

Dom turned away from the old man. "I don't know what to trust—who to believe anymore!"

"You did not believe in me so much as *you believed in his terror.*"

Cortez returned a finger of accusation himself, back toward the old man who seemed to be dying on his feet. "Don't you get it now, Dom? Like the gods of old—*the ancient magic*—he only has power and substance if you believe in him. Stand up for yourself! Be your own woman! Turn your back on him and all that he stands for, and then guess how fast he disappears!"

From her peripheral vision, she saw the old man extend a hand toward her, and she knew she didn't want to be touched, not by him, and certainly not by whatever he really was.

He only wanted to assure her that he was real, corporeal flesh and blood. She swatted at him blindly, instinctively, and the old man fell.

Dominique shrieked, realizing too late what she had done.

Cortez smelled blood and quickened his pace, closing the distance between him and Dom.

But the old swordsman, the ancient warrior, Alonso, held on by one arm. His body arced out into space, pinwheeling beneath the steel, yet his fingers—tendons screaming—held firm. His shoulder burned like fire as ripped muscle was stretched yet again, saving the rest of him as he dangled from the metal strut's slick L-beam. His other hand still clutched the precious iron spike, as if to let *that* go might sever his connection with whatever archaic power sustained his form in this time and place.

Dom desperately wanted to take back her reckless action, but knew she didn't have the strength to lift the old man back to safety. All she could think to do was offer an impotent apology. But instead, she found herself anchoring one arm firmly around the security of the main support leg, and regardless of her doubts, she extended her other hand down to him. Her eyes beseeched him to take it.

Cortez suddenly realized that Dom herself had nearly ended the ancient warrior's threat—*what irony!* He hadn't fallen far enough, however, and now she was attempting to undo her damage. *How gallant, how noble—how* **chivalrous** *of her!* The "spell" the old man wove upon "his angel" was a powerful one, and Cortez knew he had to break that hold once and for all if anything was to be salvaged from this night. He'd have to be careful, though, or he'd lose everything.

"No, Dom," he implored, "don't do it—don't risk your life on account of him. You've already given him enough, and look at how he's twisted everything you've believed—everything you know is *true!*"

Dom closed her eyes, scrunching them tight, trusting to nothing, yet still her hand stretched forth. *The old man should see her effort and use it to his advantage—save himself—throw away the stupid pole and take what salvation she offered before she changed her mind.*

The voice of Cortez kept hammering at her, "It's not too late, Dom. Wake up! Reject him, and come back to me. Even now, I can still fix everything for you!"

Keeping her eyes closed, she shook her head, no longer caring to hear all the advice being proffered on her behalf. She wanted *both* of them to shut up. *Let her make up her own mind, come to her own conclusions, and let her do it in her own good time!*

Yet still she heard, "Look with your own eyes, Dominique..." and it was the voice of the old man, soft and comforting, cutting through the howling gale and the confusion inside her head.

"See me with *your* vision...not with his."

She opened them, first one and then the other. She knew her own face was a mask of confusion, painted with agony, highlighted by uncertainty. She gazed into his face below her. Amid the ancient lines etched there by the uncounted years and the burdens of his heart she saw a peace that passed all rational understanding.

The old man was truly the mad one after all, she concluded. The proof was clear and plainly displayed by his calm demeanor: unflappable, while utter chaos whirled about him. After all of her internal debates on the substance of guilt and upon whose head it lay, she was ready to concede most of Desmond's argument. Yet, blame and madness aside, she couldn't help but look into those sad, oblivious eyes…

…and mouth the words, *"Take my hand."*

Damn him!

As he always found a way to do, the old bastard was claiming victory even as death converged upon him from all sides.

To save "his angel" for himself, Cortez mustered all the sincerity of which his kind was capable.

"Everything I did, Dom…I did it for you. You know that's the truth." The voice was tender, calm and reasoning, a refuge from the storm, a beacon drawing her back to safety and sanity. Yet she hesitated. She'd been ready to believe Desmond. But his sudden over-played, poignant profession was clouding all her certainty again.

By the very proximity of his voice, she could tell he was nearby, kneeling on the same beam and whispering words of salvation

and devotion, even as she stretched her hand into the abyss to rescue an obvious madman. She retracted the lifeline abruptly, and whirled on her ex-boss,
her former lover, and the keeper of all her deepest secrets.

"You *lied* to me!" she shrieked.

Quick as a rattler, Cortez snatched at her hand and pulled the reporter
up to him, both of them now rising from their knees. He countered her
charge without missing a beat. "And you lied to me, Dom—never forget
how many times you lied to me!"

From every side, truth was a hammer breaking her will, forcing her
submission to one cause or the other. She knew she was a liar and always
had been. Desmond knew her only too well.

Then his tone changed again, and it was just like they had returned to
those quiet whispers they'd shared so often in the dark. "But we all lie, Dom.
All of us. It's natural—it's human. From the very beginning, just like the old
man said...*we lie to get what we want.*" He pulled her body up close, and his
great bulk was like a rock, stable and sure against the gale.

He continued, "But this moment is more important than you realize. Just
come back with me...of your own volition—*your choice, Dom.* No pressure.
No strings attached. Let it be *your* decision, here and now, and we'll work
this out...*together.*"

She still didn't know what to do, whom to finally believe, and so she simply sobbed into the familiarity of Desmond's great arms. Regardless of her
qualms, she gave in, surrendering to the tangible strength he embodied.

In the end it really was all about her.

Cortez was so close to sealing the
victory he could taste it, smell it in
the wash of "his angel's" drenched
hair. The truth had been a gamble
that had nearly backfired, but Dom
was back in his arms, and she was
his. He felt her body quiver against
him. Now she was ready for the
tender lies.

"And I give you my word," he
assured her. "I'll give you everything
in this world that you've ever
dreamed of having—*I promise.*"

Chapter Thirty-Six

Billy Sanchez stared straight into the heart of a maelstrom surely born in Hell. On the rooftop, a flaming inferno spread out before him—an amalgam of helicopter wreckage and burning pools of oil and fuel—while above it all, the heavens wept as they had not done since the days of Noah.

Between Heaven and Hell stood the great WDVL transmission tower, and whipping windmill blades that threatened to bring the entire structure down upon his head. Even from where Billy stood at the threshold of the rooftop service entrance, he could feel the vibrations of the tower shaking itself apart. It was only a matter of time.

The tower had been part of his world for his entire life, standing like a watchman on the periphery of every hope and dream he'd ever had, every failure or mistake he'd ever made. He never thought he'd see it up this close. He never imagined he would see it fall.

Upon its girders, fifty feet above the flaming rooftop, amidst the fury of the storm, three desperate souls now clung as if clinging to life itself. Dominique and the monstrous station manager, arm in arm even after all that had happened between them. Beneath them hung the old man Sanchez had left for dead.

And once again, Billy could do nothing.

The nameless old man, who'd at last called himself Alonso, dangled from the strut, his ancient bones hanging helplessly as slaughterhouse beef. *If only he could **do** something.* Above him, the Biblical gardens of Eden and

Gethsemane—sister and brother set as bookends against time—played out symbolically on the human stage once again: the respective lures of their temptations and consequences revealed the cycle of the human condition.

The first seduction: *take, eat, and, I promise… ye shall be as gods.* And the latter, the agony of the midnight garden, on the eve of sacrifice and death, where sweat dripped as blood: *forsake the lost to their fate, and save yourself.*

It would be so easy to do just that: *simply let go and drop into the fire.* After all the years of pain, loss, and suffering, it would be as sweet release to lay down the mantle at long last. He thought the time had already come—*Billy Sanchez*—and he'd bequeathed the sword that now hung useless in his arthritic hand. But Billy was not the one, or, at least, he'd forsaken the Call; and weren't those two options really one and the same? *Despite all of his hopes to the contrary, Sanchez was no successor.*

As for Dom, willingly embracing the darkness above her? She was only one more, and he had fought for so many. *What was to be gained by the effort of another? How much was there to lose if he persisted in the folly of trying? He could not change the world. It was never his responsibility, his calling, to do so. What would it cost to just abandon the woman to her choice, her consequence?* The answer was simple. The cost would be the life and soul of Dominique Angel, and Alonso considered that price to be too dear to ever relinquish without a fight.

Yet hanging by one numbed arm did not make for an effective warrior. Then he remembered the Word, and knew *that* could be a sword as well—a blade that pierced the heart deeper than any edge of honed steel—and he still possessed his tongue. By God's mercy alone, he'd also retained the wit and the wisdom to use it. He cleared his throat, and entered into battle once more.

"Long ago…" Alonso began, "*his* kind promised immortality to a bitter, struggling, old scribe…." *He spoke of a poet playwright of no small renown, and yet penniless for all his fame.* "They offered him *immortality*…in exchange for ruining the reputation of one righteous man.

"For glory and for *spite* did he discredit me, his old friend…together with my servant, and the woman he felt I had stolen from him—my dearest Aldonza. But at the end of his days, I was still there for him…by Miguel's deathbed…and he confessed all the scorn and ridicule his art had made of my life, my works—all the deepest convictions of my heart…"

Cervantes had indeed written two volumes on Don Quixote…one seemingly to slander and destroy, to strike back at an old friend for perceived wrongs…and a

second volume, ten years later, almost as if to make amends for his earlier effort, an attempt to change the course of his deed and to restore some measure of noble integrity to the reputation of Alonso Quixano…

Alonso remembered well the final irony—*the true selves of Aldonza, Sancho, and he himself, all gathered about Cervantes's bed, so similar to how their fictional counterparts had come to entice the dying Quixote to rise again, to heed the eternal call and to keep the quest alive…*

And his dying friend had recanted his words. Not a confession as inspired by the Inquisition—not as one uttered unto the countless slave masters to whom the frustrated playwright had spent his lifetime indentured—but as to his brother in the faith, in adherence and devotion to the Call…

Here, in the present, however, a modern Dulcinea remained clutched in the Dragon's embrace, sobbing upon the consoling breast of evil, blinding herself to how swiftly the great beast could turn upon her tears and feast upon her soul. He had no choice now but to continue upon his present course of total admission, whether to the good or ill, to the very end.

"…All the pain Miguel had crafted with his gift and visited upon me…the aspersion, the personal treason, all by the stroke of his pen…I still forgave. And together, in his last moments…we beseeched the Christ to have mercy upon all our souls. At the very end, even Cervantes remained true to the Call. He passed from this world reconciled in peace…to me and to my lady, and most especially to his Lord above. And the only earthly 'immortality' ever ascribed to him was the now cryptic poison hidden within the words of that first book."

Desmond scoffed, "While *you* go on living century after century, is that it?"

With the conclusion of the old man's tale, Cortez now knew that he had won, and his fear dissolved as if it were merely some fragile thing left out in the rain. In this age of both reason and doubt, the sheer absurdity of old Quixote's final revelation was sure to close the door to "his angel's" heart for all time.

"If that's your story," he continued, "then I don't know whether *'my angel'* should laugh or cry!"

He felt Dominique tighten, stiffen in his grip, and saw her teary eyes close, her lips snarl, as mad Alonso played out his very last gambit upon this Earth.

Poor Alonso too must have realized that the end had finally come for himself as well, a conclusion to the ancient contest of faith versus will, as the old fool only muttered softly from his desperate one-armed perch, "Then let the woman decide. Dominique…it is *never* too late to admit the *truth!*"

Dom began to quake in Desmond's great arms.

"You know what the *truth* is…" Desmond murmured gently in her ear. "I know you do. And you don't need some madman telling you what matters to your own heart…"

With that, Desmond pulled her even closer into the most compassionate embrace she'd ever felt. Her father had held her in just such a way as this, on the day of her mother's funeral.

This was it. If her old lover was ever going to say anything to win back her heart, and more importantly, mend the damage he'd already wrought, then it was now. Whether he knew it or not, his next words had to be the most earnest, the most soul-searching he would ever utter.

"I *loved* you, Dom…" he said softly. "I always will."

It was enough. She weighed the implausible portent of everything the old man had said against the firm reality of Desmond's warmth and pledge, and came to the only rational conclusion in which she could place any faith at all.

"…And the truth shall set me free…" she whispered, almost to herself.

She looked up into the giant face of her lover/protector/betrayer, and the tears poured out in a great release from the soul she hoped she had. "He's right, Desmond. I don't know if he's really a madman or not…but his 'story' carries more *truth* than any promise you've ever made."

With her declaration, the victory Cortez had been certain was his now melted away before his eyes, through his very fingers like the proverbial snowballs in hell. *Damn the thunder, the lightning. Damn the howling storm. Damn the wind that laughed around them even now, whispering the Almighty's accursed and eternal name into his own damned ears. Damn them all!*

* * * * *

Desmond broke their embrace sharply. Dom struggled, but he still clutched her in a grip of iron, crushing the still-tender, burned flesh about her wrist where, earlier, a demon in human guise had also mixed truth with its lies in order to claim her as its own.

…We've been sent by Mr. Cortez…for your safety, Ms. Angel— you will come with us.

She looked upon Desmond Cortez with her own eyes now, sharp and clear, and willing to see and accept truth for what it really was. Although he remained unchanged in his physical form, she knew in the very depths of her being the true essence of what stood before her.

He spat his words into her face: "And what has *he* done, Dom—look at the damage *he's* caused—*lives* destroyed by *his* hand! And all for *what*—a stinkin' *whore* like you?"

Dom spat right back. "I don't understand how or why—and maybe I never will—but I believe him!" Her decision. Her rules.

Desmond's formerly loving arms now hardened into twin ratcheting claws that clamped Dom's upper arms to her sides, and lifted her bodily up off the beam. Lightning crashed around them and the natural fury reflected infernally off the shallow surface of his enraged, bloodshot eyes.

Here was an intimacy she'd never dreamed.

For one brief moment, she thought he would rip her in half, never doubting that Desmond had the strength to snap her spine in an instant. Instead, his furious dark eyes, so tender when they'd made love, now shriveled up like fatty gristle on a hot grill and she saw them fall back into his head, leaving only mocking, empty sockets.

"And to think, I almost cared about you!" he shrieked at her, and his spittle felt like acid upon her cheek. "You've made your choice—now go to your noble knight, *and the both of you be damned!*"

Like a child's dolly discarded upon the tarmac of a vacant lot, the Dragon flung the "littlest angel" off its tower, down the center shaft, toward the very pit of Hell itself.

The soulless eyes of Desmond Cortez were vacant and hollow as the reporter fell. In the end, his kind *would* have her, one way or the other.

Chapter Thirty-Seven

The rooftop had become an inferno, but Billy Sanchez was thankful for the torrents of rain that buffered the raging heat and prevented the fire from escalating any further. Amidst the helicopter wreckage, he knew there must be people, those who had possibly given their lives to provide the video footage seen down in the studio, the images that confirmed to all who saw them exactly in whose hands the desperate evil truly lay.

Billy hadn't known what to do, and perhaps it was *because* he felt useless that he stopped thinking about what he was doing and just leapt straight into the fire.

He paid no heed to his previous burns, still salved and wrapped. The flames of that vicious alleyway attack now seemed a lifetime ago. Without analyzing the minutiae of his actions, nor calculating any personal satisfaction by way of what others would say or think or judge, he simply acted.

One at a time, he found and pulled two bodies from the crash. For just an instant, the broken bodies reminded him of snuffed-out cigarette stubs, squashed, with the limbs twisted in unnatural perpendiculars. He had a moment's hesitation over moving them at all in this condition, but only a moment's worth. The aggravation of injuries was surely better than cremation. Besides, Billy couldn't even tell if either of the bodies was alive or dead—that is, until one of them moaned.

The broken man in the white helmet—actually, it was a woman, Billy noticed, with the indecipherable tag, "Jeunet," stenciled on her flight jacket—stirred, groaned, and looked blearily into Billy's bright eyes.

He couldn't help but grin and nod his head like a manic idiot. "Yes! You're alive!"

Deep down, Billy realized with great satisfaction that when the moment had come to be a genuine hero, he had performed without any thought for himself and, at long last, done the right thing. If this night ever ended, there just might be hope for lost souls like him after all.

Detective Ben Saunders arrived at the WDVL building at about the same time as the rest of downtown's finest. He wished there'd been opportunity to restock his smokes, but the Fire Department chatter he'd monitored on the way over assured him that where he was planning to go, there was already more than enough fire and smoke.

"Well, the action isn't down here…" he said, resigned to the inevitable.

"It's up *there,*" finished Nathan Creed as he looked up toward the WDVL rooftop, thirty-three-stories high.

Ben followed the big man's gaze, and thought how calm disaster always seemed when witnessed from a great distance. Now that he was actually here, he found he didn't really mind Nate's tag-along company as much as he'd feared. Wherever he went, the rescue mission founder brought along his own sense of confidence, and his aura was contagious.

Billy had dragged both of the crash victims into a small room that made up the rooftop service entrance. He checked the pulse of the second one, following the instructions of the woman in the white helmet, that which had probably saved her life. The head of this victim seemed a shattered ruin, but there was a pulse, and where the heart still beat, there was life. The tag read "McIlhenney."

Billy was startled by a sudden shout that came from the bottom of the emergency stairs: "Hey you! Freeze! Don't move!"

"These two are hurt bad!" he shouted back. "Somebody call 911!"

Detective Saunders didn't flinch. "William Sanchez?" queried the detective, his voice booming with the requisite authority the situation demanded. A complement of SWAT troopers suddenly swooped in around him, filling the staircase.

"Yeah…it's me." Billy's affirmation stemmed more from annoyance. "But, c'mon, do your job! Do some good! I ain't got all night here, y'know."

He indicated the wounded figures lying at his feet.

The detective's pistol cocked in near unison with the bevy of assault rifles that now held the new hero as their sole target.

Billy's exasperation grew as he stared them down. "Hey, I just saved their *lives,* man! What're you all gonna do…*shoot me?*"

The detective looked uncomfortably at his sidearm. Every stupid intent needed a stupid question to clarify it as such. In that same moment, Nathan Creed broke through the line of Special Weapons and Tactics, and joined Billy at the top of the stairs. The police lowered their collective aims. Now taking charge and issuing orders of his own, Nathan dropped to one knee and checked on the injured. Billy used the diversion to slip away and ran back out into the storm. He felt there just had to be more he could do.

Within seconds, Saunders joined him up on the rooftop. Billy was momentarily defensive, until realizing that the cop, like he, was inexorably drawn to the scene of mayhem.

Together, they scanned the wreckage in disbelief, through flames, heavy oil smoke, sheets of blinding rain, and blinking past seared retinas as lightning strike after strike filled their vision with flashes of electrical discharge.

"What in heaven's name happened up here?" Saunders blurted out.

"Don't ask," answered Billy.

The detective nodded in return, his pistol now weighing uselessly in his hand. In Saunders's wake, the SWAT team charged onto the roof, following procedure, fanning out in formation—and not a man among them with any clue how to process this particular situation for which no rational training could have ever prepared them.

Through the inferno, Saunders spied another body, a dark figure lying prostrate in a wet pool of rippling, reflected flames. "There's another one!"

he shouted, trying to make himself heard over a sudden increase in the roar of the gale, and he and Billy ran to rescue yet another victim of the night's ongoing insanity.

As they closed the distance, Billy slowed as, with a chill, he recognized the black fatigues of the prone figure.

The detective kept going, splashing into a deceptively deep puddle that rose to his ankles. Heedless, he squatted into the cold damp in order to overturn the black-garbed body.

"No! *Don't!*" screamed Sanchez, but it was too late.

The figure had seemed lifeless at first, but then it twitched, coughed, and hacked up what seemed buckets of oil and water that had failed to mix regardless of whose stomach and lungs they'd resided in.

Saunders let himself relish the true joy of that moment before turning to the frantic Hispanic. "He's alive!" he shouted back, his face lit by an ecstatic grin, oblivious to Billy's reciprocal cry of *"Look out!"*

Dripping, black-suited arms reached up and seized the detective by his shoulders. Saunders looked down and saw the eyes open. His first thought was that he had finally come face-to-face with the elusive *man with the scary eyes.* But then, those opened-wide orbs dropped back into its head—not rolled up to reveal the whites, but literally *dropped* back, like two small stones falling into the inky black depths of fathomless dark pools or subterranean caves. Then Saunders saw the raging rooftop fire reflected around the hollow interior of its empty, cavernous skull. It grinned, and its teeth writhed like maggots in its open mouth.

Saunders's sudden cry was cut short as one vice-like claw clamped over his throat, nails burrowing into his flesh to give it a better grip upon the detective's neck. His eyes bulged as, desperate for air, he tried to pry loose the unyielding evil that held him.

The abruptly-silenced cry still lingered in the air, and Billy's horror doubled as he realized that what he was now hearing, trailing on the cusp of Saunders's stifled voice, was Dominique Angel's piercing scream carried down on the wind from high above, from up where the great rotor was failing in its effort to harness the storm.

She screamed. Billy looked up. And the reporter fell.

Chapter Thirty-Eight

Alonso Quixano's pale fingers clutched the slippery edge of the steel L-beam. He had learned long ago, in such moments, to discard the rational, the analytical, and to follow pure instinct. Thus he dropped his precious iron spike without a thought, letting it fall into the hellish inferno far below. It was so randomly abandoned because a free hand was so desperately needed to catch the woman before she might plummet to her death. Granting Darkness a victory this night was something Alonso would not allow.

He caught one slender wrist of the shrieking reporter as she fell past him. He clamped hold with an abruptness that nearly dislocated his remaining good shoulder. Dom's scream halted with a startled yelp as the sudden stop jerked her in mid-air. Her body twitched almost comically as she found herself suspended by the haggard old man's stupendous effort.

Far below, the discarded iron clattered on impact amid the flames.

Desmond Cortez bellowed his frustrated rage at the storm, daring the heavens, the lightning itself to strike him dead, challenging Almighty God with his wrath. In moments, though, mere precious seconds, he would turn his attention back to the spasming fingers that were all that held the reporter and his accursed enemy on this side of eternity.

Dominique was terrified: two such life and death falls in less than an hour was a bit much even for adrenaline junkies, something she most definitely was not. Once she realized she'd been caught, though, she felt a stab of white pain shoot up the arm from which all her free weight dangled. She raised her opposite hand to support the quaking arm at the elbow.

When she finally felt confident enough to risk looking up, she saw the face of the old man staring down at her.

"Trust me," was all he asked.

The strain of the rescue effort gouged itself ever deeper into his quivering features. Yet his eyes were dark still pools. It seemed no tumult of this world could ripple their calm waters. Her own eyes never wavered from them.

"I trust you," she answered.

He swung her frame only twice—once to generate momentum—and on the second pendulous swing, he released his hold on the beam.

They both fell, but he pulled her into his arms as they dropped, two birds falling to earth as one. Then he twisted their impromptu embrace, correcting their course in mid-flight, a new trajectory taking them two levels and a mere eighteen feet down from their previous perch.

Once again, it was not the old man, but the warrior, Quixote, who dared the impossible and landed them safely on the lower beam. His gallant, rugged beauty had returned. The implacable sense of justice seared into the rigid set of his jaw and the righteous fury of his stern, steely eyes still burned. Dom felt she was only too deserving of the deep, fiery retribution that smoldered there.

How many times had she betrayed him, denied him, stood by to watch him die? While all she'd cared about was the next trivial move on the board, the oh-so-fragile concerns of her heart, and the ever-changing uncertainty of her own pathetic feelings. In the face of the world and all its teeming masses, spinning their merry way toward chaos and oblivion, her aspirations now seemed shallow and cold. And yet…

Here stood the dashing Hero. And his wounds were not so great as to prevent him from evening the scales, righting all the wrongs, rescuing the myriad damsels—along with their equally inept counterparts—and saving the day.

Quixote looked up at the wrath of Desmond Cortez raging impotently above them, and he smiled. "She sees my true face…" he shouted, "and she does not judge!"

In that moment, Dom knew that he had not judged her either, even though every right to have done so was his long ago. He held her, firm and sure, and she felt that he was proud of her despite all her failures and counter-accusations.

In his anger, Desmond nearly fell into the pit himself, and desperately grabbed the vertical beam for support. " 'My angel' sees only what she *wants* to see—don't you, Dom?" The argument was as hollow as his heart.

Quixote gripped her shoulder even tighter, declaring, "And *'Dulcinea'* now sees what she has become!"

Dom could no longer remain silent, nor could she stand by while the white knight fought all of her battles. She cried out, "My whole life has been a *lie,* Desmond—*all of it!* I want…I want to be *free…*"

Quixote suddenly spun around to face her directly, abruptly dismissing any of the further ranting of Desmond Cortez, as if *here* now stood a matter of greater significance than anything else in all of the long, sordid history of the world.

The moment had arrived. Dom had seen it coming two days ago, barreling down the highway at 120 miles per hour, and mistaken it for nothing more than the haunting eyes of a vagrant madman—one whom she'd thought could be twisted and controlled on her terms.

…And then, she said, the little angel would wake up in Heaven…

Everything in her life had led her to this single moment: Her mother, leaping from a window when Dom was too young to know what was really happening. Her father, only too willing to accept the blame, earning Dom's condemnation in a series of never-ending judgments against him. Her own self-righteous hatred, finally leading him to put a bullet through his head—he who could never do enough to fix all the broken dollies. Followed by a swift decision to flee into the night, leaving it all behind, her old world, escaping the scene of the crime and making for herself a new life—with a new name. And in a new life, she didn't have to accept her share of the guilt. Instead, she could let all the blame rest upon the memory of one broken man who had paid the ultimate price for all of his crimes.

*But did her father end his life for all of **her** crimes too? Or had she played a hand in the deed as well? Was it her words that loaded the chamber? Her silence that aimed the barrel? And did she pull the trigger with her hatred?*

Dom had one last chance to dodge complicity and dismiss all the charges against her as nothing more than spiritually-contrived guilt raining down on her troubled conscience. She just had to weather the storm till all of the emotions had run their course and the seas of her soul were calm again. Of course, that required acknowledgment of a soul, that which she'd spent a lifetime denying. Such was the only way she'd found to live with all the guilt. *Circular logic.* And it all brought her back to the facts she could never escape, no matter how fast or how far she tried to run.

She knew it was really about so much more than these evasive games she played. Deep inside, where it really mattered, in her broken heart and…yes, the *lost soul* she knew she had… that none of this was about the guilt of others. It wasn't even self-immolation on the altar of her own martyrdom.

In the end, it was about her after all: about Dominique Angel coming to the realization that *none of it* was about her. *It was only a matter of love and forgiveness.*

Dom wanted to run, but there was nowhere to go but down. She wanted to scream her rage at the unfairness of life to the very heavens themselves, but she couldn't even hear her own voice over the fury of the gale. She wanted to throw herself down in shame, at the feet of God Himself, but a pair of strong arms held her and loved her and wouldn't let her go. She couldn't look at anything, for her tears were streaming fast and clear, their current stronger than the falling rain. Her lips curled back because she couldn't keep them from quivering and showing the entire world the lost child she really was. From clenched teeth, she broke at last into heaving sobs, collapsing into the strong arms that lowered both of them to their knees along the thin width of the beam.

Quixote spoke softly. "Only when we are thus broken do we see within ourselves most clearly, and know the truth that hides behind the lies we tell ourselves—all the pain we've locked away so deep inside."

She looked into his eyes and saw, reflected, the love of her father staring back at her, memories of love that she'd spent years rejecting. Then words gushed out, in competition with her tears, her voice a desperate staccato through the sobs.

"He's *not* dead. My father never died. He's still alive. He lives in Chicago. I *wanted* him to be dead because…I could never forgive him…'cause I could never forgive what momma had done…what she'd done to herself, to me…

what she'd done to all of us…what he'd made her do…oh God, I've just wanted to kill myself. He tried so hard…tried so hard to explain how messed up they both were…how scared she was of living…how afraid she was of being a failure like her own momma…how he blamed himself for not being strong enough for her until it was too late. He took *all* the blame on himself—*all of it!* And I let him do it…and it was never enough—never good enough for me. But he's alive, and I love him, and I want to tell him I forgive him. Please, Quixote, let me live through this night so I can go back home and tell my daddy how much I miss him!"

Alonso took her head and laid it tenderly against his shoulder, his voice now the sweetest of all music singing over the roar of Heaven's wrath. "I cannot save your soul… but confess all, and give yourself to the only One who can."

Dominique bowed her head against his chest, and her confession wracked its way out in broken pieces through groaning sobs. Alonso closed his eyes, knowing the real battle had finally ended and whatever remained was no longer his concern. His hand rested on her head as he added what blessing he could.

"Believe," was all he said, and it was done.

Far above, the fury of Desmond Cortez boiled its way into a frothing lather that spilled from his lower lip.

"No! She doesn't get away like that! I watched her take that bite of forbidden fruit—I tempted and she did eat! She belongs to *me!* And no *sacrificial lamb* takes what is mine by right!"

As Dom's sobs dwindled with her spent emotion, Quixote raised them to their feet, encouraging

her to face her accuser and to
no longer be afraid.

To the Dragon, he said,
"We've each cast aside our masks
and revealed our true hearts. Do
you care to show us yours...
if you dare?"

"I'll not give you the
satisfaction!" Cortez sputtered back.
He seemed ready to jump, trusting
gravity to bring him down to those he hated.

"*I command it*—in the name of the Christ,
the Most High—reveal yourself, down to the
very fork of your poisoned tongue!"

"Damn you all to Hell!" shrieked Cortez.
His body abruptly convulsed, and a clawed hand
shot up as if to loosen his collar, but instead,
talons sunk deep into his chest and shredded his rain-
drenched suit from his body, stripped flesh from bone, tore
asunder the outer cage of rib...

And the spirit within Desmond Cortez ripped free of its human casing
like shucked corn. Bulging muscle burst through skin as the Dragon reared
its mighty head skyward. Scale upon scale unfolding, rippling, shuffling like
a deck of cards in a fast deal, slicing through flesh, leaving ragged streamers—
the beast revealed in its true glory, fully twenty times the size of a man.

It unfurled mighty wings, great leathery sails to blot out the very sky in
which it ruled. The Dragon's massive claws clutched at the transmission
tower, and, as scaled digits flexed, steel beams twisted in its grip, rivets popped
from sockets, and the works of man were as dry straw beneath its sway. But
the weight of the Dragon was too great, and its tower perch creaked and
groaned, bending the windmill blades to the earth, like the proud kneeling
before its lord and master.

The Dragon roared into the storm-tossed night, the lightning striking
one outthrust claw as if to reinforce its might: "Do you now see, Dominique?
Do you understand the truth? *I AM Truth—Power!* I am the *all-consuming
darkness*—the *roaring lion,* seeking whom I shall devour!"

Dom shrank before the unholy majesty.

"Behold the Prince of the Power of the Air!"

Chapter Thirty-Nine

The sound of gun shots rang out, crisp and hollow, crackling the air with miniature sonic booms.

The SWAT team triangulated their fire on the living dead *thing* that had Ben Saunders in its demonic grip. It seemed unwilling to release its hold until the last vestige of life was drained from the detective who'd spent so many of his nights for the past ten years praying to die.

Three—Seven—Ten—Fifteen—Twenty-three—

Billy Sanchez lost count of the M-16 bursts as the voices of individual shots blurred into the cacophonous roar of modern war. The five expertly-trained marksmen never came close to hitting Detective Saunders, even as the monster that held him had risen to its feet and hefted its limp victim by the throat with one arm, like a prized trophy.

The thing howled into the night, into the storm, urging the midnight tolls to sound, as if beckoning more of its kind up from Hell to come forth and feast on the bodies, minds, and souls of men.

The automatic gunfire that peppered its stout frame from all sides blasted chunks of red meat from its standing carcass. Yet the creature seemed immune and undaunted, as if it felt nothing more than the shredding of its tattered flight suit. Nothing, that is, until one keen officer dropped his aim and took off the thing's kneecap. The other four quickly took his cue, lowered their barrels, and not a man among them stopped firing till the thing was left without any leg to stand on.

It shrieked, teetered, and fell, releasing its death-grip on the detective in order to buffer its fall with both claws.

Surprisingly, Ben Saunders landed on his feet, eyes glazed, but then

staggered
and collapsed. His
throat was a savaged ruin sending a
steady gout of punctured artery pumping red into the air.
Then, the groaning of compressing steel filled the air,
accompanied by the explosive popping of rivets ricocheting in
all directions, reducing the previous gunplay to the relative bickering of
angry gnats. All eyes jerked upward as, with a screech, the entire transmission
tower, beloved and controversial to so many generations, came thundering
down in a sudden avalanche of twisting girders.

Chapter Forty

The beleaguered tower no longer possessed the engineered strength, nor inanimate will, to sustain the weight of the Dragon. The metal lattice-work of struts and crossbeams crumpled as if the tower were a child's toy. The chopper blades of the bizarre windmill shattered against an upended stray girder, leaving impotent rotary stubs spinning madly off the side of the former symbol of the media giant.

As the security of solid steel buckled about them, Quixote wrapped his body around Dom's terrified form, and clamped them both to the surety of a single beam, trusting to the Lord of Order regardless of which way the winds of chaos blew.

The great wings of the Dragon beat more powerfully than even nature's fury, the beast hovering for an instant as its perch crumpled beneath it. The Dragon then touched down atop the settling wreckage, its massive claws taking hold and declaring its dominion over all that lay crushed about its hindquarters. Scaled shoulders flexed like a bodybuilder's, as the Dragon's ten-horn-rimmed head thrust forward, stretching its neck to the fullest extent. Defying the rain and storm, it reveled in the maelstrom's failure to knock it from its chosen pedestal. It tasted the air with its forked tongue, savoring Heaven's defeat and the ultimate

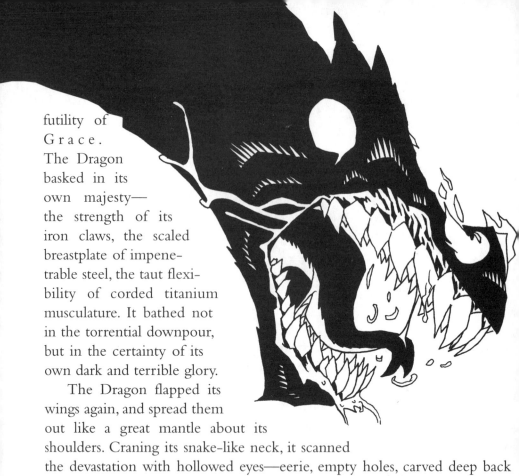

futility of Grace. The Dragon basked in its own majesty— the strength of its iron claws, the scaled breastplate of impene- trable steel, the taut flexi- bility of corded titanium musculature. It bathed not in the torrential downpour, but in the certainty of its own dark and terrible glory.

The Dragon flapped its wings again, and spread them out like a great mantle about its shoulders. Craning its snake-like neck, it scanned the devastation with hollowed eyes—eerie, empty holes, carved deep back into its skull, that saw all things nevertheless—searching for those frail mortal shells who had dared provoke its fury and despair.

"I am the *wolf* amongst lambs...*doubt* in the heart of the righteous! I am the *guilt* that haunts the tossing dreams of your restless nights!"

For a moment, Dom and Quixote hung over the edge of the roof of the WDVL building, where the beam they'd held onto had landed. The swords-man, though, never let his charge catch a glimpse of the gravity of their plight, as, with one arm, he hoisted her up onto the precarious deadfall tangle of beams. Despite the battering elements and the bellowing roar of the great beast spewing its hatred over all the inhabitants of the Earth, he followed right behind, urging her onto the rooftop proper.

The Dragon spied the two tiny figures, the current focus of its unending wrath.

They were crawling across the cantilevered beams to the sure foundation of the rooftop—back to where the beast held sway. The woman gazed up, enrapt by professional fascination in spite of the consuming terror that shook her to the core. She had been willing to give away so much of her soul in exchange for the approval and adoration of men—never realizing her soul had been forfeit long before she ever started bartering such a fragile, eternal commodity. The mortal, Cortez, was as nothing when compared to the beast that had dwelt within his shell. Still the Dragon remembered well each of his intimacies with the female.

"Gaze upon me, woman!" it shrieked, bringing relevance to their shared past in light of the present revelation. "For I am *Truth,* the reality of your own lost soul—*damned!* Everything you are—*accursed!* Everything you deny—given form and made manifest!"

…Now get some make-up on that. Clean yourself up and come back to bed.

The tiny figures then stood, small, insignificant, and powerless against the Dragon, now revealed in all of its awesome, terrifying splendor. One claw extended forward to capture the woman. The delicate shell that contained her spirit could be crushed within its grasp. While the man, the troublesome agitator—*his interference spanning centuries*—would at last be swept from the rooftop with naught but a single, dismissive swipe of the Dragon's tail…

He would hang in space, knowing in those scant seconds while consciousness remained that he had finally lost the ancient conflict for all time, before impacting with concrete and tarmac thirty-three stories below.

"You belong to *me*—" The voice of the Dragon was victorious as it stretched forth to claim one of its own by primordial right. "—And I am your *death!*"

…That's not a 'threat'…consider it down payment on a promise.

…I'll arrange that exclusive for you tomorrow.

Dominique quailed, as she realized there was nowhere to hide. Quixote, however, stood firm, tall, proud and sure, unarmed but without fear, facing the inevitable as he balanced upon the twisted beams, shielding the woman with his own body. He gestured to the great inhuman creature reaching with all of its malice toward them, and then—through hair drenched and matted in strands across his face—he *grinned*.

"Behold, Dominique Angel—the original Serpent. Understand that what you see is all the power—*the only power*—he shall ever have!" And Quixote actually laughed, loud and strong. "Stand in your faith, Dominique—for it is the *Dragon* that has run out of places to hide."

The Dragon's fury rose as the little man fairly skipped his way, sure-footed upon the girders, ever between itself and the woman, until finally, frustrated by the dance, it took up the swordsman in its mighty grasp instead. Yet, to crush its long-elusive opponent in but a single swift embrace would be as mercy to the ancient adversary, and after all of their accumulated history, such a fleeting action would lack the desired satisfaction. No, the Dragon wanted all eternity to torment his foe.

After the tower collapsed, Billy Sanchez looked up and saw the true reality of mankind's eternal enemy granted form and substance. There, atop the remains of humanity's devices and technology of expression, wreathed in lightning and smoke, the Dragon roared into the night, more powerful than the storm that raged around it.

Billy shook his head, knowing that before him was the embodiment of all his fears and failures, all of his envy, evil desire and twisted fantasy. *There* stood a dark god beyond his comprehension, and one not within a mere human's ability to vanquish.

With a concerted effort, Billy looked away from the awesome and terrifying spectacle and ran back into the crushing zone of fallen struts and girders. Somewhere beneath all the ruin were the detective and the officers that had dared challenge the Demon.

The defenseless swordsman sat in the massive claw, calm, assured, riding the talon up as if it were his own personal conveyance, and never taking *his* riveting dark eyes from the hollow, all-seeing caverns of his adversary. The Great Serpent could fling him away at any time, discarded as so much chaff, and be rid of him once and for all through whatever days of Earth remained. But the warrior knew the Dragon wished to break him instead—not in body, but in spirit. So it raised his tiny figure high into the air, bringing him face to face with its horrific maw, its silver-white fortress walls of razored teeth and the stench of dead breath.

It spoke its rage in rising decibels. "Who now, is the liar, old man? What final words of wisdom have you, to drip like honey from your impotent tongue?"

Quixote, Alonso—whomever he *once* was, whatever he was *now*—met the directed fury of the beast unwavering. His only-too-human eyes flared again with a fire that Dominique Angel had come to believe was the essence of his conviction. His voice carried, as before, above the howling gale, the crashing thunder, even over the raging roar of the Dragon itself.

"There are virtues worth living for…"

His will, indomitable—as if he spat into the very eyes of Satan; his confidence and faith, a blasphemy to everything the Serpent stood for.

"Convictions worth fighting for…"

The Dragon roared in defiance, but the voice of Quixote rose in a passion for truth that silenced even the venom of the Accuser.

"And I believe…some dreams are worth dying for!"

Quixote thrust his arms out to either side, willing to let the Devil do his worst, daring the darkness and all of the power of Death and Hell to claim a sacrifice that might guarantee its own doom.

The detective lay dying. Nearby, the leg-less Demon lay pinned beneath the crushing weight of a massive, steel-cased numeral "6"—the red neon tubes within now shattered—and it shrieked and howled blasphemy against Earth and Heaven, God and man. Between the two prostrate figures lay a rusted, iron spike.

Flames, reflected in rain-pelted pools, cradled the old, familiar rusty pole in a fiery embrace. Billy feared that if he touched it, his unworthy hands

might burn as if from holy fire.

"Make me *worthy,* Lord—not by my strength, but Thine."

He didn't know from where such words, such language, came to him. *But from whence did wisdom ever truly come?*

The massive, taloned foot of the Dragon came crashing down, missing the detective but flattening the steel-cased station number and squashing the Demon's flesh to pulp, sending its essence to damnation as the jelly of its mortal shell consumed itself to ash.

In that moment, Billy understood the reality and full scope of the battle to which he had been called: not one of flesh and blood and bone, but of spirit, darkness and light. His own life had been bought with a price, bought by blood and sacrifice, and here was his chance to return thanks, whatever the cost, by joining in that final conflict against the evil that lived in the corrupted hearts of all humanity.

Dominique screamed, knowing the end had come. The sacrifice of her savior would avail them nothing. Quixote's intended sacrifice was not the ancient one of power that saved the souls of men. His was but a symbol of that greater truth, that which lived in his heart and brought the fire of conviction to his eyes, strength to his determined will, and vigor to his ancient bones. Every day he'd remained on Earth, Alonso Quixano had lived his life as a testimony to that first sacrifice, two thousand years ago, that had saved them all in spirit, mind and soul. But the flesh...the flesh of each one would surely now perish to the Great Serpent's wrath.

* * * * *

The Dragon knew its victory had come at last, and it gloated into the face of the ancient warrior's valiance. *"Then die, old man! Die with the knowledge that you failed, and that all you fought for will follow you in death!"*

Billy Sanchez clasped trembling hands about the sacred iron and lifted the dripping spike from the fiery pool. Here was more than just some ancient relic of neglected faith, a discarded symbol from an irrelevant era. This was *Truth* exemplified, *Righteousness, Peace, Faith, Salvation,* the very armor of God distilled within a mere shaft of refined iron ore. It was a material manifestation of that discerning blade which ancient wisdom had dubbed the *Sword of the Spirit.*

Billy's hands steadied as, for one brief moment, the water's surface had stilled, and he'd caught a glimpse of his own reflected face. The fire of conviction now burned behind his own eyes. The saving of the 'copter crew had been no fluke, nor a momentary lapse in judgment.

I offer you life…

Billy raised the spike, and it became the actual sword of the Hero, three feet of gleaming, righteous steel that he thrust high into the air. And he cried out the only oath he'd ever heard that had power and truth behind its words: *"In memory of the martyrs, and in the name of the Christ—the Most High God…I cast you from this realm, now and forevermore—BEGONE!"*

Billy Sanchez thrust the blade with all the strength his thin, meager arms could manage. Two and a half feet slid into the sinew of the Dragon, and then another six inches for good measure—and he realized his blow had been struck with a strength that was not his own.

As it felt a fiery sting pierce its hindquarter, the Dragon roared in agony, losing all control of its calculated menace. It opened its claws, a reflex of flesh and pain—the way of a mere mortal beast. The hated enemy fell from its taloned hand, dropping to the wreckage below. *Perhaps the fall alone might be enough to destroy the accursed foe once and for all!*

The foot of the Dragon whipped skyward. Billy held the blade firm with two hands, and yanked downward. The momentum of the great beast's taking flight ripped its own ankle straight through the cleaving blade, doing itself even greater harm in its reflexive escape than Billy's blind stab of faith could have ever intended. Rotted, sickly ooze of yellow and green splattered from the wound and showered Sanchez in the Dragon's filth.

Quixote set foot one beam to another, discharging the energy of his fall, reducing momentum by practically hopscotching his way back to the rooftop and its sure footing.

Billy stood close by, letting the rain baptize him, cleansing the putrid blood of the Dragon from his body and soul.

Dominique Angel made her way through the gnarled forest of steel, and ran straight into the arms of her savior. Her tears fell in equal measure with the rain.

Distant, dim forms of SWAT officers were struggling to their feet and working their way through the collapsed remains of the tower.

The ancient warrior held Dom tightly for but a moment, and then broke the embrace. He skirted a short path through the wreckage, stopped, and then abruptly dropped to his knees. The others followed, and found him swiftly tending to the vicious wounds of the bleeding detective.

Ben Saunders was barely conscious. His life was fading rapidly, yet he was still cognizant enough to take in the features of the one who held him, who cradled his listless head on firm knees. He knew with full clarity that he had at last come face-to-face with the enigmatic *man with the scary eyes*. But they

weren't eyes of terror or fear. They were filled with tender compassion and love. Those eyes revealed a soul that burned with a faithful fire, a burning intensity that assured he would never let you fall into the darkness of the abyss, so far as it remained within his power to prevent it. It was those eyes that spoke to Saunders first, but the man's mouth gave voice to their message, lending credence to his miracle with actual words: *"Believe…and live."*

Chapter Forty-One

As soon as the building ceased quaking from the transmission tower's structural failure, Nathan Creed worked his way out onto the rooftop. He'd seen to the wounded pair who had been left in the service room at the top of the stairwell, and once they were tended to and stabilized, he'd orchestrated their conveyance down to street level. *The vagrant Sanchez had probably been right: his reckless action had more than likely saved the lives of the two from the helicopter.* Now, though, having no idea of what had transpired in the meantime, Creed fought through the battling elements looking for further signs of life. Scanning the rooftop, he tried to comprehend the chaos around him—the storm, debris, scattered flames, and the ghostly howl of the wind that had sounded, to those inside, so like the roar of some mythical dragon.

The reporter, Angel, and Sanchez stood close by the remnants of the tower. Sanchez held an iron spike in his hands. The strange old man was there also, at their feet, kneeling over a body. With a rush of concern, Nathan realized it was Ben Saunders.

With Creed's arrival, the old man reached up a thin, clawed hand and grabbed hold of his wrist, pulling the big man down to his knees with a surprising strength. The old man was calm, yet firm. He stared into Nathan's eyes with a tenacity that could not be ignored.

"Here," the old man croaked, "tend to this man—his life may still be saved."

One member of the scattered SWAT team, his own head running with blood and streaked by the rain, stumbled into their small clearing amidst the wreckage. Nathan Creed grabbed hold of the officer and yanked him down, just as the old man had gotten his attention a moment ago. "Here—help me.

Saunders is in bad shape, but he isn't gone yet!"

The officer stripped off his flak vest and started unbuttoning his black shirt to serve as a makeshift bandage about the detective's savaged throat.

Satisfied that everything that could be done for the detective was thus being done, the strange old man stood sharply, as if he had still other work to attend to.

"Is it over?" asked Dom. She hoped Quixote's grim bearing wasn't her answer.

He seemed ready for war.

The screeching roar of the Dragon confirmed it.

In rebuttal to the Dragon's rage, though, Billy Sanchez stood sure—taller than Dom remembered him to be. Reverently, he returned the sword to its original wielder.

The ancient warrior accepted the blade. The pride he felt in the young Latino hung palpably in the air.

"I told you, my friend…*a life worth living.*"

Billy nodded in affirmation.

Then the Hero turned to Dom with his startling, clear eyes of humility and righteous passion, and took her hand tenderly in his.

"Do not forget, Dominique," he said, "my Aldonza was *never* what the centuries have made of her. She was as flawed as you or I, and nothing more. But 'Dulcinea' was everything *holy* that, by God's mercy, she strived to be."

He gestured to include Billy. "I charge you both, from this night on…embrace your lives, live—and *believe.*"

For all of Billy's newfound strength, his face ran wet with more than just the rain.

Dom began to shake, knowing in her heart that this was the swordsman's farewell.

The cry of the Dragon again shook the rooftop and its fury resonated deep in their souls. Yet Quixote's grace and compassion were unshaken.

"Now please," he said, "stay here, both of you. Guard and protect each other…"

The Hero let go of Dom's hand. She felt its loss. His eyes darkened one last time, as if a cloud passed over him alone, reducing those eyes to dark caverns that matched the pits of his enemy. Fire and lightning then flashed together there, flames wreathing the blue-white bolts that etched across his pupils.

"*…And let me now finish what this day has wrought!*"

Then her Quixote, Dulcinea's Quixote, leapt back into battle, the raging holy storm from which only one of the two opponents would live to see the coming dawn.

Chapter Forty-Two

The Dragon circled around the remains of the once-mighty tower, having no fear of the elements raging across the night sky, laying siege to the WDVL corporate skyscraper. Its own rage kept it aloft. It swung about, prepared to bring an end to its accursed foe this night, and for all time to come. The Dragon was *Lord of this Age*. So was it ordained and so would it remain, sustained by its defiant will, its great fury, and its bitter resentment of all that walked upon the Earth—grounded, and yet destined for eternity.

It saw the small group of figures clustered upon the roof, joined steadily by others, scattered survivors of the tower's collapse. Still more came up from within the building, chancing fate, and bringing support and medical treatment for the injured and dying.

The Great Serpent would kill them all.

The Dragon *hated*. Hatred was the sole purpose in the beating of its dark heart, if indeed it had possessed one. Then it saw, high upon the uppermost peak of twisted steel, its despised enemy, Quixote, waiting to do battle once more on top of the very world it had created—the world of WDVL. There, the past and future would collide, and in so doing, they would *make news happen!*

The Dragon sucked in one great lungful of the storm-tossed night air and brought it to a boil in its vast internal furnace. Snarling, it flew directly at the warrior, rearing back only at the last instant, hovering in space, whipping the wind with its great wings into a furious gust of hurricane force, and exhaling poisonous sulfur and fire in a jet stream.

The ancient warrior met the blast head-on, cleaving the flame itself with his sacred blade, calling down lightning to his sword's tip, charging the edge

with a brilliant glow.
He cried out as if *he,* and not the
Dragon, commanded the elements. But the heavens
answered, granting the warrior a fire of his own. The sky
filled with electrical discharge, a veritable spiderweb of
ion-charged spectacle, running the Serpent to ground and
reducing the entire world once again to black and
white—a stark metaphor for the truest good and the darkest
evil, washing away any pretext of grey.

Banished from the sky, the Dragon trenchantly realized it now had to
defeat its enemy on the warrior's terms: tooth, claw, and talon to one
solitary blade. Settling to the roof, the beast landed upon its massive
haunches. But its left leg instantly buckled, as the ankle
tendon, severed by Sanchez, failed to support
its monstrous bulk. The Dragon bellowed
in agony, toppling to the rooftop.

There the ancient warrior waited, leaping down from his pinnacle to
pierce the Dragon's frame with his holy blade, crackling with Heaven's
fire. The sword entered the Serpent's gullet and exploded with righteous
energy, caustic and consuming, burning the Dragon's writhing form
from within.

With a spurting gush, poisonous blood of sickening green
spread over the rooftop. *This cannot be!* wailed the Dragon
from within its warped, blackened mind.

The swordsman, the knight of virtue and
justice, *owned* this night, and all the stratagems of
the Serpent were as fog scattered by a gale, torn
asunder by the wind of faith. The Dragon
had only rage to wield in return.

Quixote had come to wage war, to bring it to the Serpent's very stronghold, without fear, and with power in his every step. By the pressure of his sword buried to the hilt in the Dragon's flank, he forced the Serpent down to its belly to crawl upon the roof like the snake it was. The Great Beast became a marionette pulled by the tip of the warrior's steel string. All the Dragon's mighty fury frothed into impotence.

In its white-hot pain, the Dragon cursed the material world to which it was bound, all that was mortal, all that could be broken and slain. It knew that its spirit—intangible, ethereal—once untethered from the physical plane of creation, would be sucked into that inexorable whirlpool of damnation, drawn down to the pit created solely for Satan and his angels. Meanwhile *its* angel—Dominique Angel—was now lost to it forever, claimed by the realms of light.

The Dragon thrashed, twitched, and spasmed. It cursed Heaven and Grace with all the blasphemy of its soul, until it impaled its lower jaw on an upraised girder, pinning its mouth shut, so that even such sacrilege was stilled from its throat.

The ancient warrior stepped up and boldly stood before the dark, soulless stare, the desolate sockets of Desmond Cortez, one of the Great Conquistador Worms of old. Staring back from Quixote's eyes was the blazing glory of Resurrection's morning.

"*Come then, Serpent…and may there at last be an end to your vile heart!*"

Quixote rammed his sword straight through the impenetrable scales and into the defenseless, loathsome core of the Dragon's evil, releasing the consuming fire that simmered within it. He withdrew his blade, drawing streamers of flame from the wound, and the Dragon snorted yellow bile from its nostrils.

It had lost after all, and knew its accursed fate with surety.

It bucked one last time in desperation before the ancient warrior spun 'round and cleaved its Serpent's neck in twain.

The heavens, crisscrossed with bolts of electrical fire, gave final witness to the shrieking howl of the damned before drowning that feeble rage with a crack of thunder that shattered glass for miles around.

The Dragon's last thought upon the mortal coil of the world was hatred of its own kind and of itself. In the Dragon's fall, there was no pity.

Its scales smoldered, glowing like coals as skin shriveled and muscle burned away to ash. The skeletal frame was charred black by the time it was revealed, and the great bones collapsed in a clutter of death before breaking into dust, all trace washed away by the flooding rain.

Chapter Forty-Three

A final clap of thunder knocked all upon the rooftop off their feet. It echoed in their ears with a distant ringing. No further bursts followed, and the sky turned utterly black as the last discharge of lightning streaked on its journey and was gone in an instant. The torrent dwindled to an even shower.

A pair of emergency medical technicians slowly returned to their feet, and checked the gurneyed form of Ben Saunders, already secured for transport as best as they could manage under the circumstances. They were stunned the man was even alive. Considering the nature of the wound he'd sustained, he should be dead. *Something about an "old man,"* they'd heard others murmur. But the pair were content to dismiss the medical inconsistency as just one more extraordinary facet of a night that defied any rational explanation.

The detective's brown eyes opened, darting around until they fell upon the concerned features of Nathan Creed standing at his side. His mangled throat gurgled something.

Probably asking for a smoke, thought Nathan, and he smiled.

"Don't talk. You stay with us, Ben!" urged Creed. "Don't you go dying on me before you even have the chance to get on my nerves!"

The paramedics waved Creed off. Billy Sanchez took Nathan's arm and exerted just enough force—enough to catch the larger man off guard—to allow the EMTs to get on their way, hustling the wounded detective from the rooftop.

"You've done enough, man," assured Sanchez. "You helped save his life."

Creed noted the Hispanic's confident bearing and felt a stirring in his soul that bordered on respect.

Other medicos were gathering the SWAT team together, herding them to the rooftop service building where their minor wounds could be tended. Miraculously, only one officer was officially declared dead from the collapse.

Following the descent of the EMTs, a news crew burst out onto the remains of the roof, having no real understanding of what little they had actually witnessed on the newsroom monitors before the "Eye in the Sky" had crashed. The studio crew had hunkered down until all the building-shaking rattles and rolls had stopped. With the tower's complete structural failure, tech engineers below had acted quickly to reroute their signal to a landline and remote transmission station from which broadcasting could continue. The skies above the ravaged studio had now filled with the news-copters of rival networks, gathering around the seeming misfortune of WDVL like opportunistic vultures. Below, desk anchor Steven Dúmas led his own charge without hesitation, circumstances prompting this *"one-time only"* return to the beat of street reporter. His hair was still perfect. An intern kept pace, holding a large umbrella over his head.

Lights, camera, and Dúmas's intruding microphone fixed on Dom. She appeared dazed in the aftershock, pale and drenched, gazing distantly about the devastation as if looking for something, perhaps an additional sign of life.

"Dom! Our very own Dominique Angel, ladies and gentlemen," blurted Dúmas. "Are you all right?"

Dom looked at the anchor, still distracted, a slight trace of blood trailing from under her hairline. Tears sparkled in her eyes, reflecting the glare of the camera's light. Her voice was hopeful, though. "He saved me, y'know… *he truly saved me.*"

"Who, Dominique? Who saved you, and what can you tell us about what happened here tonight?"

Dom only smiled and shook her head. She turned away, leaving the news anchor to pin down one of the standing SWAT members, an officer with minimal injury, but who was only too willing to share the incredible story he had to tell.

The steady rain finally abated to a mere drizzle, then stopped altogether as the dark clouds began to break. A bright and vibrant full moon peered down from the heavens, lighting all with a pure light.

Dom's search led her back to Billy Sanchez and Nathan Creed, the smaller man trying to convey some sense of what had truly happened to the skeptical mission administrator. He appeared willing to listen, but the fantastic didn't seem to loan itself to his pragmatic beliefs.

Dom interrupted. "It's all true, Mr. Creed…every word of it. And the proof…lies scattered across this rooftop." She gestured around them—tour guide to disaster—and that was when she saw him.

The Hero stood upon an outstretched tip of the wreckage, silhouetted against the moon, as the brilliant orb forced its way through the last vestige of diminishing clouds, looking for all the world like Eden's first sunrise. He looked tired, though, and slump-shouldered, even on the heels of his victory. Perhaps for him this night was just one more step in a journey that never really ended—to reach an impossible dream.

Nathan was leery of anything the reporter Angel had to add to the already incredible story, but he followed her gesture all the same. He saw the man too, framed by the full moon, youthful, yet slouched, and a *sword* in his weary hand…

"Who is that?" he asked.

"Hey man, that's Don Quixote," said Billy, with an unexpected reverence.

"What?"

Dom answered, "Don Quixote de la Mancha…Alonso Quixano…a Knight of the Sacred Gospel and a Keeper of the Code…" She never took her eyes from his weary form.

After everything they had been through, though—the disaster and heroism in which they'd all partaken—Nathan perceived Dominique's words as some kind of ugly sarcasm, and felt his blood begin to boil. He was not of a mind to tolerate any reporter's

ridiculing spin on this night's events. His big hand balled up and extended a forceful finger of reprimand. But Sanchez shook his head, as if willing to risk his own life on behalf of Angel's honor. Nathan thought he saw something

in the small man's eyes, a simmering fire that might flare up at a moment's notice. He noticed the opposite in Dom's eyes, though, a glistening sheen of reflected moonlight—*tears.* He softened, and lowered his admonishing hand. He realized that she was, in fact, speaking from her heart, quite possibly for the first time in her life, and she, at least, believed her words to be true.

Sanchez nodded, adding conviction to Nathan's perception.

Dominique turned to look him directly in the face. "Just like *you,* Mr. Creed…a compassionate crusader who still believes that truth and virtue are ideals worth fighting for…while all around, the voices of this world—the prophets of this age—call you mad."

Her tone grew urgent. "Don't let them stop you, Nathan. Whatever they do, no matter what they say…*never, **ever** give up the fight!*"

He didn't know what to say. She'd told him nothing that he didn't

already know and believe. But he'd never
considered himself or his work to be
noble, just necessary. To suddenly receive
such encouragement and support from
such an unexpected quarter was a pleasant
shock. He looked around at the devastation again, and realized that they all had
been survivors of something extraordinary, an event that had transcended the
normal parameters of their well-ordered
tenets and perceptions. And never once
had Fate asked their permission to turn
their individual worlds upside-down.

"I hear ya," Nathan said finally,
mustering the convictions of his own
heart into action. "...And thank you." He pulled her sopping wet form to
himself, and the big man's bulk enveloped the lithe reporter in a great bear
hug. She hugged him back. Then he extended a warm, assuring hand to Billy,
clasping the vagrant's palm in both of his own.

"And we're going to have to talk about *your* future," Nathan said to Billy.

Billy smiled and nodded, not quite sure to what he was agreeing, but
shaking both big hands vigorously in return nevertheless.

At last, the three of them parted, though not until after they had each
glanced once more across the ravaged rooftop, searching for their friend to
join them. But the lone figure, the swordsman—old or young—Quixote, was
gone, as if, perchance, he had never been...

Epilogue

Morning came, just like every other since the dawning of the world. This one arrived crisp and bright, with the rising sun yellow-red and fiery as it burned away layers of early mist.

Skies were clear to the naked eye, but unseen transmissions filled the airwaves like tickertape, each lithe strand intertwining to create a tempest of pageantry from any spattering of controversy. And on this morning, as it was on so many others, *that* was *news:*

"—disaster at Network WDVL has city officials scrambling…"

"—no comment from management…"

"—transmissions down pending a full FCC probe…"

"—loss of life…"

"—seeming terrorist retaliation aimed at station manager Desmond Cortez, whose background and alleged shady dealings are under investigation by the FBI…"

"—In related news, the imminent visit of Gubernatorial Candidate Henry Devlin has been postponed. Law enforcement officials cite possible links to the tragedy…"

Far below the twisted ruin of the WDVL transmission tower, down on the streets themselves, the scattered signals were a little more tangible.

Morning newspapers were hitting newsstands, mail slots, front stoops, and suburban lawns. Unfortunately, no one would ever truly appreciate the irony that it was the camera eye of Macintosh McIlhenney III that had caught and condemned the former WDVL station manager. The city's leading daily paper had scrapped its previous plans, and plastered an image pirated from the airwaves onto the front page: a huge photo of the scowling

Desmond Cortez, holding a semi-automatic pistol to the temple of his own star reporter Dominique Angel. In sixty-point type, the headline roared with all the fury of a desperate dragon:

Media Scandal Rocks City

Dominique Angel started the new day in a quiet location far on the other side of town: a certain deserted loading bay platform, strewn with yellow police crime scene tape blowing in the morning breeze. The burned husk of an abandoned automobile lay crushed beneath the fallen weight of an old, rusted fire escape. Three chalk outlines had been washed away by the previous night's unprecedented storm. The charred auto was already beginning to rust.

Dom had parked her car and walked further on foot, retracing the previous day's steps in reverse. *The previous day,* she'd mused. *It felt more like a lifetime ago.*

Dom was running on empty now. She had spent the immediate post-midnight hours at the hospital, in the presence of the police. The remainder of the wee morning ticked away in the company of her own network's big shots, complete with a video conference to the West Coast studio headquarters, and culminating with an offer she'd be a fool to refuse.

But now, officially one hour after daybreak, she found herself back at that old bridge spanning those run-down railway tracks that no longer had anywhere to go. Just yesterday, from this very spot, she had spent one brief moment pondering her future. She'd never imagined just how diverting a single night of *destiny* could be.

She spotted a familiar soul sitting on the edge of the old trestle, swinging his legs in the morning sun.

"Billy Sanchez," called Dom, "I thought I might find you somewhere along here." She smiled as he looked up, startled.

Billy calmed himself and answered, "Yeah...it's me—I'm a free man today, after some testimony they said came from Detective Saunders himself. He made it, y'know?"

Dom nodded.

"An' those two I pulled from the 'copter crash are gonna be OK too."

"M a c k i e … a n d Madeline Jeunet," she said as she sat down next to Billy and dangled her own legs off the side like a child, or perhaps as one newly reborn. "I spoke to Nathan Creed earlier. He told me about you and Saunders—good news all

around, I'd say. Nathan said he offered you a job."

Billy's complexion darkened and he looked down in embarrassment. "Yeah…he's gonna help me get cleaned up and everything. It ain't gonna be easy, I know, but…it's the least I can do…*for him*. Y'know what I mean?"

The reporter nodded, knowing only too well of whom the former vagrant spoke.

Billy continued, "I thought if I waited 'round here long enough, he might, like, y'know—come back for me."

"Me too," answered Dom, a bit too wistfully for her own standards. "I was hoping he'd still be here. But my instincts tell me he did what he came here to do, that now he's gone and he's not coming back."

Somberness crept in at the end of her sentence, and Billy saw her lower lip quiver with the telltale sign of brewing emotion.

"You gonna be OK, Miss Angel?" he asked.

"Joe's dead…my cameraman. They found him in Desmond's office—apparently, *all over* Desmond's office." She looked as if she might break into sobs at any moment, but she willed the threatening tears back. Far on the horizon they could both see the distant WDVL building, smoke rising from the ruins of the once-mighty transmission tower. A veritable army of official investigators had already descended upon the scene, sifting through every scrap of refuse, searching for evidence that might make some sense out of the night's scandal and tragedy.

"The police want me to stick around town a little longer, but that shot of Desmond and me pretty much made coast-to-coast headlines. The network's offering me a *national* spot after all the hubbub dies down a bit… can you believe that?" Dom finally let the tears come.

"I asked, are *you* gonna be OK?" Billy said, reinforcing his concern.

She wiped at her nose with her slim right hand, the left still salved and freshly bandaged about the wrist. "The question I keep asking myself, over and over again…was any of it *real?*" She shook her head in disbelief. "I just came from the loading dock and everything's still there, just like I remember it, but…did any of that *really* happen—or was it all just…in my head?"

Billy felt less skeptical. "Well, *somethin'* happened—that's for sure." He offered her some paper napkins he'd swiped from the police station.

Dom laughed a little and wiped at her eyes. "I mean…funny as this may sound—it's not everyday that somebody…saves your soul."

"No, man…I hear you." Billy stared off into space as if suddenly lost, adrift. "It's like, nobody's ever *cared* about me before, not really, not enough to risk everything and give it all. But he gave me something to fight for—somethin' to believe in. Now… it's like—I don't know what to do without him."

Dom blew her nose into the napkin, wiped again at her eyes, and said, "I know that I can't go back to whatever I was. I—I have to call my father, let him know I'm alright."

"Your papa local?"

She laughed, and the sound was fresh and vibrant. "No. Chicago. He probably didn't even know I was still alive. But after that picture plastered all over the media…I—I have to tell him how sorry I am. I have to tell him… I forgive him. And I hope that he'll find it in his heart…to forgive me."

Billy wasn't exactly sure what she meant, but he could imagine. "I don't think that'll be any kind of problem."

"I hope you're right, my friend." She wiped suddenly at fresh tears.

"I hope you're right. So, what about you?"

"I'm afraid my Papa's dead."

"I'm sorry."

"Don't be.... It's…just another part of living." Billy rose slowly to his feet. "You know what *he'd* say to us now, don'tcha, Miss Angel?"

"Your father?"

"No…*him.*"

Dom nodded.

Billy made a wide sweeping gesture with his hands, as if bestowing some form of blessing on the proceedings. "He'd say somethin' all heavy and somber like, *'Go…and make of yourselves something new,'* or somethin' like that."

The impression was low and scratchy as if Billy was gargling small pebbles in his throat. The corners of his mouth twitched as he looked back at her.

Dom laughed again, and the sound was now warm and happy, and filled with promise. "You do him pretty well—you know that, Mr. Sanchez?"

"It's a gift…and hey, my friends used to call me Billy."

"OK then—*Billy.* My friends call me Dom."

He grinned and nodded.

The reporter said, "It's the start of a brand new day—you wanna go get something to eat?"

"You buyin', Dom?"

"You eatin', Billy?"

He helped her to her feet.

There was a catch in her throat as Dom had another sudden thought of Joe Caparelli and his fixation with *Casablanca.* She suspected her old cameraman might appreciate the end of the story after all.

Together, they wound their way back to the delivery cul-de-sac, Dom's car, and the yellow warning streamers that fluttered like a second chance in the breeze of a brand new day.

Looking down upon the two new friends, the giant smiling face of Gubernatorial Candidate Henry Devlin oversees all things like some bitter, graven idol of antiquity perched impotently upon a hilltop. The billboard proclaims him *"The Choice for a Better Tomorrow."*

Beneath the pearly white teeth, enlarged to an inhuman proportion, stands a haggard old man at the billboard's base. He is tired—infinitely tired. Yet he will go on, rising every day his Lord puts breath in his lungs, just as he's done every day for the last five hundred years or more. He will go on heeding the Call.

The old man's mind wanders, as it often does, to his old war horse, *Rosinante*—how many long generations past—and of the few brief years he'd shared with the noble, faithful beast that was nothing at all like the pathetic, spindly creature Miguel had painted with his words. He hopes there is a place in eternity for such beloved creatures, even though he's known many who scoffed at such notions, considering them akin to blasphemy. But his saintly old mother believed it was so, as she had believed God was big enough to care greatly about even the little things that didn't really seem to matter at all in the grander scheme.

Rather like people, the old man thinks. *Generation after generation, century after century, at their core, people never change.*

Seriously, he's been considering getting himself a motorcycle—*a motorized mount for these swifter times.* He suspects he might look… *"cool"* in the current vernacular, sitting astride behind its handlebars. He also knows just what name he will dub his new charger, should he make such a flamboyant investment.

He allows himself the luxury of a tiny grin. It lacks several teeth, yet would still be classified as warm and friendly. He hopes his dear mother was right after all, and so, yearns to one day be reunited with the steed he had come to love almost as dearly as his old companions: dearest Sancho, and his beloved Aldonza.

The old man wipes a lone tear from his eye. Thoughts of the past have e'er held such a grip upon him. But memories give way, as they always must, to thoughts of the present, and of the future.

He glances up at the massive image he stands beneath. Some random passing pigeon has marked the visage of the aspiring god with a potent personal assessment of his policies. The old man cannot help but agree. Yet he is saddened by how many will line up to support this politician's cause, regardless of how much of their souls it will cost them.

He has seen enough to know that politics, like what passes for religion, has been crafted by men and women down through all the misery-filled centuries of humanity on Earth, either to achieve selfish aims at the expense of another, or to inspire all to a higher goal, a loftier principle.

He takes great encouragement, however, from knowing that, underneath all the myriad machinations of a desperate human race, there *was,* and *is,* a single, great Truth. Greater than *Courage, Wisdom, Patience, Justice, Faith, Hope,* and *Love,* it stands alone, firm and immutable. It is what supports all of those classic virtues of old. Truth that has walked amongst us, telling the entire world that there is hope for mankind after all.

The old man looks down at the two distant figures far below him, his newest friends walking into the risen sun. He smiles, broad and full, and wishes them well with but a single word that captures the heart of all the wisdom he has to bestow…

"Believe."

The End

"I SAW IT FOR REAL, WITH MY OWN TWO EYES..."

"ROBIN HOOD CUT THE HAND RIGHT OFF THE GUY– THE GUY THAT WAS GONNA HAVE ME SET ON FIRE..."

"BUT SUDDENLY HE WASN'T NO GUY ANY MORE–"

"HE WASN'T EVEN HUMAN..."

"AND THEN THAT'S WHEN IT STARTED TO RAIN."